Nicky hurried forward to close the shutters.

She leaned out of the window to grasp one side. The wind was strong, blowing and swirling in gusts that threatened to topple her. She reached for the shutter, and a gust of wind caught her. The blue curtain, like a clinging wet ghost, blew back into her face, blinding her for a moment. She tried to thrust it away when suddenly it was as though a hand were against her back, shoving her forward. Pushing her...

She cried out and tried to grab the edge of the window. But the wind was strong, far stronger than before. She looked down and saw the ground below, and fought with all of her strength against the raging wind, half in, half out of the window, the rain lashing at her face while an invisible force pushed ... pushed....

"No!" she cried, and with a surge of strength she managed to pull herself back into the room.

Suddenly the lights flickered and went out.

Dear Reader,

Welcome once again to the dark side of love. This month we have two more terrific books just waiting for your reading pleasure, both of them by authors who are already well-known to readers of romance around the world.

In *A Silence of Dreams,* author Barbara Faith gifts her heroine with a dream come true. Or is it a nightmare? Suddenly love and marriage become a trap, a dangerous snare just waiting to enmesh her in inescapable peril. Read at your own risk!

In *The Seventh Night,* Amanda Stevens takes us to the Caribbean, where voodoo is more than something meant to entertain the tourists, where ghostly figures still stalk the night and carry out unspeakable rituals along the sandy beaches of paradise. For one woman, there is only one way out—if she dares to commit herself to love. Take this journey if you dare!

And keep coming back to Shadows every month, because you never know where love and danger will take you as you peruse our pages.

Enjoy!

Leslie Wainger
Senior Editor and Editorial Coodinator

BARBARA FAITH

A SILENCE OF DREAMS

Published by Silhouette Books New York

America's Publisher of Contemporary Romance

SILHOUETTE BOOKS
300 East 42nd St., New York, N.Y. 10017

A SILENCE OF DREAMS

Copyright © 1993 by Barbara Faith

ISBN: 0-373-27013-5

First Silhouette Books printing August 1993

All the characters in this book have no existence outside the
imagination of the author and have no relation whatsoever to
anyone bearing the same name or names. They are not even
distantly inspired by any individual known or unknown to the
author, and all incidents are pure invention.

Printed in the U.S.A.

Books by Barbara Faith

Silhouette Shadows

A Silence of Dreams #13

Silhouette Special Edition

Return to Summer #335
Say Hello Again #436
Heather on the Hill #533
Choices of the Heart #615
Echoes of Summer #650
Mr. Macho Meets His Match #715
This Above All #812

Silhouette Desire

Lion of the Desert #670

Silhouette Books

Silhouette Summer Sizzlers 1988
"Fiesta!"

Silhouette Intimate Moments

The Promise of Summer #16
Wind Whispers #47
Bedouin Bride #63
Awake to Splendor #101
Islands in Turquoise #124
Tomorrow Is Forever #140
Sing Me a Lovesong #146
Desert Song #173
Kiss of the Dragon #193
Asking for Trouble #208
Beyond Forever #244
Flower of the Desert #262
In a Rebel's Arms #277
Capricorn Moon #306
Danger in Paradise #332
Lord of the Desert #361
The Matador #432
Queen of Hearts #446
Cloud Man #502

BARBARA FAITH

is a true romantic who believes that love is a rare and precious gift. She has an endless fascination with the attraction a man and a woman from different cultures and backgrounds have for each other. She considers herself a good example of such an attraction, because she has been happily married for twenty years to an ex-matador she met when she lived in Mexico.

CHAPTER ONE

It was raining the afternoon Nicky Fairchild left Milan, and it was still raining a few hours later when the train pulled into the Venice railway station.

Nicky picked up her backpack, a mode of travel that would have appalled her mother. Eleanora Winston Avery Fairchild Westerly Seabrook Diaz-Enfante always traveled with at least five large Louis Vuitton suitcases, as well as her cosmetic case and jewelry case. But Eleanora wasn't here. She was in Brazil with husband number five, and Nicky wasn't traveling in style, she was backpacking her way through Europe.

She had started her trip in London and after three weeks in England, Wales and Scotland had crossed the Channel to France and taken a train to Paris. Cold and rainy Paris. The romantics who sang about "April in Paris" had very likely never been there in April. She'd caught a cold, and though she had been enthralled by the beauty of the city, after a week there she'd headed toward the Riviera on a second-class bus. She spent a few days in Grenoble before she crossed into Italy, where she was sure it would be warmer.

She had studied Italian for almost a year before her trip, spoke the language fairly well and planned to spend at least a month touring Italy.

Milan had been interesting, but just as cold as Paris. She'd found a cheap hotel that had a lovely view of the

Duomo, but no heat. She'd stayed there three days and this afternoon she'd taken the train for Venice.

When the train lurched to a stop she put on her leather jacket and smoothed her flyaway blond hair under the red plaid cap she'd picked up at a street fair in London. Hefting the backpack, she followed the other passengers down the aisle of the train to the door, and through the terminal to the exit.

And there it was. Venice, the dream city she had so longed to see, a shimmery illusion through the slanting gray rain. Exotic, romantic, implausible Venice. She stood on the steps of the train station watching the gondolas glide by. There was the sound of rain slapping wet stones, of water lapping against old wood; the smell of dampness, and of musty buildings where pigeons huddled in the eaves to try to escape the rain.

Crowds jostled about her, but she stood, mesmerized by the sight of this most fantastic of cities.

She sneezed, stepped out into the rain and headed down the Lista di Spagna, the narrow street that ran parallel to the canal, searching for the Pensione Villa Lucia, which a backpacker she'd met in Paris had told her about.

He'd said it ran about twenty-five a night, which was higher than what Nicky had planned on paying. She was running low on funds, but the monthly check from the trust fund her father had left her should arrive any day. She'd left instructions at the bank to have the next check sent to the American Express Office here in Venice. Hopefully it would arrive tomorrow and once again she'd be reasonably solvent.

The lobby of the Pensione Villa Lucia was small and shabbily Romanesque. Red velvet tasseled drapes hung from tall windows. Overstuffed velvet furniture graced marble floors. No one was in the lobby, but there was a hand bell on the carved mahogany reception desk. She called a tentative, "Hello?" and when there was no answer, tapped the bell with the palm of her hand.

"*Si, si,* I am coming." A woman came hurrying into the lobby from one of the corridors. *"Buon giorno,"* she said when she saw Nicky. "It is still raining, yes? And cold. Can I help you? You are looking for a room?"

Nicky eased the backpack off her shoulders. "Yes, if you have one."

"*Si,* I have." The woman smiled and her rather plain face became not so plain after all. In her early fifties, she had black hair with an inch-wide streak of white running through it. Her skin was pale and her eyes were a nice warm brown. She wore a dark wool dress and she had a red sweater over her shoulders.

"This is not the tourist time so we are not busy," the signora continued. "I have a nice room on the second floor. *La stanza da bagno*—the how you say...bathroom, yes?—is just across the hall. Breakfast is from seven to nine. Come, I show you."

Nicky followed the signora up a wide, winding staircase. The carpeting was worn, but the finely carved wooden banister was polished and beautiful. The corridor was dark and so was the room the signora motioned her to enter.

"Momento," the signora said, and crossing the floor, she threw open the wooden shutters.

And there was Venice, with all its sounds and smells and vibrant life. It didn't matter that the once-elegant carpet in the room was faded or that the pink-and-lavender-flowered wallpaper was peeling. Nicky hurried to the window and leaned out. From below came the shouts of the gondoliers and the splash of water from a passing vaporetto, a water bus. A flat bargelike boat had pulled up to the dock to discharge cases of beer. The man unloading looked up and saw her leaning out of the window.

"Buon giorno," he called up to her.

"Buon giorno," she called back, and with a smile she turned to the signora. "It's wonderful," she said. "I'll take it."

"Bene!" The signora held out her hand. "I am the Signora Brendisi." She handed Nicky a key. *"Ben venuto,* welcome. How long will you stay?"

"I'm not sure." Nicky sneezed. "A week. Maybe two."

"As long as you like." A look of concern crossed her face. "You have a cold, yes?"

Nicky nodded. "I picked it up in Paris."

"You must take care."

"I will. *Grazie."*

When the signora left, Nicky unpacked. Her wardrobe was simple: an extra pair of jeans, a wool skirt, a jean miniskirt, a blouse, two T-shirts, two sweaters, underwear and an extra pair of shoes. Her mother would have had the vapors.

Eleanora had, of course, objected to the whole idea of Nicky's traveling through Europe alone. She had telephoned from her new husband's Brazilian coffee plantation the moment she'd received Nicky's letter telling of the proposed trip.

"Really, Nicolina," she'd said, "if you must go to Europe, then for heaven's sake go in style."

"I don't have that kind of money," Nicky had answered.

"You have the trust fund your father left you."

"Five hundred dollars a month wouldn't last a week if I traveled in the style you'd like me to."

"You should never have quit your job."

"I don't like advertising, Eleanora. I stuck it out for a year and I saved enough money, along with the trust fund, to buy myself a year in Europe. I don't want to be a copywriter for the rest of my life. I want to write—"

"A book." Eleanora's sigh was audible over the miles that separated them. "You're just like your father. That's all he ever talked about, and talk was all it amounted to."

"He finished his book," Nicky said, breathing hard, getting mad.

"And there wasn't a publisher in New York who would touch it. If he'd stopped writing and gotten a real job, perhaps we would have stayed together."

"I doubt it," Nicky had mumbled under her breath when her mother hung up.

She hadn't seen her mother in over a year. Eleanora never wrote. She sent Nicky a check at Christmas and on her birthday. She had paid for half of Nicky's tuition at the University of Florida and Nicky had paid the rest from the trust fund and a part-time campus job. After college she'd gotten a job as a copy editor at a department store in Miami. She'd scrimped and saved for this trip, but she hadn't counted on things in Europe being so expensive.

She'd stayed at youth hostels in England and France when she could find them, at inexpensive hotels or pensiones when she couldn't. She'd been in Europe for two months and already her money was running low. Tomorrow, she would go to the American Express office to see if her next check had arrived. She'd also scout around for a cheaper place to stay.

But when Nicky awoke the following morning, her throat was sore and she had a headache. She stayed in bed as long as she could, and decided there'd be no scouting around today. Remembering that the signora had said breakfast was served from seven to nine, she dragged herself out of bed. The room was cold. She showered in water that was barely warm, then put on jeans and a sweater and went looking for the dining room.

It was in a small alcove off the lobby. An elderly couple occupied a table by the windows that overlooked the water; a single woman sat near the door leading to the kitchen. The elderly couple said in English, "Good Morning"; the single woman did not speak. Nicky had a cup of hot chocolate and a warm croissant with orange marmalade. When she finished, she asked Signora Brendisi if she knew where the American Express office was.

"But it is raining," the signora said. "Why do you not wait until it stops?" She lifted her shoulders in an expressive Italian gesture and with a rueful laugh added, "But this is April. Only God knows when the rain will stop."

She gave Nicky sketchy directions and told her what vaporetto to take.

A chill wind added to the misery of the rain as Nicky made her way down the Lista di Spagna to the vaporetto stop she had seen across from the railroad station. She waited there under the skimpy shelter, and when the water bus came, chose a window seat inside where she could look out.

In spite of the weather and her aching head, she was excited because at last she was in Venice, and that's what mattered. She watched the splat of rain through the wet windows, saw the droplets make deep circles against the sea, which lapped in foot-high waves against the long, flat boat. It was wonderful. She loved it. If she did nothing else in Venice, she'd be content to ride all day up and down the Grand Canal in a vaporetto.

By the time she got off at the Piazza San Marco, the rain had slowed to a cold, mean drizzle. She stood there in the middle of the centuries-old square and looked around her in wonder. Gondolas, like a line of floating black swans, bounced on the crests of murky green waves at the edge of the pier.

In front of her was the Byzantine-Romanesque-Gothic Church of San Marco, stunning in its magnificence of weathered domes and golden lunettes, the four bronze horses that seemed to have stopped in midgallop above the entrance, the huge doors, the faded, ancient colors.

Men in blue coveralls swept the marble slabs in the piazza. Two nuns, heads bowed, hands folded in their black habits, moved through the outside corridors of a building. The few tourists who, like Nicky, had braved the rain, fed the hundreds of pigeons with seeds and nuts sold by the vendors. Suddenly there came an explosion of sound as the mechanized bronzed figures in the bell tower began to strike the hour. The pigeons took flight, up, up into the grayness of the sky, swirling in a blur of white-and-gray wings while the bronzed figures bonged the hour.

Nicky shivered, partly from the cold and dampness, partly from the joy of being here. But finally, with a sigh, she turned away from the piazza and began to search for the American Express office.

She wasn't the only one who had come out on this rainy day. There were other tourists there to pick up mail, older people and younger people, bearded young men in torn jeans, girls in yellow slickers. They lounged against the counter or sprawled against the walls, speaking German or French, Spanish or Dutch, very likely as broke as she was, most of them waiting for a check, as she was.

"Nicolina Fairchild," she said when it was her turn at the counter.

"*Momento,*" the young woman there said. She searched through the box of mail twice, then shook her head. "No Fairchild," she said.

"Something might have come a week or two ago. Maybe you have a place where you keep old mail."

"No, *signorina.* I assure you there is nothing. Perhaps *domani.*"

Tomorrow? Nicky straightened her shoulders. She had a little less than two hundred dollars. She was paying twenty-five a night for her room at the pensione. If the check didn't arrive in the next couple days she'd be in trouble.

When she left the American Express office, she found a small trattoria where she had a hot sandwich filled with mozzarella cheese, and a cappuccino. The rain had stopped, so instead of taking a vaporetto to the pensione, she decided to find her way back through the narrow, winding streets. Midway there it started to rain again, and by the time she got to the pensione she was soaked and shivering with cold. She went up to the room, stripped out of her clothes and went to bed.

By morning she was burning with fever. Her throat was worse and her chest felt like an elephant was sitting on it. She dragged herself out of bed and made it to the alcove of the kitchen at five to nine. Signora Brendisi served her hot tea with lemon, a hard roll and a concerned look.

"It is better you stay in today," she said.

Nicky shook her head. "I have to go back to American Express," she croaked. "I'm waiting for a letter."

"But surely the letter can wait." The signora put her hand on Nicky's forehead. "You have the temperature, *signorina*."

Nicky summoned a smile. "I won't be gone long, but I really do have to go."

So once again she trudged out into the rain. And once again there was no check.

By the time she returned to the pensione she was shaking with chills and fever, so dizzy she could barely stand. She went to bed and stayed there all that day. The next morning she was too ill to get up for breakfast. When the maid, an elderly woman with a frizzed topknot of gray hair and a dark blue apron over her dark blue dress, came at noon to make up her room, she said something in a too-rapid Italian for Nicky to understand and went scurrying out the door.

A few minutes later Signora Brendisi appeared. "You are *malato?*" she asked. "Sick, yes?"

"It's just a bad cold," Nicky managed to whisper.

The signora put a hand on Nicky's forehead. "*Dio mio,* you are burning with fever. We must call a doctor at once. My friend, Dr. Raviggia, is a neighbor. I will telephone him."

"No!" Nicky struggled to a sitting position. The room tilted and she slid back down under the blanket. "I'll feel better tomorrow. Please don't call a doctor. I can't afford..."

But the Signora Brendisi had already hurried out of the room. Five minutes later she returned. "Dr. Raviggia is not in Venice," she said. "He has gone to Roma to visit his mother. But he has a houseguest, a doctor too, a specialist in the heart who is here in Venice to teach for a few weeks. I have left a message for him. The housekeeper assures me he will come as soon as possible."

"I only have a cold," Nicky started to protest. "I don't need . . ." But it was too much of an effort to speak. She closed her eyes, and as she drifted to sleep, wondered how much a heart surgeon charged for telling a patient to take two aspirin and go to bed.

"Signorina?"

Nicky opened her eyes and looked up at the man bending over her. Mephistopheles with dark Mediterranean features. A curl of dark hair hanging down over a broad forehead. A forbidding frown curving a sensuously cruel mouth. A questioning intensity in his pale green eyes.

He put a cold hand on her forehead and she winced. "I am Dr. Carlo Santini," he said in accented English. "How do you feel?"

"Not great," she whispered.

He opened the top few buttons of her nightgown and put a stethoscope on her bare chest. "Take a deep breath," he said.

She tried to, but all that came out was a wheezing cough.

The frown deepened. He raised her to a sitting position and eased the cold stethoscope down her back. "Again," he said. "A deep breath."

Was this guy kidding? It was all she could do to get air in and out, very carefully, very slowly. He laid her back down and put a thermometer under her arm. It, too, was cold.

"What is your name?" he asked.

"Nicky. . . Nicolina Fairchild."

"Age?"

"Twenty-three."

"You are traveling alone, Signorina Fairchild?"

"Yes."

"You are from the United States?"

"Florida."

"You have relatives in Europe? Someone we might call?"

"No," she wheezed. "No one."

"Do you have any allergies? To penicillin? Anything?"

"Not that I know of."

He took the thermometer from under her arm and looked at it with a deepening frown. "You have pneumonia, *signorina,*" he said. "You must go to the hospital."

"Can't," she said.

He turned to Signora Brendisi, who was hovering at the end of the bed next to the frizzy-haired maid. "Get her coat," he ordered.

"She doesn't have a coat, Dr. Santini. Only a jacket."

He swore. Then he said something else, and the frizzy-haired maid went scurrying out of the room.

He bent over Nicky, and suddenly she found herself being wrapped in the blanket that covered her bed.

"Listen," she tried to say. "I don't want to go to a hospital. I can't—"

But he didn't listen. He simply bundled the blanket around her, picked her up and headed for the door. She tried to struggle, but he was bigger than she was. Six feet, probably. Football shoulders. Broad chest.

Signora Brendisi hurried down the steps ahead of them.

"It's raining," she said.

"I'll keep her covered."

They were outside. The door closed behind them. Nicky felt rain on her face, then the blanket covered her and she couldn't see. She heard the sound of a motor-boat, words shouted in Italian. Then she was on the boat, cradled in his arms.

Waves. The sharp stinging smell of the water, the coolness of rain. And him. The beat of his heart against her cheek. Darkness.

Nicky opened her eyes. The room was clean and white. A nurse was standing beside her bed, adjusting the bottle that hung above her head. She looked down at her arm and saw the needle there, the slow drip from the tube attached to the IV.

The nurse raised Nicky's head and held a glass with a straw to her lips. The orange juice was cool and sweet and very good.

"Grazie," Nicky said and closed her eyes.

It was night when she opened them again. Mephistopheles was sitting in a chair next to the bed.

"How are you?" he asked.

She wanted to say, "You're the doctor, you tell me," but he didn't look as though he had much of a sense of humor so she murmured, "Chest hurts."

He took the stethoscope from around his neck and turned her. She felt the coldness of metal on her back. When he eased her over, he asked, "You have no relatives?"

"Mother. In Brazil with her coffee beans."

He shook his head. "I do not understand?"

"She lives in Brazil with number five."

"Number five?"

Nicky's eyes drifted closed. "Tired," she murmured.

She felt his hand on her forehead. Then the darkness came again and she slept.

They covered her head and shoulders with a plastic tent. She remembered the doctor had said she had pneumonia. Did people still die of pneumonia?

"I never get sick," she wanted to tell somebody. Sniffles, maybe. The measles when she was seven and spending Christmas with her father. He sat beside her bed. He read her stories and played games with her. She loved him, and when she was better and Christmas vacation was over, she had wanted to stay with him.

"Maybe next year when you're older," he'd said.

But by next Christmas he was dead. Her mother had been in Greece, and Nicky had spent Christmas in a Connecticut boarding school.

If her father were here now...

She said, "Daddy?" and a hand grasped hers.

"Hang on," he said. "Fight!"

Nighttime again. Her breathing hard and rasping in the silence of the room. She drifted on the edge of consciousness, and every time she opened her eyes, he was there, his pale green eyes intense, serious, probing.

"Hard to breathe," she whispered.

He lifted the plastic and leaned down so that his face was close to hers. "You must try," he said. "You *must* get well. I won't lose you again!"

She looked up at him, held by the intensity of his gaze. She felt the strength of the hand holding hers, pulling her back. Back from...

"You will get well," he said.

"Yes." Only a whisper. "Yes."

There were spring flowers in her room—lavender irises, daffodils and violets. Signora Brendisi came to visit and brought her a blue nightgown. "To match your eyes," she said.

She patted Nicky's hand. "Dr. Santini has assured me you are recovering and that in a few days you will be out of the hospital and you can return to the pensione. But you must rest when you do, yes?"

"Signora..." Nicky hesitated. "I have very little money. I've been expecting a check from a New York bank, but it hadn't come before I became ill. I'm sure it has by now. As soon as I have it I'll pay you, but I'm afraid it will be a little while before I can pick it up. In the meantime I could move to a less expensive place, a small room—"

"I will not hear of it. I will trust you, yes? And you will pay me when you can."

"But I have the hospital bill to pay. And the doctor's bill."

"Dr. Santini has assured me you are not to worry about that." Signora Brendisi smiled. "He is a good doctor. A little abrupt, perhaps, but nevertheless a good man. The nurses have told me that when you were so sick he rarely left your side."

"Yes, I remember...." Pale green eyes gazing so intently into hers. And the words, *I won't lose you again.*

Again? What had he meant by that? She had never seen him before her illness. Had she only dreamed the words?

"He is not from Venice," the signora said. "He has a home near Florence, and now that the seminar he was teaching has finished, he will be leaving Venice. But Dr. Raviggia is back from Rome. You will see him when you need to."

He was leaving. She wasn't sure why the news gave her a strangely bereft feeling, but it did.

She took a nap when the signora left, and when she awoke she saw Dr. Santini standing in the doorway, watching her with a look so deeply probing that for a moment she felt something akin to fear.

She took a deep breath and summoned a smile. "I can't thank you enough for taking care of me, Doctor," she said. "I'm concerned about the bill, for the hospital and for you, but I'm expecting money from the States and as soon as it comes I—"

"We don't need to discuss money now," he said, brushing aside her words. "We must only think about your regaining your strength."

"Signora Brendisi told me you would be leaving Venice soon."

"Not for a while."

"But I thought—"

"I have decided to stay." He came into the room. He stood over her bed and looked down at her. "I will not leave you," he said.

CHAPTER TWO

The night before Nicky left the hospital, Signora Brendisi brought her a pair of her blue jeans, a sweater and a light blue cashmere coat.

Nicky ran her fingers lightly over the soft fabric. "It's very kind of you to let me borrow your coat, *signora,* but it looks new. I wouldn't want to get it soiled."

"It is new," Signora Brendisi answered with a smile. "But it is not mine, Nicolina. It is a present for you from Dr. Santini."

Nicky stared at her. "But I can't accept a present like this. It's much too expensive."

"*Si,* it is expensive. But when I said as much to the doctor, and that very likely you would object to such a gift, he said you needed a coat and that you could discuss it with him later." She lifted her shoulders. "He is a strange man, I think. So serious, so intense. But a good doctor, yes?"

She remembered him gazing at her with his strange, impenetrable eyes, clasping her hand in his, compelling her to fight. And the words *I won't lose you again.* Had they been spoken or only dreamed.

How strange, she thought. How strange.

When Signora Brendisi left, a nurse came to help Nicky bathe and dress. She brushed Nicky's dark blond hair back off her face into a ponytail and tied it with a blue ribbon.

"You're very thin," the young woman said. "You have lost weight. You must eat very much pasta—spaghetti and ravioli, cannelloni and lasagna. You like our food in Italy?"

"I love it," Nicky said with a laugh.

"Then you must eat and get fat, yes?" She took the blue cashmere coat off the hanger and placed it over Nicky's shoulders. "How beautiful it is," she said. Then she helped Nicky into a wheelchair and wheeled her down to the lobby, where Dr. Santini waited.

He stood sideways to her, talking to a doctor in a white coat, and for the first time Nicky really looked at him. He was as tall as she had first thought, and his complexion was the dark smooth olive of the northern Italian. His thick black hair looked tousled and unruly. As she watched, he brushed it back from his forehead in an impatient gesture. An impatient man, she thought, a perfectionist. Intense about everything, cruel perhaps. A sensuously brooding Heathcliff, forceful and strong. A man unlike any she had ever known.

He turned and looked at her, and an expression she could not define came into his eyes. Without taking his gaze from hers, he said something to the man he had been talking to and started toward her.

"Your eyes are very blue this morning," he said. But he did not smile, he only gestured to the nurse, and the three of them went out of the hospital to the dock, and to the water taxi that waited there.

When he had seated her in the back of the boat, she took a deep breath of the fresh spring air and said, "You can't imagine how good it is to be outside in the sunshine. Sunshine! I can't believe it. I want to go back to the Piazza San Marco. I want to walk all around the square and feed the pigeons and listen to the bells. And

walk up every narrow street. And ride in a gondola...."
She smiled up at him. "I want to see every inch of Venice."

"But not for a while. First you must rest and get your strength back." He reached over and fastened the coat around her throat. "I have arranged with Signora Brendisi to have your meals brought in," he said. "You must eat and rest, and when you are better I will show you Venice."

She didn't understand. He was her doctor, and when she had been in the hospital he had taken wonderful care of her. But she had never seen him until the afternoon he had come to the pensione. Now he was escorting her back there and she wasn't sure whether or not the gesture was in a professional capacity or if it was something else, something more personal. As was his offer to show her Venice. Certainly his buying her what was an obviously expensive coat had not been part of his professional duties.

Carefully she said, "The coat is beautiful, Doctor. It was kind of you, but I can't accept it."

"Nonsense. You need a coat."

"I have a jacket."

"A jacket and blue jeans." He shook his head. "You are a beautiful young woman, Signorina Nicolina. You must not go out in Venice looking like a badly dressed boy."

"A boy!" Her blue eyes flashed with anger. "I like the clothes I wear."

"But I do not."

"*You* do not?" Nicky glared at him. "You have no right..." She stopped. He had gone far beyond what any doctor could be expected to do for a patient. He had stayed by her side when she'd been so desperately ill, and she knew with a deep-down gut feeling that if it had not been for him, she might not have made it. He didn't have the right to tell her what to wear, but she didn't want to be angry with him.

"Look," she said, offering a smile, "I appreciate everything you've done for me. But I've had a father—I don't need another one."

"I have no intention of being your father, signorina," he said in a deceptively soft voice. "Believe me, that is not what I have in mind."

She couldn't look away, for his eyes held her as surely as if he had captured her hands and would not let go.

"Doctor..." She took a steadying breath. "Dr. Santini, I—"

"Carlo," he said in that same deceptively soft voice. "My name is Carlo."

Before she could answer, the boatman called out, "Pensione Villa Lucia," and the water taxi bumped against the dock.

Santini took Nicky's arm and helped her up the three steps to the landing. Her legs felt weak and it was an effort to take a step.

When she hesitated, he looked at her, his face full of concern. "What is it?" he asked.

"I'm...just a little shaky."

He put his arm around her. "Lean on me, Nicolina," he said. "Let me help you." He guided her past the empty tables and chairs on the waterfront patio. "It will be pleasant here when the weather is warmer," he said. "By the end of May or the first of June it will be filled with tourists. You will enjoy it then."

Nicky shook her head. "I'll be in Spain in May," she said.

"Spain?" He looked surprised. "Why would you want to go to Spain?"

"The same reason I wanted to come to Italy. To see it."

"Italy is better. You should stay here. Besides, it is not good that you travel alone. Here you have friends."

"The only person I know is Signora Brendisi. And—and you of course."

"Of course." There was a gentle pressure on her arm, and he said, "Sometimes, Signorina Nicolina, one person is all any of us need."

She looked up at him, but before she could respond, the door opened and Signora Brendisi called out, "Here you are at last. Come in, come in. And you, too, Doctor. Bianca has prepared tea and sandwiches and wonderful little cakes. Please join us."

He looked at Nicky. "Please do," she said.

They followed the signora into a small dining room Nicky had not seen before. Three chairs had been arranged around a table set with a pretty blue-and-white tablecloth, china dishes and silver. The elderly woman with the frizzy gray hair smiled at Nicky and bobbed her head. *"Ben venuto, signorina,"* she said. "It is glad that you are well."

"Grazie, Bianca."

Carlo held a chair for Nicky, then for the signora. Bianca served the tea and sandwiches and the small cakes. Everything was delicious, but halfway through the meal Nicky felt a sudden lightheadedness. When she lifted her teacup, her hand trembled.

Carlo pushed his chair back. "It's your first day out of the hospital," he said. "You're tired and you must rest."

"I—I'm all right."

He pulled her chair out. "Come, I will help you to your room."

She wanted to tell him that she wasn't a child, nor was she an invalid, and that she could certainly get up the stairs by herself. But he had his arm around her, and almost against her will she found herself letting him help her up the stairway and down the hall to her room.

He led her to the bed and eased her back against the pillows. "We must get you well as soon as we can, Signorina Nicolina," he said. "And when you are well I will show you my Italy, and there will be no need for you to go to Spain."

Nicky looked at him, startled, not sure what to say. But before she could say anything, he murmured, *"Arrivederci,"* and softly closed the door.

Every day fresh flowers arrived—red roses, lavender lilacs, pink camellias. Every evening a different restaurant brought in her dinner—cannelloni and fettuccine, truffled chicken, lobster.

Nicky didn't know what to think or what to do. Here was a man she had met only in a professional way, yet he was showering her with gifts of food and flowers, not to mention the expensive cashmere coat that she had tried several times to return to him. His demeanor remained professional. He came to the pensione every afternoon. He took her temperature, which had returned to normal two days before she left the hospital, and listened to her breathing. If these were house calls, she thought, his bill would be astronomical.

And because it had to be talked about, she said, on a sunny afternoon when they were having tea in the garden patio of the pensione, "You've never said anything about your bill, Doctor. I have a check coming in from the States that I'll be able to pick up at the American Express office tomorrow. I'll need to pay the hospital, too."

"I've taken care of the hospital bill," he said.

"The hospital bill?" Nicky looked at him, startled. "Well, then, if you'll give me that bill, I'll add it to yours. You'll be leaving Venice soon. I want to settle up before you do."

"I'm in no hurry to leave Venice."

"But Signora Brendisi said you were only here for the seminar. If that is over..." Nicky looked at him, puzzled.

"It has been over for almost two weeks," he said.

"Then why...?" She felt a flush of color. "Did you stay in Venice because of me, because I was so ill, I mean?"

"I stayed because of you, yes."

"But I'm well now."

"I know." He took a sip of his tea. "And since you are, perhaps you would like to go out to dinner tomorrow night."

This was all going too fast. He had paid her hospital bill. He sent her flowers every day; he had gourmet meals sent in. He did all of the things a suitor might do if he were pursuing a woman. Yet Carlo Santini had not indicated by a look or a touch that he had that kind of interest in her.

She did not know how she felt about that, or about him. He was older than she was, not that it mattered. Certainly he was attractive, handsome in his somber, brooding way.

"Tomorrow night?" he asked as he rose to leave.

Nicky looked up at him. "Yes," she said. "Tomorrow night."

* * *

The next morning she took a vaporetto to the American Express office, accompanied, at Signora Brendisi's insistence, by the aging Bianca.

"You cannot go alone," the signora had said as Nicky was about to leave. "What if you feel ill and need assistance? Dr. Santini would not like it if he knew you had ventured out alone."

Dr. Santini. She wanted to say that the good doctor didn't own her, that she was over twenty-one and she would come and go as she pleased. She did not need anyone to accompany her, certainly not someone who herself might need help. But because it was easier to agree than to argue, she had left the pensione with Bianca. The check had arrived. She cashed it, and with five hundred dollars worth of lire in her purse, returned with Bianca to the pensione. The first thing she did when she got there was to go to Signora Brendisi.

"You've been very patient," she said with a smile. "But I can pay you now. Do you have my bill?"

"But it has been paid, Signorina Nicky. Dr. Santini took care of it several days ago."

Nicky's mouth tightened. "You can return the money to him when he comes tonight. Meantime I'll pay you what I owe."

Signora Brendisi held up her hands. "I cannot do that. You must talk to the doctor and straighten it out with him."

What was happening here? Carlo Santini had paid her hospital bill and he'd paid the money she owed Signora Brendisi. Why? This wasn't something strangers did for other strangers. Why had he done it?

That night Nicky dressed in her dark wool skirt and black turtleneck sweater. She looked at the pale blue coat hanging in her closet, then reached for her leather jacket.

Carlo was waiting for her when she came downstairs. He wore a dark gray tailored suit, a white linen shirt and a dark tie. "Where is your coat?" he asked.

"In the closet. I told you that I can't accept it. If you'll tell me where you bought it, I'll return it tomorrow."

"But I want you to wear it tonight."

"My jacket is warm enough."

"I prefer you wear the coat."

She frowned up at him. He frowned back at her, then to Signora Brendisi, who watched from the doorway to the dining room, he said, "Would you be kind enough to send Bianca to fetch the signorina's coat?"

"Wait just a minute." Nicky, hands on her hips, glared at him.

But before she could say anything else, the signora said, "In truth, Signorina Nicky, the jacket is . . . how do you say . . . not quite suitable for evening in Venice."

Nicky looked from the signora to Carlo. Her lips twitched, but at last she said, "I'll wear it if you'll let me pay for it."

"We can talk about this later."

"We can talk about it now."

He shrugged. "Very well. If you won't accept it as a gift, you may pay for it."

Bianca trotted up the stairs. When she returned, Nicky took off the leather jacket and Carlo helped her into the blue coat. For a fraction of an instant his hands lingered on her shoulders. Then he said, "*Bene.* Now we go."

The sun had set by the time they went out to the water taxi, but it was still light, and the sky was a brilliance of red and hazy pink, of shadowed blues and greens. Gulls swooped low over waves capped with the bronze and gold of the fading sun. It was a beautiful evening, one Nicky would never forget. If this had to be the end of her travels, then she was glad they had ended in Venice.

Sudden unbidden tears rose in her eyes, and Carlo, who had not spoken since they had left the pensione, said, "What is it, Nicolina?"

"It's so beautiful," she whispered. "I'll never forget..." She shook her head. "Some day I'll return. Some day."

He looked at her, his pale green eyes almost opaque in the fading light. "You will return, *cara mia*," he said.

And again, as she had been before, she was held by the intensity of his gaze.

When they docked by the Piazza San Marco, he put her arm through his and led her across the piazza into one of the most elegant restaurants she had ever been in. There were gold love seats and pink marble columns, green terrazzo floors, murals with delicately fading colors, crystal chandeliers. And a maître d' in a black tuxedo.

"Good evening, Pietro," Carlo said. "We have a reservation. A table near the window overlooking the piazza, please."

"*Si, si*, Doctor. Right this way."

They followed him to a beautifully appointed, candle-lit table. The maître d' seated Nicky. "Your coat, *signorina*," he said as he eased the blue cashmere off her shoulders.

She wondered what he would have said if she'd worn her beaten-up leather jacket.

A waiter brought gold-embossed leather menus. Carlo said, "Shall I order for you?" and when Nicky nodded, he glanced at the menu and ordered in Italian almost too rapid to understand.

When the waiter left and they were alone, Carlo said, "Tell me about yourself, Nicolina. What did you do in . . . you said Florida. Is that right?"

"Yes, Miami. I worked as a copywriter in a department store. But what I really want to do is write . . . novels."

She folded the white linen napkin across her lap. "My father was a writer," she said.

"You called for him in your delirium. He is dead?"

Nicky nodded. "He died when I was eight."

"And your mother? You are close to her? You also spoke about her when you were ill, but I didn't understand."

"My mother and I aren't close. My father was her second husband. She's had three more husbands since him, and now she is in Brazil with husband number five."

He frowned, but before he could say anything else the sommelier appeared. When Carlo had ordered the wine, he turned back to Nicky. "How many times have you been married?" he asked.

"Not even once, Doctor. I doubt that I ever will marry."

"You're only twenty-three. Perhaps in time you will have as many husbands as your mother."

"And perhaps not," she said coolly. "If I ever marry, and I'm not sure that I will, it will be for a lifetime."

"A lifetime." He toyed with a silver fork. "You're a romantic, Signorina Nicolina."

"Am I?" She looked at him across the table. "How many wives have you had, Dr. Santini?"

"One," he said. "She died two years ago."

"I'm sorry. I shouldn't have asked."

"Why not? I asked you, didn't I?"

The wine, a red Bardolino, arrived, and the waiter poured. Nicky took a sip. It was dry and tart. She took another sip and wondered about Carlo Santini's wife. She would have been beautiful, she thought. And sophisticated. She'd probably never worn a pair of jeans or a comfortably worn leather jacket in her life. She would have dressed in beautiful gowns. And a cashmere coat.

The dinner was served: wild-mushroom risotto, baby artichokes, sole with scampi, filet mignon, and finally a dessert plate of assorted cheeses, black cherries and wild strawberries.

Carlo refilled her wineglass. His hands were strong, competent. A surgeon's hands, she thought, fine boned, the fingers lean, spatulate. The gray suit he wore this evening was tailor-made, the striped tie conservative and obviously expensive. There was about him an almost old-world look. Two hundred years ago he would have been a Medici count, well mannered, charming, with just enough danger in his eyes to give a woman pause.

As he gave her pause.

"Tomorrow we will go to Torcello if the weather is good," he said, breaking in on her thoughts. "It's an hour's ride, but I think you will enjoy it. We can go early and stop at the lace factory on Burano."

Nicky looked at him. "Doctor..." The flame of the candle cast dark shadows on the sharp planes of his face. The light flickered and she saw in his eyes a look of mystery, and of something else she did not understand, something so compelling that for a moment she could not look away.

He had never held her hand or kissed her or looked at her in a way that said he found her desirable. His attitude was more of a possessive nature, as though he had every right to tell her what to do or what to wear. But why? She didn't understand.

He came around the table to pull her chair out, and when they left the restaurant, he led her toward the gondolas. Gondoliers dressed in white pants and blue-and-white-striped shirts waved broad-brimmed, beribboned straw hats and called out to them. Carlo selected a gondola, and holding Nicky's arm, helped her to board.

In spite of her preoccupation about exactly what his intentions were, she was excited about a gondola ride in Venice on a perfect star-filled night. She settled back against the cushioned seat and the gondolier pushed the boat away from the dock.

Lights from the hotels, from lighted moorings and old houses, reflected on the water. The sky was a dark Venetian blue. And the gondolier began to sing an Italian love song.

Nicky leaned back against Carlo's arm and closed her eyes. I'll remember this, she thought. When I leave I will remember the smell of the sea, and the songs, and Carlo Santini. I will remember the warmth of his arm around my shoulders, his dark good looks and his frown. I will remember everything.

"Nicolina?"

She opened her eyes. His face was inches away from hers, and suddenly it was as though everything stilled and waited.

"Nicolina," he said again, and then he kissed her.

His lips were firm against hers and for a moment she was too surprised to respond. But he persisted, urging her closer, demanding a response. When her lips parted under his, she heard him sigh and his arms tightened around her.

As though from a distance she was aware of the splash of waves against the black swan boat, the smell of the sea and the muted song of the gondolier. Then all sound faded and there was only Carlo, holding her close.

His mouth tasted of wine. She rested a hand against his cheek and felt the bristle of beard on her palm.

"Cara, cara mia," he said against her lips, and she felt herself melting into him, weak of will, his for this brief moment in this dark Venetian night.

"I knew it would be like this." He kissed the hand that rested against his cheek. "Nicolina," he whispered. *"Dolce amore."*

"Carlo? Carlo, I—"

"No," he said, stopping her. "Do not question. Only accept what we feel."

He kissed her again, and a flame like the first curl of red wine down a dry throat warmed in a velvet heat inside her. She put her arms around his neck to hold him as he held her, to touch and smooth the thickness of his hair. Her mouth became as hungry as his mouth, tasting as he tasted, searching as he searched.

He murmured her name against her lips, and with a shuddering sigh he let her go and held her away from him. "This is the way it will be between us," he said, and held her without speaking until they reached the Pensione Villa Lucia.

He took her hand when he told her good-night. He kissed her and said, *"Domani, cara mia.* Until tomorrow."

Then he was gone, and she stood alone in the open doorway and watched the gondola glide away into the night.

Tomorrow, she thought. Tomorrow.

CHAPTER THREE

"I want to settle what I owe you for everything," Nicky said the next afternoon when Carlo arrived.

"There's not time to discuss it right now, Nicky. I have a water taxi waiting. It's almost an hour's ride to Burano, so if we're going there and on to Torcello while it's still daylight, we really must go."

He looked at her jean miniskirt and the striped T-shirt, her bare legs and flat sandals. "Is that what you're wearing?" he asked.

Nicky flushed. "I've been traveling light," she said defensively. "I don't have room in my backpack for nice clothes."

He picked up the cashmere coat and draped it over her shoulders. "At least wear this," he said. And when he saw the thrust of her chin, he quickly added, "It will be cool on the water. You've been ill and we must take care of you." He fastened the coat about her throat. "Besides, I'm the doctor. I know what is best for you."

She didn't think she believed him, but she hesitated, torn between anger and the need to be with him again. "I promise you that I won't catch cold," she said. "I'm sorry you're uncomfortable about my clothes, but they're all I have. Most of the time since I've been traveling I've stayed in youth hostels. I've eaten my meals at stand-up counters in railroad stations or in trattorias." A slow smile softened her features. "I didn't expect to be wined and dined, Carlo. I'm afraid this is it, the skirt or jeans."

"Not jeans," he said emphatically and, looking thoughtful, added, "I cannot help but wonder how you would look in different, more elegant clothes, Nicky. You would look older, yes? More sophisticated, more—"

Nicky laughed. "Carlo," she said, linking her arm through his, "the word *sophisticated* isn't even in my vocabulary."

The boat was sleek and fast. When they left the canal and headed out toward open water, the wind blew Nicky's hair about her face in a flyaway tangle. The sun and the wind and the taste of salt spray on her lips made her feel clean and fresh and wonderful. After all those days in the hospital, days when she hadn't been sure she would ever see sunlight again, this was glorious proof that she was alive.

She turned to Carlo, wanting to tell him how she felt, but when she looked at him the words died on her lips. He was watching her, and his pale green eyes were narrowed with an intensity of passion, a look of such hunger, such desire, that for a moment she could not breathe.

Before she knew what he was going to do, he took handfuls of her hair and pulled the locks back away from her face. She felt the pressure of his fingers splayed against her scalp and knew a moment of fear. He held her like that, his eyes narrowed almost to slits, studying her every feature. Then he kissed her and his mouth was hard against hers. When he let her go, a shudder ran through his body and he turned away.

They spoke very little after that. Nicky looked out her side of the boat at the sun-crested waves, feeling uneasy, a little frightened. Why had Carlo looked at her that way? Looked as though he were trying to find the answer to a puzzling question. Why?

They passed small islands and remote fishing villages. Gulls and frigate birds flew high against the azure sky as they drew closer to the Island of Burano. Small boats bobbed against the dock there. Pink-and-white houses dotted the hillside.

Carlo told the boatman to wait. "We will only be here a little while," he said, and taking Nicky's arm, led her ashore.

Still uneasy, she moved a little away. But he spoke casually, telling her about the island and the people who lived here. When they entered a shop to watch the women work their intricate patterns, he asked one of them to explain the process. And when she had finished, he asked that they be shown the things that were for sale.

The woman brought out beautiful tableclothes and matching napkins, lace collars, doilies and mantillas.

Carlo picked up a pale blue mantilla, cobweb fine, as softly delicate as the petals of a newly opened rose. He held it to Nicky's face. "Yes," he murmured. "We will take it."

And again his eyes held that same questioning look she had seen on the boat.

He draped the mantilla over her hair and around her shoulders. "It matches your eyes," he said before he turned back to the woman selling the mantillas. "We'll also want a black one. Something to wear for evening with a fine black dress."

"I don't have a fine black dress," Nicky said. "And you can't keep giving me gifts."

He put a finger against her lips. "I have only just begun," he said.

She honestly didn't understand his interest in her. He was sophisticated, obviously well off, a man of a world far different from hers. This afternoon he wore expensive tailored slacks and an even more expensive jacket over a silk shirt. Italian casual. And here she was in a jean miniskirt and a T-shirt. Florida casual.

"Can't you see?" she wanted to say to him. "Can't you see that we have nothing in common? That I'm not at all the type of woman you should be interested in?"

He took her hand and they went back out into the sunlight and down to the boat, and in a little while they reached Torcello.

They walked along the sloping canal bank to the church that he said was the oldest in Venice, and when they had looked at it, they went farther on, through a garden of flowering blooms to a vine-trellised inn.

"The food here is among the best in Venice," Carlo told her. "There are no menus. We will leave it up to the waiter. Would you like wine?"

"Yes, please."

"A Soave to start, I think. Then we shall see."

There were a few other couples and several families in the pleasant dining room. A white-jacketed waiter led them to a table overlooking the water.

"Today we have shellfish cocktail in brandy," he said when they were seated. "Then cappelletti." He looked at Nicky over his wire-rimmed half glasses. "This is pasta stuffed with spinach and walnuts and a bit of magic, *signorina*. You will like. Also there is fresh asparagus and roast duck. Yes?"

"Yes," Carlo said. "And red wine with the duck."

"That seems like a lot of food," Nicky said doubtfully.

"You lost a lot of weight in the hospital." The suggestion of a smile quirked his lips. "I must fatten you up."

For what? she wondered, but did not ask.

The waiter brought the wine. He poured a bit in Carlo's glass. Carlo tasted it, nodded, and the waiter filled Nicky's glass.

Carlo lifted his glass and touched it to hers. "There are things you should know about me," he said when he settled back in his chair. "I told you I had been married and that my wife died two years ago."

"Yes, I'm sorry. How long had you been married?"

"Four years."

"There were no children?"

"Isabella was not ready for children." He toyed with the stem of his wineglass. "She was very beautiful, you see. Very proud of her figure. Perhaps in time..."

He shook his head as though shaking away the memory of a time long past.

"I live in Tuscany," he went on. "Not quite an hour's drive from Florence. My grandmother lives with me. Her name is Elizabetta and she is eighty-five. I think you will like her."

Nicky raised an eyebrow but didn't speak.

"The house—the Casa Santini—belonged to my father's family. It's very old, sixteenth century. There are thirty-six rooms, all of them big and almost impossible to heat in the winter. There is a garden that my grandmother, with the help of a gardener who is almost as old as she is, attends to. And there is a maze."

"A maze?" Nicky asked.

"A confusing labyrinth of tall hedged pathways, something like a huge puzzle you must try to find your way out of. I used to play there sometimes with cousins who came to visit. We would chase each other up and down the rows, separated by the green walls of the hedges, shouting back and forth to one another. Once when I was five or six I went into the maze alone. I couldn't find my way out and I became so terrified I began to run up and down, screaming for my mother and father. I could hear Luigi, the gardener, and my parents calling out to me, but I couldn't find them.'' He shook his head. ''It was the most terrifying experience of my childhood.''

Nicky watched him as he talked, and in her mind's eye she tried to see the child he had been, the little boy lost in a confusing labyrinth of tall green shrubs, trapped, unable to escape. As he spoke she could see a vulnerability she had not been aware of before, something in his eyes, the faint remembrance of terrors past. And suddenly she wanted to touch him, to reach across the table and tell him she understood how afraid he must have been. ''It's all right to be afraid,'' she wanted to say. ''It's nothing to be ashamed of.''

Instead she said, ''And the maze is still there?''

''Of course. It is part of a three-hundred-year-old tradition.'' He paused when the waiter approached with the seafood cocktail, and when they had been served he said, ''Tuscany is especially beautiful in the spring, Nicolina. I would like very much to show it to you. And my home, of course. I am most anxious for you to see it.''

''Carlo. . .'' Nicky held her hand up, stopping him. ''This is going too fast. I don't—''

''Florence is the most beautiful of cities,'' he went on, as though he had not heard her. ''There are hundreds of things there I must show you, works of art such as you will see nowhere else in the world.''

Nicky shook her head as though trying to clear it. ''But I'm going home,'' she said. ''Back to the States.''

A frown furrowed his brow. "I don't understand. You said you were going to spend a year in Europe."

"I was, but I hadn't counted on getting ill. By the time I pay for the hospital and the pensione, I'll be broke. I don't have any choice— I have to go back."

He lifted his wineglass and drank from it without taking his eyes from hers. "I realize this may be difficult for you to understand, but once in a rare while something very special happens between a man and a woman. You cannot rationalize or explain it—when it happens you must simply accept it." He reached across the table and covered her hand with his. "You've become important to me these past few days," he said. "I don't want to lose you."

"But we barely know each other. You've been wonderful to me, Carlo, both in the hospital and now, as a doctor and as a friend. I appreciate it—"

"It isn't your appreciation I want."

"Then what do you want?" Her eyes met his. She shook her head. "I don't understand."

"Don't you?" He smiled, and in a voice so low she could barely hear, he said, "It's very simple, Signorina Nicky. I want you."

Her eyes widened. Her mouth went dry. She couldn't speak.

The waiter brought their pasta.

Carlo said, "Try it, my dear. In my opinion it's the best in Italy. However, there is a restaurant in Florence that makes a cappelletti that is also good. I will take you there and you will decide for yourself which is the best."

She had a sudden urge to jump up and shout, "Wait just a darn minute! I'm not going to Florence or anywhere else with you. I'm going home...." Back to her ho-hum job in the department store. Back home where she belonged.

But before she could say anything, Carlo began to talk about his medical practice. His office was in Florence, he said, and he was on the staff of a hospital there.

"I should have been back two weeks ago," he told her. "But I have an assistant, a capable young man who is an excellent cardiologist. You will meet him when we go."

He went on, speaking as though it were a fait accompli that she would accompany him to Florence and on to his home. She could barely eat her dinner. She sipped the white wine, then the red. She nibbled at the duck and declined dessert. She felt as though she were in a dream and that any minute she would awaken.

It was dark when they left the restaurant. Carlo took her arm, and she felt a shiver that had nothing to do with the cold. When they reached the water taxi that had been waiting for them, he put the blue coat over her shoulders.

"You must wear the mantilla," he said. "To keep your hair in place." He draped it over her hair and stood back and looked at her before he nodded and helped her aboard.

She settled into the padded seat at the back of the boat. Carlo sat next to her and put an arm around her shoulders. "Rest if you're tired," he said as the boat moved away from the mooring. "The trip back will take at least an hour."

"I'm not tired."

He put a finger under her chin and lifted her face to his. "But you are upset, yes? Because I do not want you to go. And you are thinking, who is this man? I barely know him! Why is he saying these things to me?"

"Why are you?" Nicky asked. "I don't understand, Carlo."

"I'm not entirely sure I do either, Nicky. I only know that I don't want to let you go...." He wrapped his arms around her and brought her close. "I want you to stay with me, to be with me."

She stiffened, cautious and afraid. But he only held her, and in a little while her body relaxed against his. When it did, he tilted her face to his and kissed her.

His lips were cool with the flavor of salt spray, and though she had told herself she should not kiss him, her lips parted under his.

The kiss deepened and grew. They scarcely breathed, so lost were they in the sensation of mouth on mouth. He drank from her lips like a man too long without sustenance. His tongue was hot and moist, and when it touched hers she moaned low in her throat. And told herself she must not do this, that she should pull away from him. I will, she thought. In a moment I will.

His mouth tasted of the sea.

A moment more.

Once she made as though to move away, but he wouldn't stop kissing her. He kissed her eyelids, her cheeks, her nose, kissed her as though he would never let her go.

She felt his power, and the strength of the arms that were a haven in the darkness of the night. He held her against his chest and she smelled the good man smell of him, soap and warmth and musk that seemed a scent peculiarly his. Then she was lost in the mouth that devoured her mouth, in the tongue that so sweetly dueled with hers.

Hot hands reached inside the blue coat and under her shirt. He cupped her breasts and whispered soft Italian words. She tried to move away, but he held her there, held her as though this was his right, as though she belonged to him.

"Oh, please," she said. "We shouldn't. I can't—"

"Yes, you can," he murmured against her lips. "You can do anything with me. Everything with me."

She felt the sting of the spray on her face and the thump of the waves beneath the boat. She had the fleeting thought that if the boatman turned he would see them. But it didn't matter. Nothing mattered except the press of Carlo's mouth on hers. She was drowning in his kisses, lost in the sensation of his hot hands caressing her breasts.

Boats sped past, rocking their own, rocking them together so that their bodies pressed closer. The lights of Venice loomed on the horizon, and still they kissed a thousand kisses.

The boat entered the Grand Canal and slowed. Carlo held her a little away from him. Very gently, as though in farewell, he stroked her breasts one more time, then, holding her a prisoner with his eyes, he raked his nails over the aching tips.

Flame like a stinging current of electric shock zinged through her. She started to cry out, and brought a hand up to cover her mouth.

"Carissima," he murmured, then he pulled her shirt down and brought the blue coat back once more over her shoulders.

"Now do you understand?" he asked. "This is how we are destined to be, Nicolina. It is inevitable, my dear."

The boat bumped the dock. Carlo put his hands on her shoulders and helped her up. She waited as though in a daze while he paid for the taxi. Then he put an arm around her waist and together they walked up the steps to the pensione.

"Domani," he said. "Yes?"

She took a shaking breath. "Yes," she whispered. "Yes."

"For lunch. I will come at two." He lifted her face to his and kissed her. She rested her hands against his chest, holding on to him as though if she did not she would surely fall.

He took her hands. She felt the moistness of his tongue against her palm. "Go now," he said, "quickly, before I change my mind."

The tremor of a sigh ran through her body.

"Do not sigh and do not look at me like that. Because if you do..." He took her shoulders and gave her a gentle push. *"Buona sera,* my Nicolina. Go now."

She did as he asked, but when she had opened the door, she looked back at him, a tall, silent figure there in the darkness. *"Buona sera,"* she whispered.

The next morning Nicky went back to the American Express office. There was another check. She cashed it, and when she went out she walked back toward the pensione instead of taking a vaporetto.

She took her time, looking in shop windows, and when she passed a small boutique she paused in front of it. There was a white dress in the window, stylish and chic, with deceptively simple lines. She knew she shouldn't spend the money, but oh, how much she wanted to look nice for Carlo today. She didn't want to wear her miniskirt or jeans. She wanted to dress up for him.

She bought the dress, a pair of white pumps, a white purse and silk stockings. And when she paid she asked the salesperson, a handsome woman in her forties, if she could recommend a place where she might get her hair done. The woman gave her directions to a salon a few blocks away. An operator was available. She gave Nicky a shampoo, then blow-dried her hair and brushed it so that it curled about her face and over her shoulders.

And the whole time, with the shopping and in the hair salon, all that Nicky could think of was that in a few hours she would see Carlo again.

She wasn't sure how it had happened. She had heard of patients who fell in love with their doctors, and she supposed it was natural that when you were ill and vulnerable you wanted to cling to the person into whose hands you had placed your life. But she didn't think that was it. She wasn't sure whether or not she had fallen in love with Carlo Santini, but she had surely fallen into something.

No one had ever kissed her the way he had kissed her, or made her feel what he made her feel. He had overwhelmed her, dizzied her with his kisses, sent her senses reeling with his stroking touch.

But why? That's what she couldn't understand. Why had he chosen her? She wasn't a raving beauty. Her figure was good but not spectacular. She had good teeth and nice legs, but her breasts were too small and her fanny was too rounded. God knows she wasn't a fashion plate. If Eleanora couldn't get her to dress up, nobody could.

But she'd bought the white dress and high-heeled shoes and she'd gone to a beauty salon, something she hadn't done since high-school graduation. Because she had wanted to please Carlo. Because the thought of seeing him again warmed and excited her.

He arrived at the pensione at ten minutes before two. Bianca came to knock at her door. "*Il dottor* is here," she announced, breathless from climbing the stairs. "He is waiting."

"*Momento.*" Nicky held her thumb and index finger half an inch apart. "Tell him *uno momento.*"

She looked in the mirror, turning so she could study the dress, the silk stockings and the white pumps. She looked okay. No, better than okay. She had put on a bit of eye shadow and a thin trace of eyeliner, but it wasn't the eyeliner that made her eyes shine, it was because of him. Because of Carlo.

He was at the bottom of the stairs waiting for her. He looked up when he heard her and said, "*Buon giorno,* Nicolina." His eyes widened.

"*Buon giorno,* Carlo." She smoothed her hands over the skirt of her dress, suddenly shy.

"You're wearing a dress," he said, surprised.

"Yes, I—I bought it this morning."

"You look *multo bella.*" He reached for her hand and brought it to his lips. "*Bellissima,*" he said.

The restaurant he took her to was an elegant outdoor café on the Grand Canal. As he had the night before, he ordered wine. When it came he spoke of ordinary things: the changing weather and the traffic that moved up and down the canal.

It was not until they had almost finished lunch that he said, "I had a call from my office this morning. I have to return to Florence sooner than I expected because a patient of mine has become quite ill. Dr. Tacchia, my assistant, has been taking care of him in my absence, but now he feels that surgery is necessary."

"I'm sorry." Nicky looked at him, then lowered her eyes. "Sorry that you're leaving, I mean."

"Nicolina..." He took a sip of his wine. "There is something I must say to you. I had planned to wait, to give you a little more time to be sure of how you felt, but now there is no more time." He reached across the table and took her hand. "I want you to come home with me," he said.

"Carlo, I—I can't. I know this sounds old-fashioned, but I'm not the kind of woman who just goes off with a man. I'm not ready for an affair. I don't want—"

"I'm not asking you to have an affair. I'm asking you to marry me."

"Marry..." The breath caught in her throat. She couldn't speak. She could only look at him, her eyes wide with shock.

"This morning I spoke to someone at the registrar's office. We can go there now and apply for the marriage license and have the blood test. A judge I know has agreed to perform the ceremony. We will have a church wedding later but for now—"

"Wait—wait a minute! This is too fast. I can't. We can't—"

"Of course we can." He leaned across the table, his eyes intent on hers. "I will take care of you, Nicolina. You'll never want for anything. All I ask is that you be with me, stay with me, because I know that this is right. Finding you was a miracle. I will never let you go."

She felt as though the world was spinning round and round and that if she didn't hang onto his hand she would surely spin away.

"Say yes, *carissima*."

She looked into his eyes, eyes that willed her to respond. She bit down on her bottom lip.

"It will be good between us."

"We barely know each other."

"We know enough." He reached out to stroke her cheek. "Say yes," he said again.

She was trapped by his gaze, held by the fingers that stroked her cheek. "I . . ." She fought to control her emotions. "I have to think," she whispered. "I—I can't . . . it's too sudden."

"But I will only be in Venice for a few more days," he said in a reasonable voice. "When I leave I want you to come with me."

"Marriage . . ." She had to take a steadying breath. "Marriage is forever. I need time."

His eyes narrowed; his nostrils flared. She saw the searing heat of his eyes, the shadows that lay not quite hidden behind the green depths. Then, as though with an effort, his gaze softened. "I know this has come as a shock to you. I see that now." He reached for her hand and gently squeezed it. "We will talk tomorrow," he said. *"Domani."*

Nicky couldn't sleep. Every time she closed her eyes she saw his face. She touched the lips that he had kissed and felt the hot, sweet sting of desire surge through her. She thought of how it had been last night coming back from Torcello, of the smell of the sea and the taste of his mouth. She remembered the touch of his hand on her breast, and the sting of regret when he let her go.

She thought of how it would be when she said good-bye to him, and felt herself grow cold with the fear that if she refused him, she would never see him again.

Is this what love is? she wondered. This confusion, this longing and desire for a touch unlike any other touch? A kiss that is like no other's kiss?

"Carlo," her heart cried. "Carlo."

He came the next morning while she was having breakfast in the sunlit patio. He stood in the shade of a blossoming lemon tree and said her name, "Nicky?" When she looked at him, she saw an expression on his face she had never seen before, a look of uncertainty and doubt. And of something more, the same need and the vulnerability she had seen when he'd told her about being lost in the maze when he was a little boy.

She pushed her chair back and went to him. "If you still ..." She had to stop for a moment because her heart was beating so hard it was difficult for her to speak. She stood in front of him, arms at her sides. "If you still want me ..." She shook her head, unable to go on.

Relief softened his features. "Nicky," he murmured. "Oh, Nicky."

Then she was in his arms, and it was for her a sense of coming home and of a belonging she had never known before.

He rained kisses over her face. He kissed her mouth and held her as though he would never let her go.

"It will be good between us." He pressed her close and his arms were strong and sure. "I'll never let you go," he said against her lips. "You're mine now. Forever mine."

They went to the registrar's office. She gave her mother's name and her father's name. She showed her passport, and raised her hand to swear she had never been married before. A man put a legal-looking paper in front of her and she signed it.

They went into another office and a doctor took a sample of her blood. "The test results will be ready in three days," he said.

Carlo took her arm and they went back out into the sunlight.

When they passed a jewelry store, he said, "Come, I want to buy you an engagement present."

The jeweler, a portly man with a fringe of silver hair around his otherwise bald pate, looked up when they entered. He'd been inspecting a diamond ring and the loupe was still attached to one eye.

"Dr. Santini!" he said. "How good it is to see you again. It has been a long time, no?"

"Indeed it has. I'm here to buy a gift for a lady, Signor Veroni. A necklace, perhaps, or earrings."

"But of course, Doctor." The jeweler smiled at Nicky. Then his smile faded and his face blanched. His eyes went wide and the loupe fell to the floor with a crash. *"Signora!"* he gasped. "I thought...I thought you were—"

"This is the Signorina Fairchild from the United States," Carlo said quickly. "We are looking for a present for her."

"Signorina..." Signor Veroni could say nothing else. He stooped to pick up the loupe, checked to see if it was broken, then wiped it with the handkerchief he took from his pocket. "What—what would you like to see?" he asked.

"Something in gold," Carlo said.

The jeweler took several velvet-lined trays out of a locked glass case and laid them on the counter.

"The necklace," Carlo said. "The one with the small gold coins." He picked it up and held it against Nicky's throat. "Yes," he said, "we'll take this."

"There are earrings that match." The jeweler glanced at Nicky, then looked quickly away.

"Let me see them."

Signor Veroni held them up. Carlo took them and handed them to Nicky. "Put them on," he said. "They'll go well with your dress."

The jeweler held a mirror. Nicky put the earrings on. Carlo picked up the necklace and fastened it around her throat. The coins shimmered on a fine filigree chain; the gold was cool against her skin. With his hands on her shoulders he said, "It's perfect, isn't it?"

Perfect, yes. But he hadn't asked her if she liked it or the earrings. He had simply selected what *he* liked.

He paid the jeweler with a check. Though it was still difficult for her to translate lire to the dollar, she managed to figure out that the necklace and the earrings had come to over three thousand dollars. They were a splendid gift. And yet...

And yet what? Nicky asked herself when they left the shop. Carlo had wonderful taste, and very likely he'd thought she might be shy about picking out something that was so expensive. That's why he had selected the necklace and earrings without asking her.

She thought then about the strange behavior of the jeweler when he had first seen her. Had he mistaken her for someone else? Another woman Carlo had bought jewelry for?

"You'll need money for a dress for the wedding," Carlo said.

"I have enough. You still haven't let me repay what I owe you."

"Nor will I. Whatever I have is yours now. Remember that." He put her arm through his. "I'm sorry we won't be able to have much of a honeymoon, but we can spend a day or two in Siena. Later, when I can take some time off, we'll have a real honeymoon. In Greece, perhaps. You'll like Greece."

Too fast, she thought. This is all happening too fast. She was on a merry-go-round and she couldn't get off. She wasn't sure she wanted to get off.

He took her back to the pensione. He told her to rest before they went out to dinner that night. "You must ask Signora Brendisi to help you find a dress and a suitable traveling suit," he said, and pressed a handful of lire into her hand. "You really cannot go around in blue jeans now."

When he left, Nicky looked down at the lire. And knew that her life would never be the same again.

CHAPTER FOUR

The wedding was held three days later in the garden of the Pensione Villa Lucia. A judge in a pin-striped suit performed the ceremony. Dr. Raviggia and Signora Brendisi were the witnesses.

None of it seemed real to Nicky... her dress with the pale pink brocade jacket over a swirl of pink chiffon. The gold coin necklace, the earrings, high-heeled shoes. Her bridal bouquet of pink camellias and lavender violets. The stranger standing next to her.

She listened to the words spoken in Italian with a crazy what-am-I-doing-here feeling. Her stomach fluttered; her throat went dry.

Carlo took her hand. He slipped a wide gold band onto her finger. He said, *"Sposa mia."*

Nicky looked up at him with a shy smile. Then the smile faltered, for in his eyes there was a look not of love or of passion, but of triumph.

Signora Brendisi embraced her. Dr. Raviggia shook Carlo's hand. Bianca wiped her eyes and blew her nose.

They went to the restaurant overlooking the Piazza San Marco where Carlo had taken her that first night. Dr. Raviggia ordered champagne. The judge offered a toast. Carlo touched his glass to Nicky's and kissed her cheek.

He was a gracious host. He smiled when Bianca drank too much wine. He talked about medicine with Dr. Raviggia, about politics with the judge.

Signora Brendisi said, "I will miss you, Signorina Nicky."

"And I'll miss you. You've been very kind to me, *signora.*"

"Francesca, yes?" She squeezed Nicky's hand. "I wish you much happiness, my dear. Dr. Santini is a fine man. I know you will be happy."

The food was delicious, but Nicky barely touched it. When they finished their coffee and after-dinner drinks, the judge looked at his watch and announced that he had to get back to his office. Dr. Raviggia said he needed to check in at the hospital.

"I'll take the ladies back to the pensione," Carlo said. He took Nicky's arm. "Are you ready, Signora Santini?"

Signora Santini. No longer Nicky Fairchild, she was Signora Santini now. Carlo's wife.

She looked up at him, wanting an answering look that said he loved and cared about her. An intimate look that told of remembered kisses and of bliss yet to come. Instead she saw only cool formality.

They took a gondola back to the pensione. When Carlo escorted the three women to the door, he said to Nicky, "I've made reservations for tonight at the Gritti Palace. Tomorrow we'll go to Siena. Why don't you rest for a bit? I'll return for you at seven." He kissed her cheek. His lips were cold.

After he left, she went upstairs. She took off the pale pink dress, lay down on the bed and looked up at the high ceiling. "Carlo?" she whispered, and felt a chill that was as cold as his lips had been.

It was a splendid room. The walls were pale yellow, the gossamer curtains and the drapes a deep golden shade.

The carpeting was soft and thick and white. There was an apricot brocade chaise longue near the windows, a small table and two chairs. A dresser and a four-poster bed.

There were two bathrooms; a dressing room opened off one of them. That's where Carlo had put the new suitcase that held Nicky's new clothes.

"I'll use the other bathroom," he said. "There's no need to dress for dinner. We'll have a light supper here in the room."

"That would be nice." Nicky twisted one of the buttons on her new gray suit.

"And champagne." He frowned. "Don't do that," he said. "You'll wrinkle the jacket."

She curled her toes inside her new gray pumps.

"Look," he said. "It's been a busy day and we're both tired. Why don't you have a bath and change into your... into something more comfortable."

"Yes, all right. I won't be long." She went over to the dresser, where she laid down her bridal bouquet, then turned uncertainly and looked at him.

He went to her and put his arms around her. "It's going to be all right, Nicky. Between us, I mean. I'll be good to you. I'll give you anything you want."

"I want your love," she almost said. "I want your caring, because I've had so very little of it in my life."

"Maybe I should call Eleanora. My mother."

"Yes, of course. I should have thought of it myself. If you have the number in Brazil, I'll have the hotel operator place the call."

"It will be horribly expensive."

"But I'm horribly rich." He smiled, for the first time that day. "Go and take your bath," he said. "You can take the call in the bathroom."

Nicky nodded and some of the tension eased. "I won't be long," she said.

"There's no hurry. I'll place your call, then order dinner. Cold lobster and a salad, yes?"

"It sounds wonderful." She took a deep breath. "I'll be back soon."

She ran a bath while she undressed. There was a phone next to the tub, and a tray filled with perfumed soaps and bottles of perfumed oil. She selected a scent and poured it in, and when she had pinned her hair up, eased herself into the hot water.

The words of a song, "Sadie, Sadie, married lady," ran round and round in her brain. That's what she was now, a married lady. Married to an older man, a doctor who very likely traveled in a social circle she knew absolutely nothing about. The days of blue jeans and T-shirts were over. No more backpacks and sandwiches at stand-up counters. No more barefoot walks along a beach at sunset, or pastrami on rye with a pickle on the side. That part of her life had finished. Her home was in Italy with Carlo. Tonight she would sleep in the same bed with him and they would make love.... She took a deep breath. What would it be like with him? Would he be a tender lover? Would he...?

The phone rang. She picked it up and her mother said, "Nicky? Nicky, is that you?"

"Yes, Mother. How are you?"

"I'm fine, but why are you calling? Is something wrong?"

"No, nothing's wrong."

"Where are you?"

"I'm in a bathtub in the Gritti Palace in Venice."

"In Venice? But I thought you'd be in Spain by now. At the Gritti Palace? Did you say the Gritti Palace? But that's expensive, Nicky! You don't have that kind of money. What are you—''

"I'm married, Eleanora. I was married this afternoon."

"—doing in a place like that? What...?" Eleanora Winston Avery Fairchild Westerly Seabrook Diaz-Enfante gasped. "Married!" she shrieked. "You're married? To whom?"

"His name is Carlo Santini. Dr. Carlo Santini."

"He's a doctor?"

"Uh-huh." For the first time today Nicky was actually enjoying herself.

"But—but... How long have you known him?"

"Almost a month."

"A month! My God!"

"You only knew your new husband for two weeks."

"That's different. I'm more mature than you are. I've had more experience."

"Being married five times will do that."

"Really, Nicolina!" Eleanora sounded outraged. Then, in a change of tone, she asked, "Where will you live?"

"Carlo has a home near Florence. Sixteenth century. With thirty-six rooms. I'll send you the address as soon as I know what it is."

"Well, I—I simply don't know what to say. You have my best wishes, of course, but I really wish you had talked to me about this first. You hardly know this Dr...."

"Santini," Nicky said. Then, "Look, Eleanora, this is terribly expensive. I'll write you as soon as I'm settled."

"Yes, well, all right. I suppose I should offer my congratulations."

"That would be nice."

"You have them, of course."

"Thank you, Mother."

Nicky lay back in the tub, smiling because she'd knocked Eleanora's socks off. Then she heard the outer door open, and voices. Dinner had arrived. She had to get out of the tub. She looked at the white nightgown and peignoir hanging on the back of the dressing-room door. Her stomach fluttered and she felt as though she had a lump the side of a golf ball in her throat.

"Be calm," she told herself. "It will be all right."

She got up out of the tub, and when she had dried herself, she put on the white nightgown and the white lace peignoir. She brushed her hair and touched lipstick to her lips. And taking a deep breath, went to Carlo.

He was standing in front of the floor-to-ceiling windows that overlooked the Grand Canal. He wore a long velour robe.

Black, she thought. Of course.

The champagne was open and cooling in a silver bucket. He filled two fluted crystal glasses and handed one to Nicky. "To my bride," he said. "You look very beautiful, Nicky."

"Thank you, Carlo." She took a sip of her champagne. "It's a pretty room," she said.

"Yes." But he wasn't looking at the room, he was looking at her. Her peignoir was elegant, of simple lines, lace-ruffled with an off-the-shoulder neckline and a long sweeping skirt that opened to show the sheerness of the gown beneath. Her shoulders were pale. He saw the outline of her small breasts, but his expression did not change. "You spoke to your mother?" he asked.

"Yes."

"What did she say when you told her you were married?"

"First she shrieked. Then she wanted to know who you were and how long I'd known you."

"I can understand her concern." He looked at Nicky over the rim of his glass. "You may invite her to visit if you wish."

May? He was giving her his permission to have her mother visit? Troubled now, as well as more nervous than she'd ever been in her life, Nicky walked to the windows and looked out. The night was mauve, cloudy, starless. Streetlights from the three-cornered stanchions reflected on the water and she could see the gondolas floating like silent swans. One of the gondoliers began to sing and the melancholy of the song brought unexpected tears to her eyes. How many couples over how many years had floated up and down the canal? How many loves had been lost? How many dreams had faded?

Carlo put his hands on her shoulders. "It's beautiful, isn't it?"

"Beautiful and sad," she said.

"Sad?" He turned her to face him. "But Venice isn't sad. It's a city filled with life, Nicky."

That's how she'd first seen it. But now... She looked up at Carlo, looked for reassurance that everything between them was as it should be. He loved her. Surely he loved her. Why else would he have married her?

The cold lobster was delicious; the salad was crisp. She sipped her champagne while Carlo talked about Siena.

"It's one of the most beautiful places in Italy," he said. "A town already steeped in language and art and commerce in the thirteen hundreds. It has charming narrow, crooked streets, a beautiful central piazza and a quite wonderful cathedral."

She pretended to be interested. And in a way she was, but there were other things she wanted to talk about: their life together, how it would be when they came to his home. What his grandmother was like.

She wanted him to kiss her like he had kissed her that night coming back from Torcello. She wanted to feel the way she had then. She wanted him to say something, to do something that would ease the cold knot of fear in the pit of her stomach.

Carlo poured more champagne for her and for himself. She took small sips. He drank two glasses. And when they had finished with the champagne and the dinner, he phoned for a waiter, and someone came to wheel away the dining table.

"It's getting late," he said. "We had better get some rest if we want to get an early start in the morning."

Nicky nodded, but the knot of fear was in her throat now and she couldn't speak.

He took her hands in his. "Come," he said. "It's time for bed."

She stood before him while he unfastened the peignoir and slipped it from her shoulders. "You really are very beautiful," he said.

Her heart beat hard against her ribs. She wanted him to kiss her, to hold her and tell her that he was glad they were married.

He caressed her shoulders and she shivered. "What is it?" he asked. "You are nervous, yes?"

"Yes." She tried to smile. "A little."

"But why? We are husband and wife. There is nothing to be nervous about."

"You haven't told me..." Nicky shook her head, afraid to ask what she so desperately wanted to ask.

Then, gathering her courage, she said, "Why did you marry me, Carlo?"

He smiled. "Why do you think, Nicolina?" He stroked the hair back from her face. "Because we are so good together. Because when I kiss you I can forget."

"Forget?"

"Unpleasant things." He cupped the back of her head and brought her close. "I can get lost in your kisses," he said. "I can drown in your mouth."

"Carlo, I—"

"Shh," he whispered. He kissed her and it was as it had been. He drank from her lips, tasting her as he would taste spring wine, supping from her mouth while his arms tightened around her and a sigh shuddered through him. He cupped her breasts through the silky sheerness of her gown, and when she murmured against his lips, he picked her up and carried her to the bed.

"Wait," Nicky said. "I—"

But Carlo didn't wait. He tore at the sash of his robe and she saw that he wore nothing beneath it. He threw it aside and stood naked before her. But only for a moment. Then he was kneeling beside her, tugging at her gown. She heard something rip and he said, "Lift your arms." And when she did he pulled it over her head.

"Carlo," she said. "There's something I—"

He stopped her words with a smothering kiss.

"Please . . ." she tried to say.

He came up over her and covered her with his body. She felt the hard man length of him against her thigh. She was pinned by his body, unable to move.

"I've waited so long," he said against her lips. "But no longer. No longer."

He gripped her hips.

She said, "Carlo, wait, I—"

He thrust himself into her and she cried out with the abruptness of it, cried with shock and pain.

He froze. "My God! Why didn't you tell me?" His body quivered with barely restrained passion. "You should have!" And in a voice so low she could barely hear, he whispered, "What have I done? *Ay, Dio,* what have I done?" Then a shudder ran through him, and with a low cry he began to move against her like a man possessed.

He plunged hard and his big body shook with an emotion he could not control. Like a conquering warrior he battered against her tender walls, ravaging, plundering, making her his with the dark fury of his movements.

"Put your arms around me," he cried. And when she did he thrust hard against her. "Like that. Yes! Because you're mine. Forever mine."

He took her mouth and kissed her with a fierceness that hurt and bruised. He raised his head and looked down at her, his eyes narrowed with a passion that threatened to consume him. His lips were drawn back, the cords of his neck taut as bow strings. He thrust himself against her again and again, then suddenly he cried out, a primitive cry that seemed to come from the very depths of his soul.

She didn't move.

His heart beat like a wild thing against her breast and his breath came in strangled gasps. When his breathing evened, he rolled away from her and said, "I'm sorry. I didn't mean it to be that way."

And when she did not answer, he said, "You should have told me you were a virgin." He raised up on one elbow and looked down at her. "I thought all American girls—"

"Not all," she said.

"I didn't mean to hurt you." He kissed the lips that he had bruised. "I'll make it up to you. The next time it will be different."

The next time. Her body felt bruised. Unloved. That was the worst of all, for she knew now that Carlo did not love her. He had married her because he had wanted this from her. He had taken her, not with love but as a man conquering an enemy.

Without a word she got up and went into the bathroom to bathe, and when she came back into the room once more, she put the nightgown on and slipped into bed beside him. When he made as though to gather her in his arms, she stiffened.

"I'm very tired," she said, and turned away from him.

Through the open window she could hear the slap of waves from passing boats, and as though from a distance the song of a gondolier. "O Sole Mio," he sang.

Nicky drew her knees up to her chest and squeezed her eyes shut. And knew that never, ever, had she felt as alone as she did now.

When she opened her eyes the next morning, Carlo was not with her. She pushed herself up on her pillows and looked around the room. It was a beautiful room, filled with sunlight now. She saw the white peignoir folded over a cushioned chair. And her bridal bouquet, faded and withered on the dresser.

She turned away from it, wanting to block out the memory of the day before, and of the night. She did not know where Carlo was and for the moment she did not care. She threw back the satin sheet, anxious to dress and bathe before he returned, and saw the note he had left on his pillow.

It read, "I'm going out for a little while. I've ordered your breakfast to be delivered at nine."

The clock on the bedside table read eight-thirty.

She hurried into the bathroom and drew her bath, and when the tub was full she eased herself into it, wincing when the hot water touched her body. What should have been the happiest night of her life had been a nightmare. If it happened again... She thought of his words: *You're mine. Forever mine.*

In spite of the hot water, a chill quivered through her. She had fallen in love with Carlo, and though he had not said the words, she had thought he was in love with her. Why else would he have wanted to marry her?

She tried to tell herself that it would get better. Now that "the deed" was done, it would be fine. Carlo would be more patient. They had only just begun. They had their whole lives ahead of them. It would be easier the next time.

She stepped out of the tub and dressed in the suit she had worn the day before. As soon as she went out into the room, a waiter knocked and brought her breakfast in: strawberries with cream, hot chocolate and buttery-soft croissants. She ate by the windows overlooking the water, and had just finished the last of her chocolate when she heard the door open.

"Buon giorno," Carlo said.

"Buon—buon giorno."

"Your breakfast arrived on time?"

"Yes, thank you."

"You were sleeping when I left. I didn't want to wake you."

"I found your note."

"Good." He crossed the room and, sitting in the chair across from her, took a small, tissue-wrapped package out of his breast pocket. "I've brought you a wedding present," he said.

Nicky put her cup down. "You didn't need to do that."

He handed it to her. "Open it."

Her fingers fumbled with the tissue. She opened the box and folded back more tissue. Diamond earrings winked up at her. She looked at them, then at Carlo. "They're very beautiful," she said. "Thank you."

"I'm glad you like them." He looked at his watch. "It's almost ten," he said. "If you're ready, we really should be going."

"I'm ready."

"We'll take a taxi to where I've left my car. With luck we'll be in Siena for a late lunch." He looked at her. "You are all right? Yes?"

Nicky nodded. "Yes, I'm all right."

"Then we will go."

He went in to get their suitcases. A bellman came to take them, and Carlo stood by the door, waiting.

Nicky looked at this room where they had spent their wedding night, and a feeling of such despair, such overwhelming sadness gripped her that for a moment she could not move.

"Come along," Carlo said.

And together they went out and closed the door behind them.

CHAPTER FIVE

The rolling hills of Tuscany were green with the promise of summer. Chestnut trees and dark patches of cypress added strength to the contours of the landscape. Vineyards flourished under a searing blue sky; old olive trees budded with new fruit.

They'd had little to say to each other since they had left Venice. Carlo looked straight ahead, capable hands on the steering wheel of the black Ferrari. His face in profile was serious, almost stern.

What was he thinking? Nicky wondered. Was he remembering last night, how inept she had been, how inexperienced? She had wanted so badly to please him, but she hadn't. He had taken her in anger, as though wanting to punish her. But for what? she asked herself. What have I done to displease him?

She had come into this marriage ready to give Carlo all of her love, for love was something to be given, not purchased with a gold necklace and diamond earrings. Was that what love meant to him? Something that could be bought and sold?

Troubled and unhappy, uncertain about the future, Nicky settled back against the fine leather seat and tried to enjoy the countryside, surely some of the most spectacular she had ever seen. They passed through small towns and villages with steepled churches and old stone houses. Farmers worked in newly sown spring fields.

Small boys tended herds of goats. Old women, dressed in black from head to toe, looked at them with curiosity as they passed.

It was a little before two when they arrived in Siena and found the villa in the hills where Carlo had made reservations. Their room was spacious and well appointed, with windows and a balcony that overlooked the town.

"We'll have lunch here," he said. "Then we can drive into town."

"All right."

"Nicolina..." He hesitated, his brow furrowed, his eyes troubled. "I know this is all very new to you—my country, the language." His mouth quirked in something that might have been a smile. "And me. You are feeling like a stranger, yes? But that will pass, you will adjust."

She looked at him, her eyes level, her expression serious. "Will I?"

A muscle in his cheek jumped. "Of course. Once we have settled into our life at Casa Santini, everything will be all right. Elizabetta isn't well, but we have maids so that the burden of caring for her will not be on your shoulders. You will have the whole day to do as you please. And I will return to you at night."

He put his hands on her shoulders. Her body stiffened. He reached out to cup her chin, and when she flinched, his mouth tightened and he let her go. "I'll wait for you downstairs," he said.

She closed her eyes when he shut the door behind him. The man she had married was a stranger, and she didn't know what to do about it.

They had lunch on a shaded patio. The cannelloni was delicious, the garden salad fresh. From inside the restaurant came the sweet, sad music of mandolins. They spoke to the waiter but not to each other, and Nicky was relieved when an American couple who had the table next to them began to chat. They were Mr. and Mrs. Adamson from Atlanta, the gray-haired woman said. Daddy had just retired, their children were married and this was their first trip abroad.

They were nice people, and Nicky enjoyed talking to them because they symbolized a bit of home. Several times Carlo looked at his watch, but it didn't matter. She wanted to hear her own language spoken, to learn the latest news from Washington, to laugh at American jokes again.

It was after four when Carlo finally said, "It's getting late, Nicolina. We must be going if we want to see anything of Siena." He pushed back his chair, and to the Adamsons said, "It's been nice meeting you."

They drove into town without speaking, but when they parked and he took her hand to help her out of the car, he kept hold of it. As they started down one of the narrow, crooked streets, he said, "Much of what was medieval survives today in Siena. Twice a year, in early July and mid-August the Palio festival is held. Everyone wears sixteenth-century costumes. There are blaring trumpets and banners, and a horse race through the center of town. It's a wonderfully colorful pageant, and if I can schedule it, we will come back in August."

If I'm still here, she thought.

Like a tour guide he showed her to the Palazzo Pubblico and the cathedral with its striped facade. She wished she were a tourist. Wished she could thank him at the end of the tour and go back to her hotel room alone.

When evening came they had a sandwich and a cappuccino at an outdoor café. A little after nine Carlo said, "You're tired. We should go back to the villa."

"No," she wanted to say, "I want to stay here. I want to sit in this quiet café in this quiet town. I don't want to go with you. I cannot bear another night like last night."

She picked up her purse and went with him back to the car. When they reached the hotel, she said, "I'm going to take a bath."

Carlo nodded. "It's been a long day and you're tired. A bath will help."

Nicky stayed in the tub until both she and the water grew cold. When at last she came out and dried herself, she stood in front of the mirror to brush her hair. Blue eyes that seemed almost too big for her face looked back at her. There were bruises on her waist, her hips and her thighs, and she turned away from the mirror so she wouldn't have to look at them. She took a pale blue nightgown out of her suitcase and put it on.

The only light in the room came from a small bedside lamp. Carlo was out on the balcony, and from the garden below, Nicky could hear music. She stood uncertainly, then, taking a deep breath, went to stand by the French doors.

He turned. "Come," he said, beckoning with his hand. "It's a beautiful night."

She stepped out onto the balcony. In the distance she could see the lights of Siena, the rolling hills, dark patches of trees. And in the sky the golden slice of a new moon.

"This is the soul of Tuscany," he murmured. "I hope some day you will love it as I do." He looked at her through the darkening night. "It's getting chilly," he said. "Let's go in."

Nicky clasped hold of the railing. He covered her hand with his. "Come," he said.

They went inside. He turned to look at her and, smiling, said, "I like your gown."

"The other one was torn."

He recoiled as though she had struck him. For a moment he didn't speak, then he said, "We've gotten off to a bad start and I'm sorry. I'll make it up to you."

With another pair of diamond earrings? she thought.

He kissed her. She didn't respond.

He hesitated, then he took her hand and led her to the padded rocking chair near the balcony doors. He sat down and, pulling her with him, settled her on his lap. Her body was stiff, unbending. "Let me up," she said.

"In a little while." He put a hand against the back of her head and brought it to rest on his shoulder. He stroked her hair and held her there, gently rocking. The night air was soft. From down below came the sound of the mandolins, and somewhere in the distance a church bell tolled.

Nicky shifted against him, her body resistant, but he would not let her go. He only stroked her hair and held her, and in a little while, though she had vowed she would not, her body began to relax against his. And when she did he kissed her.

For a moment she didn't respond, but he persisted, his mouth gentle on hers until finally her lips parted and the kiss became a tentative sampling of each other's mouths. He held back, not insisting, letting her give what she wanted to give.

They kissed for a long time, kissed until the kisses became deep and moist and hungry. After a little while he touched her breast through the silk of her gown, and for a moment the fear came again, fear that once he had touched her like this he would take her to the bed. And hurt her as he had last night.

But he only continued to kiss her and stroke her, and soon her body warmed, and without conscious thought she moved closer. He ran the tips of his fingers across the hardened peaks and gently squeezed. She murmured her pleasure, and he slipped the straps of her gown over her shoulders, and cupping a breast, bent down to kiss her there.

Warmth, like thick, rich syrup, trickled through Nicky's body. She kissed the top of his head and began to stroke his hair. If it could just be like this, she thought, just this holding and touching and kissing, just like this without the other part. The hurting part.

He sought her mouth again and kissed her with deep, slow kisses. Her arms crept up around his neck. She ran her fingers through the thick dark curl of his hair, stroking his skin as he stroked her breasts. She moved closer, but when he eased the blue gown up over her thighs, she stiffened.

"It's all right, *cara mia,*" he whispered. "Just let me touch you this way. I won't do anything you don't want me to do."

He soothed her to quietness. He caressed her legs, her inner thighs, and all the while he kissed her, kissed her until she was weak and pliant in his arms.

Time stood still. The music from below faded and died, and all that was heard was the night song of a bird calling to its mate, and the squeak of the gently rocking chair.

His robe fell open. He turned her so that her breasts could touch his chest. She felt the tickle of chest hair against her hardened nipples, the smoothness of his skin and the beat of his heart against her hand.

He kissed her again and she was lost in him, unmindful of anything except his mouth on hers and the hands that so gently caressed her.

He stood and, still holding her, walked to the bed and put her down. He took off his robe and came in beside her. Before she could protest, he gathered her in his arms and began kissing her again.

"Carissima," he whispered, and eased his body over hers.

And though her body was hot and yearning with need, she stiffened, remembering how it had been the night before.

"Give me your mouth," he said as he nudged her legs apart with his knee.

He kissed her, then he eased himself over her and joined his body to hers, slowly, carefully, and did not move until her body accommodated him.

She was still afraid, even when her arms came up to encircle his shoulders. He began to move against her. Sensations she had never before experienced spread like liquid fire and she moaned, not with pain but with pleasure. She lifted her body to his and let his warmth fill her. He kissed her breast and a tremor of pure pleasure ran through her. He rocked her as he had rocked her before, but now their bodies were joined, one, as he urged her toward a moment she had never experienced.

"This is the way it should be, *carissima,"* he whispered against her lips. "Let go, my Nicky, let me lead you."

His cadence quickened. She clung to him, awash in a sea of pleasure unlike anything she had ever known. Reaching, reaching...

And it happened, powerful, shattering, lifting her to a height of emotion she hadn't thought possible. She cried out, and when she did, Carlo covered her mouth with his. He thrust against her once, twice, and his cry mingled with her own.

He kissed her closed eyes, her nose, her cheeks, her mouth. And when at last he said, "I must move, I'm too heavy for you," she shook her head.

"No," she whispered. "Stay like this for a little while."

Carlo lay with his face against her throat. He breathed in the scent of her hair, and knew a peace he had not known for two years.

A patch of sunlight awakened Nicky. She lay on her side, close to him, the sheet low over her hips.

"Good morning," he said. "Did you sleep well?"

She nodded, suddenly shy. "Have you...have you been awake long?"

"Only for a little while." He brushed the dark blond hair back off her face and kissed her. "I like to look at you when you're sleeping."

She blushed. Sometime in the night the blue gown had come off and she had slept naked in his arms. Now she pulled the sheet up to cover herself.

He pulled it back down. "Let me look at you," he said with a smile. "I want to see . . ." He sucked in his breath. There was a faint yellow bruise on one breast, other bruises on her waist and on her thighs, marks he had made when he'd gripped her that first time. *"Dio mio,"* he whispered. *"Ay, Dio mio."* He dropped his head upon her breast, ashamed to look at what he had done.

Nicky touched his hair. "Don't," she said. "Please don't."

He raised his face. "I did that to you," he said. And when she didn't answer, he shook his head. "I didn't mean to. Something happened to me. I've wanted you for so long. I'd waited—''

"But we'd only known each other for a few weeks." Nicky looked at him, puzzled. "I don't understand."

"I know you don't," he said. "I'm not sure I do, either." Then, because he didn't want her to ask questions he couldn't answer, he began to kiss the places he had bruised. They made love again, slowly, gently, and when it was over Nicky went in to bathe and dress.

But Carlo lay there in the bed with his eyes closed, as though to blot out the sun and the memory of the marks on Nicky's body. He had taken her with force and he had hurt her, because for a few moments she had reminded him of a past that had been and was no more. Poor Nicolina, poor innocent. She was the answer to everything he had looked for. She . . . No! He pounded the bed with his clenched fists. He must not allow himself to think about the past. He had another chance at happiness now; he must not let a memory ruin it.

But when he closed his eyes he saw her face, that other face. Isabella, he thought. Isabella.

They stayed one more day and night in Siena. Little by little they became more at ease with each other. Nicky told him about her mother and the father she had known for such a brief time, about her job in Miami and the friends she had there. He told her that his mother and father had died several years ago. He had no brothers or sisters, so his grandmother was the only family he had. He told her that he had always wanted to be a doctor and spoke about his work at the hospital.

She longed to ask him about his wife and how she had died, but she didn't.

On the morning they left she put on the gray suit. "The color doesn't suit you," Carlo said. "You should wear bright reds and blues, deep pink, dark purple, sharp black and white."

"But I don't feel comfortable in bright colors. They're wonderful on beautiful, vibrant women, but that's not me, Carlo. I'm more subdued, more—"

He reached for her hand and pulled her toward him. "If I remember correctly, you were anything but subdued last night."

Embarrassed, not quite meeting his eyes, she toyed with a button on his shirt. "You bring out the beastie in me," she said.

"Do I?"

She opened two buttons and rested her palm against his chest. "So it seems."

"Undo the rest of the buttons."

"We have to leave."

"There's time."

She put her lips against his chest. "I like the way you taste," she whispered.

"I like the way you feel." He opened her jacket, and when he saw the bra, he shook his head. "Your breasts are small," he said. "You don't need a bra. I prefer that after this you don't wear one." He reached around behind her and unsnapped it, then took off her jacket.

"We're ready to leave," she protested. "We—"

He stopped her words with a kiss. He unzipped the gray skirt, and when it fell about her ankles, she stepped out of it, then her shoes. "The rest," he said, and waited while she pulled off her stockings and her panties.

Quickly, then, he stripped out of his clothes, all but his briefs. "I want you to take them off," he said.

"Carlo..." She swallowed nervously, for though they had grown closer these past two days, she was still shy with him.

He cupped the back of her neck and drew her to him and kissed her. "Do it," he said against her lips.

She touched his waist. She put her fingers under the navy briefs and slipped them down over his hips. He moved his legs and they slid down the rest of the way. He brought her closer and kissed her again, then took her hand and guided it to him. "Touch me, Nicky," he said.

With trembling fingers she began to caress him, and he said, "Like that. Oh yes, like that."

This was a part of him, this essence throbbing like a beating heart in her hand. In this moment he was vulnerable, and she loved that vulnerability.

He picked her up and carried her to their bed. They made love quickly, passionately, and when it was over he held her close. And smiled a smile she could not see.

He knew now that he had been right to marry Nicolina. She was warm and giving; she was malleable. When he had finished she would be exactly the woman he wanted—loving, honest, and above all, faithful.

He felt a pang of conscience and brushed it aside. It would all work out. He would be good to her. He would give her anything, everything. As long as she loved him the way he wanted to be loved.

He kissed the top of her head. "Come," he said. "It's time to leave."

They arrived at the Casa Santini that afternoon. There was a private road leading to the estate and a high iron fence that encircled it. Poplar trees lined either side of the driveway, and as they rounded a curve, Nicky saw sloping, manicured lawns, tall dark hedges and the house of weathered yellow stone.

It looked, she thought, like a Renaissance mansion, a place where men had schemed their Machiavellian schemes, where dark plots had been hatched, where lovers had lived and died. More forbidding than beautiful, it rose three stories high past gaping, shuttered windows. Giant gnarled-with-age trees grew close to the house, but instead of adding softness, they seemed to intensify the look of mystery.

Carlo drove into the wide circular driveway and stopped. *"Ben venuto,"* he said. "Welcome to your new home."

He led her up three marble steps. As he reached for the door, it was opened by a man in plain black livery.

"Buon giorno, Sergio," Carlo said.

"Buon giorno, Doctor. *Buon giorno,* Signora San—" The servant's watery blue eyes widened. He took a step back, his thin white hands held up in front of him as though warding off a ghost.

"Our bags are in the car, Sergio," Carlo said. "Would you get them please?"

"Of—of course, Signor Doctor. Your—your grandmother is in the library."

When the servant, with a last startled look, turned and hurried out to the car, Nicky said, "What a strange man." She chuckled. "Maybe he just doesn't like American women."

Carlo didn't chuckle. His face looked tense, his eyes anxious. "Come along," he said. "I want you to meet Elizabetta, my grandmother."

They went into a hallway lined with dark paneled wood. Nicky caught a glimpse of a broad, curving staircase, a living room with heavy dark furniture, Oriental rugs and ancestral paintings, carved doors and faded tapestries. Farther down the hallway, Carlo opened a door and motioned her inside the room.

Bookshelves lined the oak-paneled walls. A brown carpet covered most of the polished wood floor. Brown velvet drapes hung from floor-to-ceiling windows. There was a fire in the fireplace. Above it hung the portrait of a bewigged ancestor.

Carlo said, "Grandmother?"

And from a love seat placed in front of the fire, a voice said, "Carlo? Is that you?"

He took Nicky's hand and they crossed to the love seat. The lady seated there was elderly and beautiful, with delicate, aristocratic features. Her eyes were a deeper green than Carlo's, and though her skin showed the lines of age, it was easy to see that in her younger years she had been a beauty. Her white hair was arranged in soft waves about her face. She wore a black silk dress, softened at the neck with a string of pearls.

Carlo went to her and kissed her cheek. "I'm so glad to see you," he said. "You're looking well. Has Dr. Glannini been in to see you?"

"Almost every day. What a pest he is!" She frowned, which made her look very much like Carlo, and said, "Where have you been? You were due back weeks ago. What..." She saw Nicky standing in the shadows a few steps behind Carlo. "Is that someone with you? Who...?" She hesitated, eyebrows furrowed, questioning.

"Grandmother..." Carlo gripped Nicky's hand and brought her forward. "Grandmother, this is Nicolina. My wife. We were married a few days ago."

"Married? Good heavens!" Elizabetta motioned Nicky forward. "Come closer, girl," she said. "Let me have a better look at you."

Nicky came forward into the light. "I'm very glad to meet you, *signora*. I—"

Elizabetta gasped. A pale hand clasped at her chest. "No," she whispered. "It isn't possible. It—"

"Nicolina is an American," Carlo said quickly, cutting her off. "We met in Venice."

Elizabetta looked at him, her eyes wide with disbelief. Then, as though pulling herself together, she turned to Nicky and said, "How—how do you do? It's a bit of a— of a shock. I didn't know Carlo was planning to marry."

"It happened very quickly," Nicky said. "I'm sorry that Carlo didn't let you know."

"Yes, it would have been better if he had." Elizabetta looked at him again, then at Nicky. "I was just about to order tea. Will you and Carlo join me?"

"That would be nice, *signora*. But I'd like to clean up a bit first."

"Of course." The elderly lady reached for the silver bell on the table next to her. Almost immediately, a maid entered, and Elizabetta said, "This is Signora Santini, Rosa. Would you show her to..." She looked up at Carlo. "I presume to your rooms?"

"Yes, Grandmother. Of course."

"To the doctor's rooms," Elizabetta said. "Then please tell cook we will be three for tea."

"*Si*, Signora Santini." The maid nodded to Nicky. "If you will follow me," she murmured.

"I'll only be a minute," Nicky said, and turned to follow the maid out into the corridor.

"Carlo!" she heard Elizabetta say as she started out of the door. The old woman's voice was hushed with disbelief. "*Dio mio!* It's too incredible! I thought for a moment it was . . . *Ay, Dio,* I cannot believe it. How could you have done such a thing?"

Nicky hesitated. What were they talking about? Why was Elizabetta so upset? Because she and Carlo had married so quickly, and without telling her?

The maid, who was a few steps ahead of her, said, "This way, *signora.*"

Nicky hesitated, then, with a puzzled look, turned to follow the maid. They went back to the stairway Nicky had seen earlier, up the winding stairs.

What had Elizabetta been talking about? Why had she been so upset?

And suddenly Nicky was filled with a terrible sense of foreboding. This house, everything, was all so strange, so foreign. Did she really belong? What was she doing here?

CHAPTER SIX

"These are Dr. Santini's rooms," the maid said. "I will unpack for you while you're having tea. If there is anything you wish, please do not hesitate to ask." She indicated the telephone on a carved mahogany desk. "Simply pick up the phone. Either I or Graciela will come."

When the young woman left, Nicky put her purse down and looked around. A black leather sofa was placed beneath a painting that she thought might be a Gauguin. There were floor-to-ceiling bookshelves and carved end tables, one with a scattering of medical magazines. An armchair stood on either side of a fireplace.

It would be a pleasant place to relax when the nights were cold, Nicky thought, and with a pang found herself wondering what it had been like when Carlo had shared this room with his wife. She could almost see them here, sitting together in front of the fire, Carlo reading his medical journals, Isabella with a novel or perhaps knitting a sweater, something dark and soft for him. Then having a brandy perhaps, or a warm, dark sherry before they had gone to bed.

She didn't want to think about that.

It was strange that there were no feminine touches to brighten the masculine feel of the room, but perhaps after his wife's death the memories had been too painful for him and he had made it his room, a very masculine room.

And suddenly Nicky knew that she wanted to take away the pain his wife's death had caused him. She wanted to make up for the lonely years and fill his life with love and joy because she loved him. She knew that now, she'd known it the second night of their marriage when he had cradled her in the rocking chair and afterward had made such tender love to her.

It's going to be all right between us, she thought when she went into the bedroom. I'll help him to forget the pain of losing her. One day he'll forget and love me as he loved her.

She went into the bedroom. Like the sitting room, it, too, was so definitely a man's room that she smiled. The furniture was dark and heavy. The big bed was covered with a quilted spread the same color of beige as the rug. There was a leather chair with a matching hassock, a bookcase and a smaller desk than the one in the other room. There were no photographs, nothing that told of a life shared with the woman who had been his wife.

She looked up and saw the mural on the vaulted ceiling: mythological warriors with spears and shields and the big-breasted, terrified women they had captured. The colors of the mural were faded with time, but the strength of the scene was there, frightening and impressive. How many men and women had made love under this vaulted ceiling? she wondered, and thought again of the woman Carlo had shared his bed with.

But that was before, she told herself. This is the now and I'm Carlo's wife. I belong here. Ghosts from the past do not.

She went into the bathroom, where she admired the marble counter and double sink. At the far end of the room was a sunken black-marble tub beneath a large window. Through the window she could see a garden of greenery.

Nicky washed her hands and face and brushed her hair. Soon she would have to go and face Elizabetta. The elderly woman had so obviously been shocked and angry when she had learned of the marriage. Nicky didn't blame her, for surely Carlo should have told his grandmother about their marriage.

Elizabetta intimidated her; this house intimidated her. House? Good grief, it was as big as a department store, as forbidding as a mausoleum. How could she ever feel comfortable here? With a sigh, Nicky put the brush down. Then, stiffening her shoulders, she turned and left the room.

They had tea in the library. Over a very dry Spanish sherry Elizabetta Santini asked Nicky about her parents. The sherry was followed by small sandwiches, slices of mozzarella, crisp brown sausages and questions about Nicky's job and why she had come to Italy.

"How did you meet Carlo?" she asked when the cherry tarts were served.

"I became ill while I was in Venice," Nicky explained. "Signora Brendisi, the owner of the pensione where I was staying, called the doctor who lives next door to her. But Dr. Raviggia was out of the city and Carlo was kind enough to attend me." She smiled at him, then at Elizabetta. "He's a very good doctor," she said. "And that's how we met."

"I see." Long delicate fingers tapped the top of the table in front of her. "It was all quite sudden though, wasn't it? Your marriage, I mean?"

"Yes, I suppose it was."

"I had to return to Florence sooner than I expected, Grandmother," Carlo put in. "I have a patient at the hospital that Dr. Tacchia is concerned about. I'll see him—the patient, I mean—tomorrow." He took Nicky's hand. "We knew how we felt about each other. I saw no reason to wait."

"Didn't you?"

His mouth tightened. "No, I didn't."

"You were not married in the church?"

"No, we had a civil ceremony. We'll be married in the church later."

"I see." She turned to Nicky. "I'm sure your mother was disappointed not to be able to attend your wedding. Perhaps she will come when you are properly married."

"Perhaps."

"You said your father died when you were young. Has your mother remarried?"

Again and again, Nicky thought, but because she knew that would upset the already upset lady, she simply nodded and said, "Yes, *signora.*"

"You have no other family? No brothers or sisters?"

"No, ma'am."

"Carlo, too, was an only child. But he has many aunts and uncles, and cousins, of course. Dozens of them."

"And you, Grandmother." He reached out to pat her hand. "How have you been feeling?"

"Well enough." She withdrew her hand. "But I'm tired. If you will excuse me, I will rest for a little while." She turned to Nicky. "I hope you will be happy here," she said. "It can be a gloomy old place at times, and you're very young, aren't you?" She looked at Carlo. "Very young," she repeated.

She picked up her cane, a stout hickory stick with a lion-head top. "We will have a chat tomorrow at lunch, yes? If there is anything you need, do not hesitate to call Rosa. She's a new girl, but most helpful."

Elizabetta started up out of her chair and Carlo went to help her. But she shrugged him away. "I'm not feeble," she snapped. "I can help myself." And with that, with the tapping of her cane against the hardwood floor, she left the room.

"She's upset about the marriage," Nicky said.

Carlo shook his head. "With me, not with you."

"No, more me, I think. When you introduced me to her, she looked as though she'd seen a ghost."

"You're imagining things. She was surprised, but she'll be fine once she gets to know you." He brought her hand to his lips and kissed it. "I know this is all very new to you—our marriage, Grandmother, the house."

"Tell me about the house."

"It has been in my father's family for generations. He was born here and so was I. It has belonged to the Santinis' for almost four hundred years. Through wars won and lost, through famine and plague and financial reverses, somehow the Santinis managed to hang onto it. We can trace part of the family back to one or two counts, a branch of the Medicis and a couple of the Machiavellis."

"Somehow that doesn't surprised me." Nicky grinned. "It looks like the kind of a place where dark plots were hatched. I wouldn't be surprised to find a dungeon in the cellar and a mad maiden locked in the tower."

"We only keep wine in the cellar, and unfortunately, there is no tower."

"But you do have a third floor."

"Yes, we do, but it's closed off."

"Why?"

"It would be next to impossible to heat all three floors. We only heat the part we live in."

"What's up there?"

"Other bedrooms. A playroom."

"I'd like to see it sometime."

"I'd really prefer you didn't go up there." His voice was suddenly cool, testy. "There are thirty rooms on the first two floors—that should be enough for you to explore. Then there's the garden. If you like that sort of thing, you might enjoy working in it. I'm sure the gardener would welcome your help."

"Yes, I'd like that. It would be fun to help out." She hesitated. "I'd like to help care for your grandmother, too, if she'd let me."

"We'll see how it goes." He got up and went to stand by the fireplace. "You'll have to be patient with her, Nicolina. I'm afraid she's something of a matriarch and used to ruling the roost."

"What about when your wife was alive? I mean, did she take care of running the household or did your grandmother?"

"Isabella was busy with other things." Carlo turned his back on her and stared into the fire.

"I didn't mean to pry."

"Didn't you?"

"No, I..." Nicky twisted her hands in her lap. "I'm sorry. I was just ... well, just trying to see where I will fit in. I mean, do I order the groceries and plan the meals?"

"The cook plans the meals."

Nicky looked down at her hands, and in a quiet voice asked, "And what do I do, Carlo?"

He went to her and, taking her hands, pulled her to her feet. "You will take care of me," he said. "You will be everything I want you to be. My wife, my lover. Everything."

She looked into his eyes searchingly, trying to see beyond the mask that hid his emotions, and said, "This happened so fast between us. We haven't talked about... about things."

"What things?" he asked with a smile.

"About our different styles of life, our backgrounds." Nicky took a deep breath. "About children," she said.

"Children?" The smile disappeared.

"How you feel... about having them, I mean."

"I hadn't thought about it." He shook his head. "It's much too soon. We need time alone. I want to be with you without the burden of children."

"I've never thought of children as a burden."

"You're young, Nicolina. We can discuss the idea of children in a year or two. Meantime, you will begin taking the Pill." He ran his hands down over her breasts to her belly. "I don't want you to change," he said. And when she did not answer, he put his arms around her. "We need time to get to know each other. We will talk about this again, yes? In the meantime, let us enjoy each other." He kissed her. "Shall we start now?"

"Carlo—"

"No," he said, stopping her. "Now we kiss and make love."

He took her mouth again and held her so that she could not move away from him. Only when her lips parted under his did he let her go. Then, arm in arm, they went up the curving staircase.

The minute they reached his rooms, for that was how she thought of them, he undressed her and carried her to his bed. He laid her down there, and when he was naked, came to cover her body with his.

"At last you are here where you belong," he said. *"Cara. Cara mia."*

He began to kiss her. His breath came faster, his mouth more frantic, his tongue searching, plunging. He grasped her hands and raised her arms above her head, and with a low cry he joined his body to hers. "You're mine again," he said against her lips, his voice harsh with an emotion she did not understand.

"Let me go," Nicky cried, and struggled to free her hands. But he held her there, pinning her with his body, silencing her with his mouth. "Promise..." He raised himself over her, his eyes burning with the intensity of all that he was feeling. "Promise you will never leave me. Say the words. Tell me!" His face was tortured, anguished.

She stopped struggling. In a gentle voice she said, "I love you, Carlo. Of course I'll never leave you."

He released her hands. He kissed her wrists. He took her mouth again and held her close until it seemed as though their bodies merged and became one. He began to move against her, and her body flamed with a passion that rendered her helpless in its intensity. It was like being in the middle of a storm, tossed about by wind and thunderous waves. It was the most of living, a little like dying.

"Give me your mouth!" he said, and when she did, he kissed her. "Now," he whispered, holding her while she rode the crest of passion, and wept against his shoulder, helpless in his arms.

Afterward, when their breathing had slowed and their hearts had stopped racketing in their chests, he smoothed her tousled hair back off her face and stroked her body, which was filmed with perspiration. And when she had quieted, he went into the bathroom and filled the black-marble tub with scented water.

"Come," he said when he returned, and before Nicky could protest, he picked her up and carried her into the bathroom.

They sat facing each other in the warm, scented water. He soaped her breasts and bathed her as tenderly as he would a child. And when she relaxed against the back of the tub, her eyes closed, almost asleep, he moved closer and eased her up onto his thighs.

"Carissima sposa. Amorosa mia." He lifted her face to his and spread his fingers through the tangle of her hair as he had done that day on the boat. He kissed her, and when she sighed against his lips, he slowly entered her.

She caressed his shoulders and his back. He brushed soap bubbles off one breast so that he could kiss her there. But when she began to move against him, he said, "Go slowly, *cara*. Slowly. Slowly."

Adrift in a sea of sensation, she followed where he led, offering her mouth for his kisses, her breasts for his touch. And when at last it became too much, he moved so fast, so hard against her that water splashed over the tub. He filled her, he drove her to an edge where she could no longer keep silent, and when she cried aloud he took her mouth, smothering her cry with his own cry of "Isabe—"

"What?" Stunned, shocked, she tried to draw away. "What—what did you say?"

His eyes went blank, unfocused for the barest fraction of a second. He looked at her, startled. "I—I spoke in Italian. I'm sorry. I—I forget and speak it in moments of—of great emotion. It means nothing. Only an expression."

Nicky pulled away from him.

He tried to draw her back into his arms, but when she resisted, he eased himself up out of the tub and said, "Come. The room is cold. We must dry ourselves and get into bed."

They got out of the tub, and when they were dry, they went back to bed. He lay on his back, a little away from her, and in a short while his breathing evened and she knew that he slept.

But she did not.

Isabella. Dear God, he had called out his dead wife's name.

He was gone the next morning when Nicky awoke at seven. She lay in bed looking up at the high, vaulted ceiling, at the mythological warriors and the terrified women. Her soul had been bruised; she was empty, defeated.

For the first time in her life she understood the pain of women whose husbands had been unfaithful. A friend to whose wedding she'd gone a year ago had asked to meet her for lunch a few months before Nicky had left for Europe.

"Eddie's having an affair," Kay had said over her second glass of wine. "She's a girl from his office. I found out. It's driving me crazy."

"What are you going to do?" Nicky had asked.

"Everything I can to get him back," Kay said. "I'm going to fight her, Nicky. I'm going to fight her with everything I've got."

But how did you fight a dead woman? Nicky lay back against the pillows and closed her eyes. How he must have loved his Isabella. How he must have grieved. Poor Carlo. How could she hate him for the feelings he still had for his dead wife? He and Isabella had been married for four years. She must have meant everything to him.

Nicky didn't think he was a promiscuous man. When, early in their relationship, he had told her that he had waited so long, had he meant he had not been with a woman since Isabella's death? Was it so unusual, so terrible, that in a moment of passion he had made a mistake and called out his dead wife's name?

He needs time, she told herself. If I love him enough, if I'm patient and understanding, it will be all right. He loves me—why else would he have married me? I'm his wife. I can make him forget.

She got up and dressed, and when she went downstairs, she found the dining room, and Carlo. He was reading a newspaper, but he put it down when he saw her and said, "Good morning. This is a pleasant surprise. I thought you might want to sleep in..." He frowned. "You're wearing jeans," he said.

"Yes, well..." She looked down at the worn blue jeans. "I'm just going to be here. In the house. I can put on my skirt if you'd prefer it."

"The miniskirt?" Carlo folded his napkin, and with deliberate care, put it down on the tabletop next to his cup and saucer. "We'll go into Florence in a day or two," he said. "Just when will depend on my patient. Until then I suppose you'll have to wear the clothes you have. However, we're accustomed to dressing for dinner, so I would appreciate it if you would wear something besides the jeans. Your white dress, perhaps, or your suit."

Her temper flared, but she managed to restrain herself and say, "Very well. What time will you be home for dinner?"

"I'm not sure. It depends on what happens at the hospital. I have a lot to catch up on." He pushed back his chair and stood. "I'll try to call later," he said, and glanced at his watch. "It's late. I have to leave."

He came to her and kissed her cheek, then stepped back. "We really must do something about your hair," he said.

Nicky stood where she was. She heard his steps retreating down the hall toward the foyer. And then his voice, and the voice of the elderly man who had opened the door for them yesterday. She looked down the length of the polished table, with its twelve straight-backed chairs. Like the other rooms she had seen, it too was formal, almost severe. There was a tapestry above the sideboard depicting pilgrims and strange, wild-looking animals among the gnarled trees of a shaded forest. To her it was every bit as forbidding as the mural above their bed.

Their marriage bed. She thought of the passion they had shared the night before, of the fierceness of his gaze when he had grasped her wrists and held her, the strangled plea that she never leave him. The gentle kisses afterward.

And the sound of his dead wife's name upon his lips. The coldness in his eyes just now when he had seen the way she was dressed.

What manner of man was he? What passions, what grief and pain, what in his past had made him who he was? Because she loved him, she wanted to please him. If her manner of dress bothered him, she would change it. But she would not change who she was. Her name might be Nicolina Santini, but inside she was still Nicky Fairchild, the Nicky who loved hot pastrami sandwiches, barefoot walks along the beach at low tide, forties' movies and rock and roll. The Nicky who now loved a man named Carlo Santini.

These were the thoughts that troubled her while she ate the breakfast served by a maid she had not seen before. She wondered where in this great house Carlo's grandmother lived. Elizabetta had said she would see her for lunch today, but she had not said at what time, or what, if anything, Nicky was to do until then.

Nicky finished her breakfast and went to stand in front of the French doors that led out into the garden. She remembered that Carlo had suggested she might enjoy working there, and opening the doors, she stepped outside.

The grass was still wet with morning dew and the air felt cool and fresh. Sloping green lawns gave way to a stand of trees, hearty green shrubs and the garden below. Off to the right she saw tall hedges. Was that the maze Carlo had told her about, the place where he had gotten lost when he was a little boy?

Curious now, she started toward it. When she came closer, she saw that the shrubby hedges, trim and tough, were almost seven feet high. She started in. The green tunnel was perhaps twenty-five feet long before it turned. If she went down to the end of it and made only one turn, surely she would not get lost.

It was cool and quiet inside the maze. She went a few feet and turned around to make sure she could see the way she had come in, then ventured on. At the end of the row there were paths leading to both the right and the left. She hesitated a moment, then turned to her left, sure that it would be easy to retrace her steps and find her way out.

The row ended. She turned right. Just to the end of this row, she told herself, then she would go back. But when she turned and came to the end of the row, she knew a moment of confusion. Left or right? she asked herself. And turned right. Down one row, up another. And knew that she was lost.

Okay, she told herself, it's only a lot of tall hedges in a garden. Obviously there's a way out. All I have to do is find it.

Thirty-five minutes later she was still walking up one row and down another. Great going, Nicolina, she told herself. Your first morning here and you've managed to get yourself lost. Carlo will come home tonight hoping to find a decently dressed woman waiting for him and here you'll be, still wearing these damn jeans, lost in a maze of seven-foot shrubs.

In another fifteen minutes she gave up and started to yell for help. "Hello?" she shouted. "Is anybody there? Can anybody hear me? *Buon giorno!* Help! *Aiuto!*"

There was no answer.

She tried again, hands cupped to her mouth. "Hello? Hey, somebody help me. Get me out of here! Get me—"

"Hello?" a voice called out in Italian. "Is someone there?"

"Yes! *Si!* I'm in here! In the maze."

"What are you doing there? You have no business on the property."

"I have every right to be here," she answered, then stopped. She could argue with whoever it was later; right now she had to get out of the maze. *"Per favore!"* she cried. "Get me out of here!"

"Stay where you are." He sounded cross, old. "I will find you. Keep talking."

She counted in Italian, *"Uno, due, tre, quattro..."* Then in English. He answered, his voice sounding closer. She began to sing snatches of songs: "Baby Love," "Outlaw Women," "Onward Christian Soldiers."

"Si, si," the voice called out, and she turned to see a man at the end of the row.

"Thank God!" she said in English, running toward him.

"What are you doing in here?" he asked, challenging her. "You have no right..." His voice died. The color faded from his face. He crossed himself and started backing away from her.

"Wait!" Nicky cried out. "Don't go! Please don't go!"

He spoke garbled words in Italian, his eyes wide, hands up in front of his face as though to shield himself as she advanced.

"It's all right," she said, trying to calm him. "I'm the doctor's wife. My name is Nicky. Nicolina. We've just been married."

"But you..." He shook his head as though trying to clear it. "I thought—I thought..."

"What?" Nicky asked.

He turned his back on her. "Come," he said. "It is this way. I will lead you out."

She followed him, puzzled, not understanding. He was an old man—well over eighty, she thought—confused, maybe not right in his head.

They came out into the sunlight. Bushy white eyebrows hung low over his faded blue eyes. "You must not go into the maze again," he said. "It is easy to become lost."

"Yes, all right." Nicky offered her hand. "My name is Nicolina," she said. "Are you Luigi?"

He barely touched her hand. "*Si, signora.* Luigi." He looked at her, then quickly lowered his eyes and hurried away.

What in the world was the matter with the man? Nicky stared after him. Then, with a shake of her head, she started back toward the house.

CHAPTER SEVEN

They had lunch in a smaller, more intimate dining room overlooking a rose garden.

Once again Elizabetta, dressed in black as she had been the day before, was every inch the grande dame, matriarch of the family, still in charge in spite of her venerable age.

When Nicky came downstairs at twelve, the maid, Rosa, showed her where lunch would be served. Nicky had hurried toward the room, entered, then hesitated when she'd seen Elizabetta in front of the windows facing her, both hands gripping the carved lion head of her cane.

"Buon giorno," Nicky said.

"Buon giorno." The elderly lady looked at Nicky from head to toe, taking in the red-and-white-striped shirt, the blue jeans and the sandals. The corner of her mouth twitched. "You slept well?" she asked.

"Very well, thank you."

"Luigi told me he found you in the maze this morning."

Nicky blushed. "I meant to go only a little way in. I thought I could find my way out, that it was simple."

"Nothing here at Casa Santini is simple. If you want to explore the maze or the garden, ask Luigi to accompany you." She tapped white fingers against the head of the cane. "I suppose you'd like to see the rest of the house. If you would, I'll tell one of the maids to show you around." She motioned toward the table. "Come," she said. "If we're ready, I'll ring for the cook."

Nicky stepped forward. "Let me help you." She pulled out the chair Elizabetta had moved to and eased it out. Elizabetta looked up at her, a questioning look followed by a frown. *"Grazie,"* she said.

She rang a delicate silver bell. A middle-aged woman in a white uniform entered with a tray laden with plates of fruit salad and a basket of warm rolls.

"Would you care for wine?" Elizabetta asked.

"No, thank you."

"Then what would you like to drink? Something stronger?"

"Just tea, please."

Elizabetta nodded to the middle-aged woman. "We will both have tea, Maria," she said.

Nicky did not remember ever having been so uncomfortable. She searched for something to say, cleared her throat and finally said, "I must apologize for the way I'm dressed, *signora*. You see, I've been backpacking through Europe—"

"Backpacking? What is that?"

"Instead of a suitcase, I traveled with only a small pack and very few clothes."

"How uncivilized."

Nicky smiled. "That's what my mother said."

"You stayed in hotels?"

"In youth hostels mostly, but sometimes in small hotels or pensiones."

"And you traveled alone? Without a relative or a friend?"

Nicky nibbled her bottom lip. "Uh, yes," she said.

"How courageous of you." For the first time, Elizabetta smiled. "Tell me all about it—about where you've been and what you've seen."

So Nicky told her about trekking through Britain on second-class buses, and how in Scotland, when she'd come to the last stop of a local bus and stood all alone on the side of a road as the afternoon waned into evening, a family in an old car had stopped to offer her a ride.

"They took me home with them," she said when the veal piccata was served, "and insisted I spend the night."

"Strangers?" Elizabetta asked with a lift of her eyebrow.

"Yes." Nicky smiled at the memory of sleeping in a room with three little girls who giggled at her accent, and having strong tea and fresh-baked scones for breakfast the next morning.

She went on to tell Carlo's grandmother of tramping the moors in the rain, and how she had felt one sunbright morning as the ferry she was on came in to the Isle of Skye.

She told about crossing the English Channel and of the landing in Le Havre and the train trip to Paris. "I loved Paris," she said, "but I almost froze there, and that's why I decided to come to Italy."

She said she thought Milan was a beautiful city, and told of the view when she'd climbed to the terrace atop the Duomo. And of how she had felt when she'd come out of the railroad station and seen Venice for the very first time.

"It was raining," she said, "and through the rain I saw the narrow street, and the canal like a liquid boulevard. The rain didn't matter. I was in Venice and it was instant love."

"And was it instant love when you met Carlo?" Elizabetta asked in a quiet voice.

Nicky looked at the older woman, drawn abruptly out of her reverie. "I—I..."

"Don't stutter, child. Just tell me, were you instantly attracted to him?"

"I don't really know. The first time I saw him I was ill with pneumonia and Carlo was bending over my bed in the pensione." The trace of a smile curved Nicky's lips. "I thought he was Mephistopheles. He was looking at me so intently, almost as though we'd met before and he was angry with me for being ill."

"I see." Elizabetta's face was still, her eyes watchful. "Go on," she said.

"He was very kind to me when I left the hospital, *signora*. The first few days he insisted on having my meals sent in. He sent flowers. He—"

"Began to court you," Elizabetta finished.

And when Nicky nodded, Elizabetta said, "It was all rather sudden, wasn't it? You know almost nothing about him. He's thirty-six and you are, what...twenty, twenty-one?"

"Twenty-three."

"A thirteen-year difference. That's quite a lot."

"I realize that, but if two people care about each other, do the years really make that much difference?" Nicky leaned forward, her eyes serious, as though pleading for the older woman to understand. "I know I'm probably not the kind of woman you would have chosen for Carlo, *signora*. I'm not sophisticated or glamorous or any of the things a man like Carlo should have in a wife. But I love him and I'm going to do everything I can to make him happy."

Elizabetta's eyes narrowed, and she looked at Nicky so piercingly that it seemed as though she were trying to see beyond Nicky's eyes into the very depths of her soul. Then she sighed and said, "I'm suddenly quite tired. If you will excuse me, I believe I'll ring for Rosa and ask her to help me to my room."

"Let me help you." Nicky pushed her chair back from the table, and when Elizabetta looked about to refuse her help, she said, "Please, *signora*. I'd like to."

She helped the elderly lady to rise and offered an arm for her to lean on. "Is your room upstairs?"

"No, I'm downstairs now. It was too difficult..." Elizabetta stopped and pressed a hand to her chest. "A moment," she said, tightening her hand on Nicky's arm.

"Do you feel ill?" Nicky asked, concern written on her face. "Shall I telephone Carlo?"

"No, no. It's nothing. I have an eighty-five-year-old heart. At times it gets tired." She nodded. "We can go now."

Together they went out into the hall and down a long corridor. On one side were gilded mirrors and recessed niches graced with vases and delicate figurines. Family portraits in heavy frames lined the other side of the hall—elegant women in eighteenth- and nineteenth-century gowns, and men, one in a suit of armor, another in the red vestments of a cardinal, others in frock coats, and the last one, in a military uniform, astride a black stallion, a sword raised in his right hand. His expression was fierce, warlike.

When Nicky hesitated in front of the portrait, Elizabetta said, "That was my father, Carlo's great-grandfather, Giorgio Santini."

"He's very handsome."

"All of the men in our family are handsome. I'm not sure whether that is a blessing or a curse."

"What do you mean?"

"Things come too easily for Santini men—money, profession." Elizabetta hesitated. "And women, of course."

Women. Nicky hesitated, then, gathering her courage, said, "Are there any portraits of Isabella?"

Elizabetta's mouth pursed in a thin, tight line. "Why do you ask?"

"I—I suppose I'm curious." And because she had to know, she asked, "Was she very beautiful?"

"Very," Elizabetta snapped, then, pointing to a closed door at the end of the corridor, said, "These are my rooms. You may leave me now."

"Please let me help you in."

"I'm quite capable of taking care of myself." The tone was acerbic, cutting off any further offer of help.

Nicky stiffened. "Then if you'll excuse me," she murmured.

But before she could turn away, Elizabetta put a hand on her arm and in a softer voice said, "Forgive me for being abrupt. I did not mean to be. It was kind of you to offer to help me and I appreciate it." She started into her room, then paused. "I hope you will be happy here, Nicolina. I realize that things must seem very different for you, but if you love Carlo and he loves you..." She looked at Nicky, the same piercing look she had used before, then quickly lowered her eyes. "We dine at eight. I will see you then."

"Very well, *signora*."

"Elizabetta," the elderly woman said. "I would like you to call me Elizabetta." And with a nod, she went in and closed the door behind her.

Nicky walked back down the corridor alone, and this time she stopped and really looked at the portraits that hung there.

All of the men—the gentlemen in their frock coats, the knight in his suit of armor and the dour-faced cardinal—bore a resemblance to Carlo. But it was the man in uniform astride the black stallion that looked the most like him. In his face was the same determination, the strength, the pride that was in Carlo's face. The same sensuous cruelty of his mouth, the same passion blazing in the pale green eyes. This was a man who would take what he wanted. A man who would kill an enemy without remorse or guilt. A man who could love and hate with equal passion.

A shiver, like a chilling presentiment of things to come, ran through Nicky, a feeling so strong that for a moment she felt almost faint. But she could not turn away, for she was mesmerized, caught by the searing intensity of the gaze of this man who looked so like the man she had married. What secrets and what sins lay hidden behind the pale green eyes? What passions burned through that strong, masculine body?

And why, among all of these portraits of the Santinis, were there none of Isabella? In not one of the rooms she had seen had there been a portrait or a photograph, anything to remember the woman who had been Carlo's wife.

Why? Nicky asked herself as she left the corridor and climbed the stairs to the second floor. Why?

Carlo and his grandmother were having a sherry in a sitting room off the dining room when Nicky appeared that evening.

"How nice you look," he said when he saw that she was wearing the white dress, and going to her, he kissed her cheek. "Shall we go in to dinner?"

They went into the formal dining room. Elizabetta, dressed in elegant black silk with a baroque necklace of pearls around her throat, sat at one end of the table, Carlo at the other.

Nicky asked him about his day and he told her about the patient Dr. Tacchia had been so concerned about.

"I've changed his medication," he said. "I don't think surgery is called for right now. I'd really prefer to monitor him for a few weeks before we decide on anything drastic. So..." He smiled at Nicky. "I thought that tomorrow we could go to Florence for a day or two of shopping."

"Shopping?"

"We discussed it this morning." He shook his head. "You really cannot go about looking like a...how do you say in English? A beachcomber?"

Her anger flared and bright color spotted her cheeks. "I should be receiving a check this week or the next. When it comes I'll go shopping."

"Nonsense. You're my wife. I'll buy whatever you need." He tapped his fingers against the side of his plate in a nervous, staccato rhythm. "You have to realize that we have a more formal life-style here in Italy than what you've been accustomed to in Florida."

Nicky looked down at the chicken cacciatore, which had suddenly lost its flavor.

"You do understand?" he asked.

"Yes," she said. "I understand."

"*Bene*. Then it is settled. Tomorrow we go to Florence."

Elizabetta had looked from one to the other while the exchange took place. Now, in a kindly voice, she said to Nicky, "While you are there you must insist that Carlo take you to the Uffizi, my dear. And of course you must see Michelangelo's *David*."

"Of course." Carlo sounded impatient. "I intend showing her everything."

"If she is dressed correctly." Elizabetta frowned. "Frankly, Carlo, I see no reason why Nicky cannot wear the clothes she chooses to wear, especially during the day when she and I are here alone. I quite like the informality of blue jeans."

"I don't. And since Nicky is my wife . . ."

Nicky was more grateful than she could say to Elizabetta for defending her, and furious with Carlo for treating her like a child. She resented his high-handedness and the assumption that blue jeans were her normal style of dress. They weren't. When she went to work, she wore business-type dresses or tailored suits. She attended meetings and went to business luncheons with executives who in their own fields were every bit as important as Carlo was in his profession. She might be young, but she wasn't a ninny. Last year she had won an award for having come up with the idea for a successful ad campaign. When she'd left her job to make this trip to Europe, the president of the store had called her into his office and told her that her job would be waiting for her whenever she returned.

Backpacking was the only way she had been able to afford to travel in Europe. It would have been ridiculous to carry heavy luggage packed with fancy clothes. She resented Carlo's assuming she was a Florida beachcomber who did little more than loll on the beach all day.

When coffee was served she excused herself and went up to their rooms. When he came up thirty minutes later, she was curled up on her side of the bed, pretending to be asleep. He got in beside her and lay without touching her.

"Are you asleep?" he asked, and when Nicky did not answer, he moved closer and rested a hand on her waist. "I'm sorry if I offended you at dinner. I didn't mean to. It's only that I want you to be..." He hesitated. "To be the best that you can be."

He moved closer and fitted himself against her back. And though her body warmed, she did not move or speak. In a little while she heard his even breathing and knew that he slept. But she did not.

The first shop he took her to was one of understated elegance. A tall, beautifully dressed woman greeted them. She introduced herself as Madame Fernanda and escorted them to a small salon and offered tea. There she looked at Nicky and said, "You are a size eight?"

"Yes, *madame.*"

"And your style is casual elegance, yes?"

"But that isn't what we're looking for," Carlo said before Nicky could answer. "We want a more-sophisticated, a more-glamorous look."

One finely arched eyebrow raised, but before she could speak Carlo said, "We'd also like to purchase lingerie. Perhaps you could have one of your assistants select some things for us to see."

Madame Fernanda nodded. "Very well, Dr. Santini. I'll take care of it. Now if you will relax a few minutes, I'll select some things for our models to show you."

And what am I supposed to do? Nicky wondered. Sit here like a prize poodle while he selects my dog collar?

They'd had very little to say to each other that morning. Carlo had gotten up before her and had almost finished his breakfast by the time she came down. He'd nodded approvingly at the suit she was wearing and said, "We'll have a splendid time in Florence."

"Carlo..." Nicky tried to speak calmly, reasonably. "Carlo, I appreciate what you're doing. It's kind of you to want to buy me things, but—"

"No," he said, holding up a hand to stop her. "I want to spend money on you. I'll take great pleasure in it, so please, let me do these things. Let me be good to you."

Now he reached to take her hand and said, "We're going to be terribly extravagant today, so don't object if you think something is too expensive. I enjoy spending money on you."

Nicky returned his smile, for while there was still a part of her that resented his taking over her life, there was another part of her that thought, he's doing this because he loves me and because he wants me to look nice for him. And isn't that what I want? To please him?

She settled back in her chair and the fashion show began.

The first model appeared wearing bright purple pants and a splashy, flowered overdress. It looked fine on the dark-haired, dark-skinned Italian model, but it wasn't Nicky's style. However, before she could voice an opinion, Carlo said, "Yes, that's perfect. Please put it aside for us, *madame*."

A strapless red evening gown was next. Once again he nodded approval. Nicky sank lower in her chair.

Then came a succession of other clothes. Several times Nicky murmured, "Oh yes, that's pretty, isn't it?" But each time she did, Carlo shook his head and said, "That really isn't your style."

He chose a bright blue embroidered gown with a shockingly low neckline, a short silk floral print, a bright coral suit with a skirt that came to the top of the model's thighs, a pale blue flowered silk, a blue evening dress with a plunging neckline and a slit in the skirt, an off-the-shoulder red organza, a shimmering gold-sequined dress so short it left little to the imagination, a short backless black silk. And finally something that Nicky actually liked—a white silk blouse with a scooped, ruffled neck and long full sleeves, and a long black velvet skirt.

He asked that their purchases be delivered to the hotel, then, taking Nicky's arm, hailed a taxi to take them to a salon specializing in casual wear. There he seemed more inclined to ask her opinion. "For while I don't especially approve of pants," he said, "I know you feel comfortable in them and I see no reason why you shouldn't wear them during the day."

He bought a dozen pairs in black, gray and varying shades of beige and cream, silk shirts to go with them, and because Nicky liked them, several bright Gypsy skirts and blouses.

Her head was spinning. Carlo had spent a small fortune on her. Ten thousand dollars, twenty? It was like an incredible dream, every woman's fantasy of walking into a Saks or a Neiman Marcus and saying, "Show me your size eights, I'll take them." And while she hadn't liked many of the styles he'd chosen, she realized that the world Carlo lived in was much different than what she had been accustomed to. Perhaps because of the difference in their ages, he wanted her to look older than she was.

But she balked when he said, "Now we'd better get you some shoes. I really can't abide your sandals. You'd look much better in high heels."

The shoes they were shown were of Italian leather as soft and smooth as cream. But she was damned if she wanted three-inch heels.

"I'd fall flat on my face with heels that high," she said indignantly. "Besides, I'd be too tall."

"Nonsense. You're what, five-five? You need a bit of height, Nicky."

"But I don't like—"

"The red shoes are perfect," he said, overriding her objections. "Look how beautifully they slim your legs."

At last she compromised. He chose several pairs of the three-inch heels; she settled for five pairs of two-inch and a pair of flats, and vowed to herself that she would never wear the shoes with the higher heels.

They had lunch, and for the first time that day, after a few sips of red wine, Nicky began to relax.

"You've spent a great deal of money," she said.

"A great deal." He grinned. "Tonight, when you're wearing one of your new outfits, I'll take you to the finest restaurant in Florence." He leaned across the table and took her hand. "Afterward I will make love to you and you will forget that you were angry with me last night." He brought her hand to his lips and kissed her palm.

She felt the warmth of his tongue against her skin and a flush of unbidden heat ran through her body. "Carlo?" she whispered. "Carlo?"

"Think about tonight," he said. "Now come, I have a surprise for you."

He took her to a beauty salon where, without her knowledge, he had made an appointment the day before. A man in his early thirties, wearing a white jumpsuit with several gold chains around his neck and gold rings on his fingers, greeted them. He was well built, with a trim mustache and neatly clipped flaming red hair.

"Dr. Santini," he said. "And this is your wife." He held out his hand. "*Buon giorno,* Signora Santini. It is my pleasure to be of service to you." He lifted a strand of Nicky's hair. "Very good," he said. "Thick and healthy. It will be a pleasure to work with."

Nicky looked inquiringly at Carlo. "Work?" she asked with a raised eyebrow.

He laughed. "Just put yourself in Enrico's hands. He knows what we want."

"We?" she said in English, her voice rising an octave. "I don't recall discussing my hair."

"Don't you?" He put a hand on her shoulder. "You have beautiful hair, *cara,* but you don't do anything with it. I've instructed Enrico to lighten it a bit and to cut it in a more stylish fashion."

"Cut it?" She put a hand to her hair as though to protect it. "I don't want to cut my hair."

He smiled. "Trust me, Nicky, and trust Enrico. He's one of the most famous hairstylists in Italy." He turned to the other man. "You know what to do," he said. "I'll be in the café across the street. Send someone for me when my wife is ready."

"Of course, Doctor. And do not worry, Signora Santini will be even more beautiful when I am finished with her."

Carlo squeezed her shoulder, then turned and hurried out of the salon. Enrico took Nicky's arm. "You can put a smock on in the room on your left," he said. "Roberto will shampoo you and bring you to me."

Like a lamb about to be sheared. What was she doing here? She didn't want her hair lightened or cut. On the other hand...

Oh Lord, why was there always another hand? It might be fun to have a different look. She'd worn the same style since college. Maybe she'd look good with a short cut. And after all, she was a married woman now, the wife of a doctor. She should have a more-sophisticated, a more-European look. Shouldn't she?

When her hair had been shampooed, conditioned and hot oiled, she was led back to Enrico, who studied her face for a few moments, and with a gleefully maniacal look, picked up his scissors. Nicky closed her eyes. When she opened them again she'd been shorn.

Enrico clapped his hands and said, "Yes? It is perfect, no? Now we will lighten it."

She had a pedicure and a manicure while the color was applied to her hair. And when she said she preferred plain polish, the manicurist said, "The red would be much better, *signora*," and before Nicky could stop her she'd begun.

Another shampoo. Her hair was blown dry and styled back off her face with a wisp of bangs over her forehead. She looked different. Pretty and stylish. But not me, she thought. Not me.

Enrico sent a young woman to look for Carlo. He came into the booth, but for a moment he didn't speak. He looked at Nicky's reflection in the mirror and his eyes went wide. He put a hand on the doorjamb as though to steady himself.

"Just as I imagined," he whispered. A sigh shuddered through him. "Incredible. Incredible."

But he wasn't looking at Nicky. He was looking at her image in the mirror, almost as though he were looking at another woman, a different woman. For that fraction of time he seemed not even to be aware of her.

CHAPTER EIGHT

Nicky lay in the big, canopied bed, and though the curtains were drawn to diminish the light in the room, she could not sleep. Every time she closed her eyes she could see the expression on Carlo's face when he had walked into the booth of the beauty salon. If he had been shocked by the sudden change, she would have understood. But it had been more than that. It was as though she herself had become invisible and he saw only her reflection in the mirror. She had wanted to say, "It's me, Carlo. My hair may be a different color and a different style, but I'm still me. Look at *me*."

There were so many things about him she didn't understand. He was generous, he was kind, he was autocratic. There were times when he treated her as though she were a child, or a doll that he wanted to dress up and show off. At other times he acted more like a father or a bad-tempered professor with a recalcitrant pupil. He could be a gentle lover who took her to heights of passion she had never even dreamed existed. He had only to look at her in a certain way, to touch her as he had today at lunch, and her body would go weak with desire.

What manner of man was this husband of hers, this man she had promised to love, to honor and to obey? He had never told her he loved her, yet surely he did. Surely he could not be with her as he was if he did not.

These were the thoughts that troubled Nicky as she lay staring up at the red-velvet canopy above the bed. When Carlo had insisted she rest before dinner, she had said that, yes, she was tired. But more than tired, she needed time to be alone to sort out her thoughts about all that had happened today.

The clothes he had purchased were hanging in the closet. Tonight he would want her to wear one of the dresses he had chosen. And she would, because she wanted so desperately to please him, to be the woman he wanted her to be.

At last, exhausted by the busyness of the day, she slept. And when she awoke and showered, she slipped into a new peach teddy.

"How do you feel?" he asked when he heard her stirring and came in. "Did you rest?"

"I'm fine. And yes, I rested."

He went to the closet and took the gold-sequined dress off the hanger. "Wear this tonight," he said, handing it to her.

Obediently, Nicky slipped it over her head. It felt silky smooth on her body, and shimmered like golden stardust in the light of the room. But the skirt came just to the top of her thighs and she said, "It's awfully short, isn't it?"

"Not for a woman with legs like yours." He picked up the gold high-heeled shoes and brought them to her. "Sit down," he said. "I'll put them on for you."

He cupped her foot in his hand and slid the high-heeled pump onto her foot. "Your bones are so fine, so delicate and fragile," he mused as his hand moved up to the top of her thigh. "It will be difficult to wait." He looked up at her. "But there will be pleasure in the waiting, for every time I look at you tonight I will know, as you will, *cara mia,* that when the evening is through we will come back into this room and lie naked together." He slipped her other shoe on. "Think about that, Nicky. Think of how it will be later when we're alone."

He took her hands and brought her to her feet. She felt dazed, warmed by the flush of desire that crept like liquid velvet through her body. She didn't want to wait. She wanted him to make love to her now.

"Come," he said with a slight smile that said he knew exactly what she was thinking, and taking her hand, he led her from the room.

They had an aperitif at an outdoor café in the Piazza della Signoria. The night was soft, scented with springtime and warmed with the sound of mandolins from a nearby restaurant. He bought her violets. He held her hand and told her how beautiful she was.

When they went into the restaurant, he motioned for her to precede him. Other diners, particularly the men, turned to look at her, and when they were seated, there was a glow of satisfaction on Carlo's face. "You see?" he murmured. "I knew it would be like this."

He ordered champagne. Nicky sipped without tasting it, and looked at him through the flickering candlelight. He was a devastatingly attractive man. At times his brooding El Greco eyes were shadowed by mystery and, as they were now, by a smoldering sensuality that made her tremble.

He wore a dark suit of the finest cashmere, a white silk shirt and a conservative tie. His face was smooth from his recent shave, and except for his thick black hair, which seemed always rumpled, he was the epitome of the well-dressed Continental man. But for all of his perfection, it was the tousled hair that endeared him to Nicky, for when she looked at it, it reminded her of that small boy who had been lost in the maze.

They had antipasto with hot, salty breadsticks, cannelloni that melted in the mouth and a rack of lamb that was crisp on the outside and tender pink on the inside.

Carlo talked about the hospital and his work there. He told her about Florence and the places they would visit the following day. He was as pleasant and charming, as polite and correct as though this were their first date. But once or twice, when she raised her glass to take a sip of her champagne, she saw him watching her, and there was in his eyes an almost haunted look that made her uneasy.

It was toward the end of the meal that he said, "I like the name Nicolina. Nicolina Santini. It has a pleasant ring, yes?" And without waiting for a reply, he said, "Let's drop the 'Nicky,' shall we?"

"But—" she tried to say.

"It makes you sound like a schoolgirl." He smiled. "You're not a schoolgirl, you're a married woman, and I prefer that from now on we use Nicolina."

"No," she wanted to say. "You've changed my wardrobe, you've changed my hair, you've put me on the Pill so I won't get pregnant, and now you want to change my name. Pretty soon there won't be a me anymore."

She cupped her fingers around her wineglass, needing to feel the coolness, and said, "I've been Nicky all my life, Carlo. That's how I think of myself—that's who I am."

"No," he said in a patient voice. "That's who you were."

It was after eleven by the time they returned to the hotel. When Nicky started into the bedroom, Carlo said,

"Put on the new blue nightgown, Nicolina. I'm very partial to the color."

She went into the bathroom and closed the door. From the bedroom she heard the sound of music and knew he had turned on the stereo. She didn't move, but stood there in front of the closed door and looked at her image in the mirror, at the glittering dress and the high heels, the short, too-blond hair. And knew that it was Nicolina who looked back at her, that somehow the person she had been—the young woman everyone had always called Nicky—had disappeared.

"Nicky?" she whispered, as though trying to call back the girl she had been. "Nicky?"

But no one answered.

She bathed and put on the blue nightgown that Carlo had selected, and after she had brushed her short blond hair, she went out into the other room.

As he had the first night of their honeymoon, he was wearing the long velour robe, and she knew there would be nothing under it. He was at the window looking out at the Arno, but he turned when he heard her.

"There you are," he said. "I was wondering where..." He stared at her, his gaze suddenly intense, nostrils fluted, full lips parted. A shadowlike expression veiled what lay hidden behind his green eyes. He held out his hand. "Come here," he said.

Slowly, pale hand to her throat, Nicolina went toward him.

He clasped her shoulders and she felt a shudder run through him. "Yes," he said. "It's exactly as I knew it would be." And with a strangled cry he brought her into his arms.

His heart beat hard against the thin fabric of her gown, and she felt a moment of fear because she sensed the barely restrained passion that lay coiled and ready to spring. He kissed her, grinding his mouth so hard against hers she felt the press of his teeth. And when she tried to protest, he thrust his tongue past her lips, searching, tasting, frantic in a need she didn't understand.

"Open my robe," he cried, and when she did he pulled her close and she felt the male hardness of him against her body.

"Carlo..." she tried to say. But he wanted no words. He blocked them with his mouth and took her lips, her breath. He gripped the back of her head, holding her so that she could not escape while he ravaged her mouth. His body shook with need and he groaned with pleasure.

And slowly, slowly, though she was frightened by the intensity of his kisses, her body warmed. She moved closer, both hands flat against the broadness of his chest, then on his shoulders, holding him as he held her.

Her knees went weak and a flame raced like wildfire through her body.

She moaned into his mouth, and when she did, he said, "At last. At last."

She lost all sense of time and place. There was only Carlo, only the mouth that covered her mouth, the body that pressed so close to hers.

He swept her off her feet and carried her to the bed. He thrust his robe aside, and when she struggled to a sitting position to try to take the blue gown off, he gathered the silky material in his fists and ripped it down the front.

Shocked, she made as though to cover her breasts, but as he had done that other time, he captured her wrists and urged her down onto the bed.

"You're so beautiful," he said. "So like..." A shiver ran through him and he let her go. He kissed her mouth, her eyelids and her cheeks. He trailed a line of kisses over her throat, her shoulders. He cupped a breast and held it poised as he began to kiss her there. He took a nipple between his teeth and held it while he lapped with his tongue.

"Carlo!" She gasped and began to move against him, wanting him now as much as he wanted her, her body frantic with need, on fire with desire, ready to be filled by him. "Please," she said. "Oh, please."

He raised his head and looked at her. His eyes were narrowed, alight with a passion that stopped the breath in her throat. "I've only just begun," he said.

He held her there, writhing under the hands that would not let her go while he lapped at her breasts. And when at last he left them, he burned a line of kisses down over her belly, down to her thighs.

"No," she whispered. "Please..."

He nipped the tender skin there, and when she cried aloud, he healed it with his tongue. She struggled, trying to get away from him, trying to escape.

But he wouldn't let her escape. He held her hands to her sides. He kissed her thighs again and nibbled love bites as he drew ever closer to that small heart of her.

She fought against the flame that threatened to consume her. She heard the sounds of whimpers and of cries, a litany of, "Please oh please oh please," and barely recognized the words as her own.

He let go of her hands, and though she had meant to push him away, she did not. Her pleas became not pleas of escape but of supplication. She was out of control, on the threshold between agony and ecstasy, helpless, racked by sensations she had never before experienced. Unable to hold back, she cried out, and her body shook with all that she was feeling.

He came up over her and with a triumphant cry joined his body to hers. He said, "Hold me! Touch me! Give me your mouth!"

And when she did, his body exploded in a paroxysm of feeling. He collapsed over her, and his breath came in sobbing gasps.

Too spent to move, he lay over her, his face against her throat. "Love," he whispered in Italian. "Sweet wife."

She stroked his tousled hair, his shoulders and his back, so filled with love she could not speak. For surely Carlo loved her. She heard it in his voice; she'd felt it in his hunger for her, his passion. For me, she thought. Only for me. And what does it matter that he calls me Nicolina, or changes my hair and the style of my clothes? All I want in this world is to please him, to be everything he wants me to be.

At last he eased himself away from her, and in a voice once again calm, almost dispassionate, he said, "Are you all right? If I was rough, I didn't mean to be."

"No, of course you weren't rough." She kissed the side of his face. "I love you, Carlo. I want to please you."

"Nicolina...?" His expression softened. He shook his head as though to clear it, and taking a deep breath, said, "You do please me, Nicolina." Then it was as though the veil she had seen earlier once again shadowed his eyes. He patted her shoulder and said, "It's late. We'd better go to sleep."

And he turned on his side away from her.

Nicky lay without speaking, feeling as though he had deserted her, wanting so desperately for him to cradle her in his arms, to warm her and tell her that he loved her.

In a little while she heard his even breathing and knew that he slept. But it was a very long time that night before Nicolina, who had been Nicky, went to sleep.

* * *

He showed her as much as he could of Florence in the next few days: the Cathedral of Santa Maria del Fiore, which had been consecrated in 1436, as well as Giotto's Campanile, the Palazzo Vecchio, the Boboli Gardens, the Uffizi Gallery and the Pitti Palace. She stood before Michelangelo's *David,* awestruck, tears misting her vision, unable to believe the genius that had created this miracle.

"I, too, felt like this the first time I saw it." Carlo squeezed her hand and they stood there together, silent before the magnificence of this work, before they moved on to see the other treasures of Florence.

He told her wonderful stories about the artists who had lived in this most beautiful of cities, and she began to see, through his eyes, the way it had been so long ago. He made history come alive for her; he showed her things she had never seen before—sculptures, statues, paintings by some of the greatest artists the world has ever known.

Whenever she showed any sign of being tired, he insisted they stop for a glass of wine or a cappuccino. When they crossed the Ponte Vecchio, he bought her a fine leather handbag and gloves, and a pair of silver filigree earrings.

Every morning after she had had breakfast in bed, he selected what he wanted her to wear that day. "The coral suit," he would say. "The flowered silk."

On their last evening there, he insisted she wear the red organza when they went out to dinner. It was strapless, nipped in at the waist, with a short, flaring skirt, and cut too low in the front for Nicky's taste.

"The bodice is awfully low, isn't it?" she said, putting the palm of her hand against her chest as though to disguise the décolletage. "I feel half-naked."

"Nonsense." He took her hand away and ran his fingers across the rise of her breasts. "You have beautiful breasts. It does no harm to show them."

He sat close to Nicky in their dimly lighted corner booth of the restaurant. He took her hand and kissed her palm; he caressed her leg under cover of the linen tablecloth. And his eyes promised that the evening was not yet over.

When they went back to the hotel and into the empty elevator, he pushed the button to start it, and when the doors closed, he pulled Nicky close and with his lips against hers said, "You've never been more beautiful. More desirable." His breath was hot, his body hard with barely restrained passion.

The doors opened, and with his arm around her waist, they went down the corridor to their room. As soon as they were inside, he kissed her again, his mouth hungry against hers, hands pressed against the small of her back to bring her closer.

"Amore," he whispered. *"Amore."* He reached around the back of her dress for her zipper.

"Wait," Nicky whispered. "Carlo..."

The dress fell to her waist. He pulled it down over her hips and kicked it aside, then stepped out of his shoes and tugged his trousers and his briefs down.

"Nicolina." He tore at her satin panties. "Nicolina!"

He put his arms around her and, sinking to his knees, took her with him. Then he was over her, grinding his body against hers, and before she could speak or move he had grasped her hips and joined his body to hers.

She encircled his shoulders and lifted herself to him, the shock of his taking her like this mixed with gladness because this was proof that Carlo loved her, that he wanted her so urgently he couldn't wait.

She opened her eyes and looked up at him. "Darling," she whispered. "Dar..." The words died on her lips, for in his eyes there was a look of almost Mephistophilean triumph. "Carlo?" she whispered. "What—"

He covered her mouth with his and drove hard against her like a man possessed. His cadence quickened. He put his hands around her back and lifted her closer. *"Si!"* he cried. *"Si, cara mia!"* And his body went wild with a passion he could not control.

He sought her mouth and kissed her hard and deep. She answered his kiss and lifted her body to his, as lost as he was in this immensity of feeling that surged between them.

He said, "Yes? Yes?" She cried his name into the silence of the night and clung to him as though she would never let him go.

It was not until later, when he lay sleeping beside her, that she remembered the look of triumph in his eyes. And something else. A frightening something she did not understand.

The next morning he checked in at his office and then went to the hospital. When he returned to the hotel, they started the drive back to the Casa Santini.

It had been an exciting few days and Nicky felt like a new woman. Actually I am a new woman, she thought with an inward smile. I have a new wardrobe, a new look and a new name. She smoothed an imaginary wrinkle from the skirt of her new coral suit and glanced at Carlo. My husband, she thought with love and with pride. He was a strange and a wonderful man, a man who could be as fierce as a lion, but who could also be gentle and considerate. He had frightened her last night, but afterward he had held and soothed her, and she had forgotten that brief moment of panic.

He was very good to her. He had insisted that she have breakfast in bed every morning, and twice when he thought she was tired, he had run a tub of hot water for her, and kneeling beside the tub, had bathed her as gently as though she were a child.

At other times . . . No, she wouldn't think about those other times. She loved him and that was all that mattered.

They turned off the highway onto the private road that led to the Casa Santini. He smiled and said, "We're almost home."

Home. Nicky rested her hand on his knee. "I love you," she said.

And told herself she did not mind that he only answered, "Dearest Nicolina."

He pulled into the circular driveway and stopped. As before, the man Sergio hurried down the front steps.

"We have a good bit more luggage than when we left, Sergio," Carlo said with a smile. "Would you and Rosa take it up to our rooms, please?"

"Certainly, sir." The elderly man looked at Nicky, raised white eyebrows, then quickly turned away.

"Come along." Carlo took her arm and led her into the house. "I want to check on Grandmother. Perhaps you'd like to go up and rest a while before dinner."

But Nicky shook her head. "I want to say hello to Elizabetta before I do," she said.

"You like her, don't you?"

"Yes, Carlo. I like her a lot."

He squeezed her hand. "That pleases me, Nicolina. More than I can tell you."

The maid Rosa came out of the kitchen and smiled when she saw Nicky. "Welcome home, *signora,*" she said. "You, too, Doctor. Your grandmother is in her rooms. I've just taken a cup of tea in to her. I'm sure she'd like to see you."

"Then we'll go and say hello." He put an arm around Nicky's waist and together they went down the corridor to Elizabetta's rooms.

He knocked, called out, "Grandmother?" and when she answered, he opened the door.

"We're home from Florence," he said.

She was in a chair by the window, her cup of tea on the table beside her. She smiled at her grandson, and to Nicky she said, "How I've missed you. Did you enjoy..." The color drained out of her face. "Nicky?" she said. "Is—is that you or..." She started up from her chair. "Your—your hair! The way you're dressed..."

White hands fluttered against her chest. *"Dio mio!"* she cried. And before Carlo could reach her, she fell back, unconscious, into her chair.

CHAPTER NINE

"It's her heart!" Carlo said, and sent Nicky running for his medical bag. When she returned, breathless and frightened, he made her wait outside the door while he ministered to Elizabetta.

Nicky paced the hall. She thought of how frail the older woman was, how white Elizabetta's face had gone, as white as though she'd seen a ghost. Had it been her heart or had something else brought on the attack? She was all right one minute, Nicky thought, then the next, when she saw my hair and the way I was dressed, she suddenly went pale. Do I remind her of someone she's known before? A friend from the past? What is it?

Almost thirty minutes went by before Carlo came out from his grandmother's room. "She's resting," he said. "She's going to be all right."

"But what is it?" Nicky whispered. "What's wrong with her?"

He led her farther down the hall. "Elizabetta had a serious illness ten years ago and it left her with a weakened heart." He hesitated, as though debating with himself whether or not to tell Nicky the truth, and finally, in a gentle voice, said, "She's been living on borrowed time for the last several years. There really isn't very much medical science can do to help her. All any of us can do is to try to make whatever time she has left as pleasant for her as we can. She's going to need a lot of looking after in the next few months, Nicolina, but don't worry. I'll arrange for a private nurse. I don't want Elizabetta to be a burden for you."

"A burden?" Tears welled in Nicky's eyes. "But I want to help. I know I'm not a nurse, Carlo, but I'd like to spend as much time with Elizabetta as I can. If you think that it's necessary to have a nurse for a few days, that's fine. But after that I can take care of her. And Rosa can help. She can sleep in Elizabetta's room at night and I can attend her during the day."

"You have other things to do," he said with the beginning of a frown.

"Like what? You're in Florence all day. We have maids to clean and a cook to make the meals." Nicky straightened her shoulders and looked him square in the eye. "I want to help take care of your grandmother and I'm damn well going to."

"Don't swear," he said.

"I damn well will if I damn well want to!"

"Nicolina . . ." The beginning of a smile softened his mouth. "I don't know why we're arguing," he said. "Of course you can help with Elizabetta. It's only that I hadn't expected you'd want to. Isabella . . ." He stopped. "A lot of women wouldn't want to be bothered with an elderly person."

"I'm not a lot of women."

"No, I don't suppose you are." He looked at her, and there was an expression in his eyes she had never seen before, surprise and something she could not quite define.

"Very well," he said. "I'll arrange for a nurse until we know that Elizabetta is out of danger. After that I'll leave it up to you. But if you change your mind—"

"I won't," Nicky said.

The nurse, a pleasant-looking, rather large woman in her early sixties, arrived that afternoon. Nicky, who had been sitting beside Elizabetta's bed, stood when Rosa brought the nurse in.

"I'm Sophia Cadute, Signora Santini." She pumped Nicky's hand before she turned to Elizabetta and in a loud voice asked, "And how are we feeling?"

"I have no idea how you're feeling," Elizabetta said with asperity. "And there's no need to shout. I may be ill but I'm not deaf."

Sophia Cadute took a step backward, then with a grin, she said, "I see we're a bit feisty. That's a good sign, isn't it? Now let's take our blood pressure and then we'll have a nice nap."

Elizabetta muttered under her breath and cast a despairing look at Nicky, who took her hand and said, "I'll be back a little later. Is there anything you want? Anything I can get you?"

"A bit of sherry, perhaps."

"Sherry!" The nurse shook her head. "Oh, no," she said. "Absolutely not."

"I always have a sherry before my dinner," Elizabetta protested.

"Not any more, I'm afraid. Dr. Glannini wouldn't approve, nor would Dr. Santini."

Nicky squeezed Elizabetta's hand. "Try to rest. I'll come back in a little while." She leaned to kiss the older woman's forehead and to whisper, "I'll see what I can do about the sherry."

Elizabetta slept, and when she awakened, Carlo went in to check on her.

"Her blood pressure is better," he told Nicky when he joined her at dinner. "She's going to be all right."

"But what brought on the attack, Carlo? Why did she react the way she did when she saw me? It was the same the first time you introduced me to her, but today it was an even more violent reaction. Was it the clothes I was wearing? My hair?"

"Of course not. You're imagining things. Perhaps when I first brought you here she was surprised, but that was only natural, wasn't it?"

"Yes, I suppose it was, but..." Nicky shook her head. "That docsn't account for her reaction today."

Carlo reached across the table and took her hand. "Elizabetta is a very old lady with a bad heart, Nicolina. The fact that she had an attack today has nothing to do with you."

She wasn't sure she believed him, but rather than argue, she decided that as soon as Elizabetta was feeling better, she would ask her. There was something strange here and she was going to find out what it was.

Elizabetta couldn't stand the nurse, and so after four days, when both Carlo and Dr. Glannini agreed that Elizabetta was better, Sophia Cadute was dismissed.

"And tonight I'll have a sherry before dinner," Elizabetta announced with a wicked gleam in her eye.

"We'll both have one," Nicky responded with a laugh.

That night, at Nicky's suggestion, she and Carlo had dinner in Elizabetta's room. The cook prepared one of Elizabetta's favorite dishes, and Rosa set up a table beneath the floor-to-ceiling windows. There was a fine white tablecloth, candlelight, a nosegay of flowers that Nicky had picked earlier. And sherry.

Elizabetta took a sip and closed her eyes with a satisfied smile. "Delicious," she said. "You can throw away all of your medicine, Carlo. This is what I need to get me back on my feet again." She smiled at Nicky. "And a visit from you, my dear, whenever you have the time."

"I have all the time in the world," Nicky said.

And meant it. She wanted to get to know Carlo's grandmother, partly because she loved Carlo, and Elizabetta was an important part of his life, but also because she had no grandparents of her own.

Her mother and father had been married for such a short time that she'd had very little opportunity to become acquainted with his parents. She'd spent a month with them on their Ohio farm one summer when she was six. All that she remembered of her grandfather was that he was tall and spare and that he'd showed her how to reach under the hens for eggs. Grandmother Fairchild had been a round dumpling of a woman who wore her gray hair back in a tight little bun and whose skin smelled like freshly churned butter. Nicky had loved them both and she'd cried when her father had come to take her away.

Of her mother's parents she knew almost nothing. Eleanora had left home when she was sixteen to marry Herbert Avery, a man ten years her senior, and she'd never looked back. By the time Nicky was old enough to ask about her mother's parents, Eleanora told her they'd died when Nicky was three.

Nicky had listened to schoolmates tell stories about their grandparents and she'd been filled with envy. What would it be like, she'd wondered, to have a grandmother or a grandfather to bring you little presents and hold you on their lap? One special person who loved you unconditionally, someone you could love back with all the love that was in your heart?

For Nicky, Elizabetta had become that person.

Each morning after breakfast Nicky would join her, and if the day was sunny, they would sit in the garden that opened off the sitting room. Sometimes they would talk. At other times Nicky would read aloud. When she stumbled over a word, Elizabetta would help her.

"Your Italian is better every day," the grandmother told her. "You have an ear for the language and you'll be talking like a native in no time."

She spoke often about her husband, Gianfranco. "I loved him from the moment I saw him," she told Nicky one day. "We met at a fair in Fiesole when I was eighteen and he was twenty-six. There was music and dancing, the smell of all kinds of food, children racing about, people in sixteenth-century costumes, blaring trumpets, banners streaming." Her eyes sparkled with the memory. "It was just before the start of the horse race that I first saw him. I had become separated from my sisters, and suddenly, when I looked up, I saw this young man standing at the edge of the crowd gathered around the fire-eaters. He was watching me, his dark eyes intent, frowning the way Carlo sometimes frowns.

"When he started toward me, I thought about running away, but I didn't. He held me with his gaze and I stood there, my heart beating so hard I didn't think I would ever breathe properly again.

"He stopped in front of me and said, 'I am Gianfranco Santini. I'm going to ride in the horse race and I would like you to give me something of yours to carry as my standard.'

"I said, 'I don't know you,' and he replied, 'But you will, because very likely I'm going to marry you.' While I was still gasping for breath, he held his hand out and said, 'Give me your mantilla.' And I did."

"And did he win the race?" Nicky asked, as excited at hearing the story as Elizabetta was about telling it.

"Of course." Elizabetta smiled. "He came riding around the town square, my white mantilla held aloft, and when the officials declared him a winner, he rode straight toward me. My sisters were with me by that time, and I can still remember the shocked look on their faces when he stopped in front of me and said, 'Your mantilla, my lady.'"

"And you married him."

Elizabetta nodded. "Scarcely two months later. We lived together for forty-six years, Nicky, and there was not a day of it that I ever regretted." Tears filled her eyes and for a few moments she couldn't speak. Then, with a sigh, she said, "Would you like to see a picture of him?"

"Yes, I'd love to."

"I have later pictures here that I'll show you, but I'd like you to see him as he was when we were younger. Those pictures are in my album in the sewing room on the third floor. Would you mind getting it?"

"No, but..." Nicky hesitated. "For some reason Carlo doesn't want me up there." She smiled at Elizabetta. "Are there any crumbling ceilings, family ghosts, cobwebs or mice?"

"Indeed not! It's just that...that we keep the rooms up there closed off." Elizabetta tapped impatient fingers on the top of her cane. "I see no reason why you can't go into the sewing room." She waved an imperious hand. "Run along. I'm anxious to show you my pictures."

"All right," Nicky said. "I won't be long."

She went up to the second floor, but at the foot of the stairs leading to the third floor she stopped. Carlo had asked her not to go up. But Elizabetta wanted her photo album. And she herself was so curious to see what was up there she could hardly contain herself. Still... Elizabetta and curiosity won out. Nicky went up the stairs.

There was a door at the top, and when she opened it, she saw a spacious entry hall, almost like a salon, with a faded brocade love seat and two brocade chairs. The hall opened onto a long corridor, and as she started along it Nicky saw that there were four doors, all closed. She opened the first door. It was a small bedroom with a single bed, a dresser and two straight-back chairs. When she touched one of the chairs, dust came off on her fingers.

The sewing room was next, and on a table by the old-fashioned treadle sewing machine she found the leather photo album. She picked it up and went out and closed the door. But instead of going back toward the stairs, she hesitated. It would do no harm as long as she was here to have a look around.

The room next to the sewing room was also a bedroom, but unlike the other room it was very large. The furniture was massive, the canopied bed on a raised dais. It was covered with a dark purple spread, the same color as the velvet drapes that hung from the tall windows. Royalty, Nicky thought, imagining the Medici prince who had slept here.

The room next-door was a playroom. She went in and, because she was curious, went directly to the windows and pulled open the drapes. Along with a small table and chairs, there were all kinds of toys here, including a rocking horse, and in one corner toy train tracks complete with bridges, signal boxes, a miniature mountain and a switchman's house.

This was the room where Carlo had played when he was a boy—a room where some day, God willing, her own children would play.

Some day, but when? Carlo had insisted she go on the Pill. Every day he asked her if she had taken it, as though afraid she would forget. She could understand his wanting to wait for a while, to give them time to become accustomed to each other and to enjoy each other without the responsibility of children. But for how long?

She gazed around the room, picturing how it would look with new wallpaper and curtains. She could repaint the rocking horse and the table and chairs, put in bookcases for new toys and storybooks—so many things to make this a wonderful children's room.

With a sigh, and resolving that she would ask Carlo how long they must wait before they could start a family, she left the playroom. Farther down, the hall turned a corner. Nicky saw a door and tried to open it, but it was locked. Why? she wondered. The others doors hadn't been locked. Why was this one?

Clasping the album to her with a puzzled frown, Nicky stood for a moment in the deserted hall. Then, with a shake of her head, she went back downstairs.

"I went up to the third floor," Nicky said that night when she and Carlo were having dinner.

Very carefully he put his fork down on his plate. For a moment he didn't speak, then he frowned and said, "I distinctly remember asking you not to go up there."

"I know, Carlo, but Elizabetta was telling me about your grandfather and she asked me to get her a photo album from the sewing room."

"And naturally, while you were there you had a look around." His dark eyebrows were drawn together. His voice was cold.

"Yes. I was curious. I saw the two bedrooms and the playroom." She smiled, wanting to ease the look of tension on his face. "It's a lovely room, Carlo. I could almost see you there as a little boy, playing with your train set. Does it still run?"

"I have no idea."

"We could fix it up," she said. "The room, I mean. Put new wallpaper on the walls, paint the furniture. Get new curtains."

"And why would we want to do that?" he asked in a coolly polite voice.

"To use for our children. When we have them, I mean. Some day, perhaps next year—"

"I've told you how I feel about having children, right now at least."

"I know you have, Carlo, but I thought—"

"When the time is right we'll discuss it again, but right now I have other things on my mind. In the meantime, I'd appreciate it if you would stay off the third floor."

"But why? The rooms are dusty, but nothing is falling down or crumbling. I think it would be a good idea to have the maids clean up there once a week, air the rooms out—"

"Leave it alone!" he said angrily. "Just leave it alone!" He shoved his chair back from the table, and before Nicky could say anything, he strode out of the room.

She sat there, stunned by his reaction. Something was very strange. What was there about the third floor of the Casa Santini that made it off-limits? When they had first come here Carlo had told her the third floor was closed off because of the difficulty in heating up there. She could understand that. But he had also said it was in disrepair, and it wasn't. There wasn't anything that a good cleaning and dusting wouldn't make as good as new. And why, if the other rooms were unlocked, was the room at the turn of the corridor locked?

The following morning Nicky did not get up to have breakfast with Carlo as she usually did. Instead, she pretended to be asleep when she heard him get out of bed. They'd had little to say to each other the night before. He had stayed up late, reading in the sitting room, and she had fallen asleep before he came in.

When he left their room she got up and showered, but not until she heard him leave did she go downstairs for her breakfast. She was thoughtful as she sipped her coffee and gazed out into the garden. It was a warm summer's day, and she wondered as she looked around this perfect room and out at the perfect garden why she had such a feeling of discontent. She had everything she wanted—a beautiful home, jewelry and clothes, a handsome husband. Why then did she feel restless and unhappy?

Because there's something here I don't understand, she thought. Because Carlo is holding a part of himself away from me. It wasn't just because he had never confessed to her that he loved her, for she told herself that in time he would. It was more than that. It was as though he had built an invisible wall around a part of himself, and behind that wall there were things that he would forever keep from her.

She thought of the way he had looked at her when he had first seen her with her hair shorn and blond. She'd seen the shock, and something else. Surprise? Triumph? Henry Higgins gloating over the creation Eliza Doolittle had become?

If Carlo had wanted a glamorous wife, why had he chosen her? Why, out of all the women in Italy, had he chosen her?

Nicky pushed aside the breakfast she had barely touched, and with a look of resolution, went down the hall toward Elizabetta's rooms.

"It's a beautiful day," she said when she went in. "I thought that if you're up to it we might have a walk in the garden."

"Lovely." Elizabetta smiled up at Nicky from her chair. "It's time I see what that old rascal Luigi has been up to."

Nicky took her hand to help her up, and when Elizabetta had her cane they went out through the French doors into the garden.

The grass was still dew fresh, so they kept to the garden path, walking slowly, with Nicky holding Elizabetta's arm. The garden was a riot of color, with whole beds of purple irises and calla lilies, violets and lily of the valley, black-eyed Susans, blue gentians and a magnificence of roses.

"I miss working in my garden," Elizabetta said with a sigh. "These Tudor roses were here when I first came to the Casa Santini as a bride. I can remember strolling in the evening with Gianfranco. How soft the air seemed, and so sweetly scented with roses. Once we..." She looked at Nicky and a blush of color rose in her pale cheeks.

"Once you what?" Nicky prompted.

Elizabetta shook her head, but when Nicky said, "Tell me," she lowered her voice.

"Once we made love here, very late at night, when the house was quiet and the children were asleep. I didn't want to. I thought that making love out-of-doors..." The blush deepened. "But Gianfranco insisted and it was...it was quite wonderful and I will never forget."

Tears rose in Nicky's eyes. She kissed Elizabetta's cheek and said, "Thank you for telling me. I will never forget, either."

In a little while they sat in the shade on one of the wrought-iron benches. Luigi found them there. He said, *"Buon giorno,"* to Nicky, then, after wiping his hands on his work pants, came to shake Elizabetta's hand and say, "I have missed seeing you in the garden, Signora Santini."

"You mean you've missed my ordering you around."

"That, too," he said with a chuckle. "Cook told me you were ill. I hope you're better now."

"Much better, Luigi. Thank you. My granddaughter is taking very good care of me."

He glanced at Nicky, surprised, then excused himself and went back to trimming the roses.

"That was a very nice thing for you to say," Nicky said when Luigi was out of earshot.

"But it's exactly the way I feel about you, my dear. I couldn't feel closer to you if you were my own flesh and blood." She patted Nicky's hand. "I'm glad Carlo married you. You will be good for him."

"Elizabetta..." Nicky took a deep breath. "There are so many things I don't understand, about Carlo and about the house." She hesitated. "And about you. The first time we met you were shocked. It was almost as though you recognized me."

Elizabetta stiffened. "Nonsense, girl. You're imagining things."

"And a few days ago, the day you became ill, you looked at me as though you'd seen a ghost. I thought..." Nicky shook her head. "I almost thought it was the shock of seeing me with my new hairstyle and clothes that made you faint." She took Elizabetta's hand. "Why did you look at me the way you did when we came back from Florence? Do I remind you of someone? Is that it?''

"No! No, of course not." Elizabetta pulled her hand away and struggled to her feet. "I'm tired," she said. "I want to go in."

She looked at Nicky, then quickly away. But not before Nicky had seen the same shadowed expression in her eyes that she had seen before in Carlo's. She knew that Elizabetta had not told her the truth, but she didn't know why.

CHAPTER TEN

"We've been invited to a party Saturday night," Carlo said one morning at breakfast. "It will be an opportunity for you to meet some of my friends." He drummed a nervous staccato beat on the tabletop. "It's at the Andrettis'. He's an industrialist. Sicilian. She's from a rich Roman family. Very attractive. You might like her. Dr. Raviggia and his wife will be there. And my assistant, Dr. Tacchia. And about fifteen or so others, I should imagine. It will be formal and I'd like you to wear something special. Perhaps the blue evening dress we bought in Florence."

The one with the alarming décolletage and the slit skirt, Nicky thought with dismay. "It's pretty daring," she said. "I mean, for the first time I'm meeting your friends. What about the white blouse with the black velvet skirt? It's a lot more conservative."

Carlo shook his head. "No, I want you to wear the blue. You've never worn it."

Because we never go anywhere, Nicky almost said. And it was true. Since their shopping spree in Florence they hadn't gone out at all, not even to dinner. Part of it, of course, was because Carlo often worked late at the hospital or at his office in Florence. When he returned to the Casa Santini, he checked first on Elizabetta, then he and Nicky had their dinner. Afterward they retired to their rooms, he with his medical journals, Nicky with a book. Very often she went to bed before he did.

"I'm sleepy," she would say, hoping that he would put the journal down.

But most of the time he only nodded and said, "Sleep well."

There were times when she was tempted to say, "Please, come to bed with me. I'm lonely, I need you." But she did not.

If it had not been for Elizabetta, her days as well as her nights would have been filled with loneliness. She spent long hours with the woman every day, not out of a sense of duty, but because she was coming to love Carlo's grandmother. Though at first she had been reticent about speaking of personal things, she now found herself sharing bits and pieces of her childhood with the older woman. She told Elizabetta what little she remembered of her father. She confessed her ambivalent feelings about her mother, and the deep sorrow that troubled her because she and Eleanora had not been closer.

And once she spoke of her uncertainties as to her role as Carlo's wife.

"I want to measure up to his expectations," she said, "but I don't know what he wants of me. There's so much of his life I don't know anything about—his medical practice, what he likes, what he doesn't like. I want him to need me the way I need him." She looked at Elizabetta, her eyes serious, her expression intent. "Sometimes I have the feeling that Carlo doesn't need anyone."

"But he does, Nicky." Elizabetta patted her hand. "Carlo is a difficult man at times, and perhaps that is his strength, as well as his weakness. He's strong and he is determined, yes? Once he has made up his mind to do something, he doesn't look back. He knew from the time he was a boy that he wanted to be a doctor. He graduated first in his class at the university, and when he got to medical school, he thought of nothing except learning to be the best doctor he could be. For four years he worked harder than I've ever seen a young man work. It is the same now with his practice and his work at the hospital. He's totally devoted to his profession."

"I understand that," Nicky said. "I don't resent the time Carlo spends away from me, but when he's with me I feel as though..." She shook her head, trying to find the words to express all that she was feeling, and said, "As though he were holding a part of himself back."

Elizabetta covered Nicky's hand with her own. "Carlo has known great pain, and I'm afraid that has made him very guarded, very careful of his emotions. But I truly believe that if you are patient and if you continue to love him, you will break through that wall he has built around himself." She squeezed Nicky's hand. "Patience and love, my child. Remember that."

Patience and love, Nicky silently repeated. And the hope that someday Carlo would love her the way she loved him.

On the morning after Carlo told her about the party, she said to Elizabetta, "Carlo and I have been invited to a party at the Andrettis' on Saturday night."

"Oh? Well...that's nice, isn't it? You and Carlo go out so rarely. I'm sure you'll have a splendid time." She reached for one of the hard candies she kept on the table near her chair, and there was a hesitancy in her voice when she asked, "Who else is going to be at the party? Do you know?"

Nicky shook her head. "Carlo said there'd be twenty or so guests. I think I'm a little frightened at the prospect of meeting so many people."

"Nonsense, child. All you have to do is be yourself."

"That's just it..." Nicky began to fold thin pleats in the fabric of her bright red Gypsy skirt. "I'm not myself. I'm turning into someone else, a someone that Carlo wants me to be, glamorous and sophisticated...." She shook her head and there was a look of desperation in her eyes. "That's not who I am, Elizabetta. It's not who I want to be."

"My dear, I—I..." Elizabetta looked away from Nicky and lowered her gaze. "There's something...something you should know, but I—"

"What is it, Elizabetta?"

The older woman looked at her. "I—I can't," she said. "Perhaps in time Carlo will..." She shook her head, unwilling to say more.

"Will what?" Nicky leaned forward in her chair. "Please, Elizabetta. What is it? I need to know."

Elizabetta closed her eyes. "I'm tired," she said in a shaky voice. "I must rest."

"But..." Nicky choked back her questions. Elizabetta looked pale and the hand that gripped her cane trembled. "All right, dear." She kissed Elizabetta's cheek. "Rest now. We'll talk again later."

Elizabetta only nodded. And Nicky knew that the subject was closed.

Carlo had little to say on the drive to the Andretti party. He had looked at Nicky with an appraising eye when she had come down the winding staircase. The rise of her breasts showed above the décolletage of the blue dress. One slim leg was exposed every time she took a step.

"Yes," he'd said, going forward to take her hand as she descended the last step. "You look beautiful. Stunning."

"I feel half dressed."

"Nonsense."

"Maybe if I put a mantilla over my shoulders—"

"No, the diamond earrings are all you need. Nothing else. You're perfect just as you are." He took her hand and led her out to the car, and did not speak until they reached the Villa Andretti.

The private road leading to the villa was lined with ancient sycamores. Through the trees Nicky could see the house and the colored lights that played on the spray of water bubbling from a large stone fountain at the rise of the sloping gardens. Lamborghinis, Ferraris, Maseratis and Alfa Romeos were parked in the curved driveway.

An attendant in a smart red jacket and dark trousers ran to open Nicky's door as soon as Carlo stopped. He helped her out, then hurried around to Carlo's side and said, "I'll take care of your car, *signor*."

Carlo took Nicky's arm and they went up the broad stairs of the Andretti mansion. She felt the tension of his body and turned to look at him. His face was pale, his expression tense.

A butler greeted them in the foyer. From the room in front of them Nicky could hear the sound of music and of laughter, the tinkle of crystal glasses. People were grouped together beneath a sparkling chandelier, and suddenly she was excited, eager to join them, to meet new people and be a part of their happy group.

"Here you are at last." A short, balding man hurried toward them. "I was afraid you weren't coming, Carlo, but now you are here and all is well, yes? I'm so anxious to meet your wife." He turned to Nicky, hand extended, then froze, hand in midair. "I..." His mouth opened and closed. He looked at Carlo, then back at Nicky. "I'm— I'm happy to—to meet you," he managed to say. "I'm Pablo Andretti. Come let me introduce you to my wife and to our guests."

Carlo tightened his grip on Nicky's arm. She looked up at him, puzzled. But he didn't return her look, only stared straight ahead, his mouth a firm, hard line, his pale green eyes expressionless.

An attractive woman in her early forties hurried toward them. Pablo Andretti said, "Ah, here is my wife."

The woman said, "Carlo! How good it is to see you." She turned to smile at Nicky. "How do you..." She stopped, took a step back and sucked in her breath. She looked at her husband, at Carlo and finally back at Nicky again. Regaining her composure, she said, "I'm Claudia Andretti. I'm so glad you and Carlo could join us. Please come in and meet our guests."

What is this? Nicky wondered, feeling herself begin to panic. The two of them had looked at her as though they'd seen a ghost. Was it her dress? It wasn't any more daring than Signora Andretti's. What was it?

The four of them stood at the top of the steps leading into the salon. Someone turned to look and smile up at them. Then others. Suddenly all conversation stopped. Expressions were stunned, curious.

"Here they are at last," Claudia Andretti said in a too-loud voice. "Carlo and his new bride."

For a minute there was only that terrible silence, then a woman Nicky's age stepped forward and shook Nicky's hand. "I'm Signora Tacchia," she said. "My husband works with Carlo. How nice it is to meet you."

Normal talk resumed. Nicky was introduced to Dr. Raviggia and his wife, to Dr. Glannini's wife, to Signor and Signora Bazzano, Dr. Marconi. So many names, so many faces. Polite but curious. Oh, so curious.

Cocktails were served. Nicky sipped a glass of champagne. When Carlo left her to speak to Dr. Tacchia, a man she hadn't yet met approached. He was in his late forties, handsome with salt-and-pepper hair, a trim mustache and dark Italian eyes.

"We haven't met," he said with a slight smile. "I'm Stefano Ponti. I live next door to Casa Santini. May I get you another glass of champagne?"

"No, thank you." Nicky offered her hand. "I'm happy to meet you, Signor Ponti. You said you live next door?"

"In a house that's completely hidden by high stone walls and thick hedges," he answered with a laugh. "These sixteenth-century places are like armed fortresses, hidden away from the world as though they were a separate entity unto themselves." He looked at her over the rim of his glass. "Sometimes I don't think we've changed in all these years. We still hide our nasty little secrets and plot our Machiavellian schemes." He took a sip of his drink. "Did you know there's a tunnel between the Casa Santini and my place?"

"A tunnel?" Nicky looked surprised.

"Undoubtedly used for clandestine meetings. I'll show it to you sometime. Whenever you—" He looked up and said, "Oh, oh, here comes your *marito.*" He grinned at her and lowered his voice. "Fire in his eye because I've been monopolizing you, no doubt." He held out his hand. "Well, there you are," he said to Carlo. "I've been getting acquainted with your wife."

"So I see." Carlo ignored the extended hand. "We're going in to dinner," he said to Nicky. "Come along."

She ignored Carlo's scowl and the pressure on her arm. Holding her hand out to Stefano Ponti, she said, "It was very nice meeting you. I hope we can talk again later."

"You may count on it, dear lady." He tilted his drink toward Carlo. *"Salute,"* he said.

Carlo wheeled Nicky around. "I don't like your flirting," he snapped.

"Flirting? Don't be silly. We were only talking."

"I'd rather you didn't."

"Mr. Ponti's a guest here the same as we are. Why shouldn't I speak to him?"

"Because I don't want you to."

Nicky stopped and pulled away from him. "And that's a reason?"

"You're damn right it is." He took her arm. "Come along. People are staring."

"They've been staring ever since we walked in here tonight."

"That's your imagination."

"It isn't. It..." Signora Andretti was beckoning to her. "Over here, Nicolina," she said. "I've put you between Dr. Raviggia and Signora Tacchia. She speaks perfect English and is anxious to get to know you. Carlo, you're here next to Signora Davazati."

The dinner was delicious. White wine was served with the cold lobster cocktail and the vichyssoise, a dry red with the beef. As Claudia Andretti had claimed, Signora Tacchia spoke excellent English, and after months of speaking only Italian, it was a relief for Nicky to speak her own language again.

"Call me Annamaria," the woman said. From Verona, she had only recently married her husband. "I know so few people around Florence," she told Nicky. "I hope we will be friends."

The other guests had little to say to Nicky. Now and then she caught them watching her, and once when she glanced up and saw two women with their heads together, they looked away, embarrassed. So in spite of Annamaria Tacchia's friendly chatter, Nicky was glad when dinner was over and the guests returned to the salon.

Couples began to dance, and when Dr. Tacchia came to claim his wife, Nicky was left alone.

"We can't have this." Stefano Ponti took Nicky's hand. "Carlo is talking to some of his doctor friends, so I have every right to ask his wife to dance."

Nicky smiled. "All right," she said. "I'd love to."

He led her out to the other dancers. "I'd heard about your marriage," he said when he put his arms around her. "It was rather sudden, wasn't it?"

Nicky nodded. "Carlo and I met in Venice. I became ill with pneumonia and he took care of me."

"And how long did it take for him to...what is the American expression? Take you off your feet?"

"Sweep me off my feet," Nicky said with a smile. "Actually, we married very quickly. Less than two weeks after I recovered."

"I see." Imperceptibly, Ponti's arms tightened around her. "Carlo always has had a taste for exquisite women." He looked down at Nicky. "And you, my dear, are exquisite." He shook his head. "It's absolutely amazing, you know. I simply can't get over the resemblance."

"The resemblance?" Nicky asked, and felt her stomach tighten. "To whom?"

"Why, to Isabella, of course. Everyone noticed it the moment you came into the room. She was taller than you are, but she wore her hair almost exactly as you're wearing yours. Even her facial structure was much the same."

He looked down at her, his dark eyes curious, searching. "She was also partial to blue, much the same color as you're wearing. She had a marvelous flare for clothes. Actually, she set the style for half the wealthy women in Italy."

A cold chill crept down Nicky's spine. She felt frozen, numb, unable to speak.

"I've never seen a man as much in love with a woman as Carlo was with Isabella," Ponti went on. "He was obsessed, absolutely besotted with love. And of course he was devastated when she died. It was terrible, a tragic accident." Ponti paused. "You do know how she died, don't you?"

Nicky swallowed hard. "No," she made herself say. "I don't know."

"She fell from one of the windows on the third floor and broke her neck. It was during a storm. The police thought that very likely she'd tried to close the shutters and had either stumbled or been pulled out by the wind." He cocked one eyebrow. "At least that was their theory."

"I—I see." She felt sick, dizzy. She had to get away from here, somewhere where she could be alone.

"But things have turned out nicely for Carlo after all," Ponti went on. "When he found you, he found an almost exact replica of Isabella. Wasn't that fortunate for him? To find someone so like her, I mean."

Nicky stopped and pulled away from him. "I—I'm awfully warm. I—I'd like to get some air."

"Oh, I'm sorry. Perhaps I've been talking too much. Here, let me help you." He put an arm around her waist and started with her toward the open doors leading to the terrace.

"I can manage," Nicky said. "Really, I—"

"Where are you going?" Carlo, his face tight with anger, stepped in front of her.

"I'm afraid your wife isn't feeling well," Ponti said before Nicky could answer. "She felt the need for some air. I was going to take her out to the terrace."

"I'll take her." He took Nicky's arm and drew her away from Ponti. Once they reached the terrace he said, "What's this about your not feeling well? You were perfectly all right a few minutes ago. What—"

"Get away from me!" She shoved at him as hard as she could, both hands flat against his chest, her face contorted, her eyes burning with anger.

His eyes went wide with shock. "What's the matter with you?"

He took a step toward her but she backed away. "Don't touch me!" she cried. "Don't you ever touch me again!"

"What in the hell's wrong?"

"I know! Damn you to hell, Carlo. I know about Isabella. I know why you married me."

"Nicolina..." His face in the light of the crescent moon was ashen. "Nicolina, I—"

"Nicky!" she screamed at him. "My name is Nicky. I'm Nicky Fairchild. I live in Florida and I wear blue jeans and I go barefoot and I..." She was sobbing now, great gulping sobs that tore from her throat in an agony of rage. Before he could stop her she turned and ran down the steps of the terrace.

He ran after her. "Wait!" he called out. "Nicolina, wait!"

But she ran on, almost unable to see because of the tears streaming down her face, and when she stumbled he caught her.

"Stop this!" he said. "Stop it at once!"

He grabbed her arm, and when she struggled, he put his arm around her waist and half carrying, half dragging her, led her to where the cars were parked.

The attendant hurried over. "The black Ferrari," Carlo said. "Quickly. My wife isn't feeling well."

"Let me go!" Nicky tried to break free, but his arm tightened around her waist.

"Behave yourself," he ordered. "Or—"

"Or what?" Defiant, enraged, she looked up at him, her face streaked with tears. "What else can you do to me that you haven't already done?"

The attendant brought the car to a stop in front of them. Carlo said, *"Grazie."* He pushed Nicky in and hurried around to his side of the car.

"I can explain," he said as he wheeled the Ferrari out of the driveway.

"I don't want your explanation. I don't want anything from you."

He shot her a look, then, grim-faced, stared straight in front of him.

Dio mio, what had he done? He'd known this would happen some day, that someone like Stefano Ponti, damn him to eternal hell, would see and make the comparison between Nicolina and Isabella. God help him, maybe he'd taken her to the party tonight hoping they *would* see the resemblance.

What was wrong with him? There were times lately when he thought he was losing his mind, when he told himself he must have been insane to do what he had done, to think that he could replace Isabella. Mad. He was totally mad.

He looked at Nicolina. Her face in the dim glow of the dashboard light was anguished, tortured. "I'll talk to her," he told himself. "I'll make her see that it's her I want. I'll make her believe me."

He pulled into the driveway of the Casa Santini. Before he could turn off the ignition, Nicky was out of the car and running toward the house.

"Damn!" he swore under his breath. Then he, too, was out of the car and running after her. "Wait!" he cried. "Stop!"

But Nicky didn't stop. When she realized he was after her, she veered from the path and ran toward the garden. She didn't want to wait or stop or ever have to see him or speak to him again.

She stumbled in the high heels, and with a muttered oath stopped long enough to kick them off. Then she was running again, and suddenly, in front of her, she saw the maze. She darted into it and kept running.

A green darkness surrounded her. She ran to the end of the tunnel, turned and ran on. Turn after turn, getting deeper and deeper into the labyrinth of high hedges. She heard Carlo calling out to her, and all she could think of was that she had to get away from him, that he would never find her here in the maze. It didn't matter that she was lost or that she might never find her way out. All that mattered was that she get away from Carlo.

The moon disappeared behind the clouds and the night was dark. She stumbled and fell against the hedge wall, fought a rising panic and ran on, arms out in front of her because she could barely see.

Ahead of her there was another turn of the maze. The darkness was closing in on her—the darkest dark she'd ever known—and she was afraid.

She rounded the corner, and suddenly a figure loomed in front of her. She screamed and tried to turn back the way she had come. But Carlo grabbed her and pulled her up against his chest.

"No!" she cried. "Let me go! Let me go!" She shoved hard against him. "No, no, no! I never want to see you again. I hate you."

He tried to put his arms around her, but she writhed away from him and started running.

She bumped into the tall hedge, spun away from it and kept running. She could hear him behind her. She looked over her shoulder, and when she did she stumbled and fell.

Before he could stop himself, he tripped and fell over her. She struggled to sit up, but he held her there. "Are you hurt?" he panted. "Did I hurt you?"

"Let me go!"

She struck out at him and he said, "Listen to me! Listen to me!" He straddled her and gripped her wrists, holding her so she wouldn't hit him again. But she struggled, wrenching from side to side, her slender arms flailing against him.

The breath came hard in his throat. He flattened his body against hers, and suddenly it was as though every nerve ending in his body was on fire.

"Stop!" he said again, and when she screamed at him he covered her mouth with his.

The more she struggled, the more intense became his passion. He gripped her jaw with one hand, holding her so that she couldn't move, and pressed hot kisses against her mouth.

"I hate you!" she screamed, but the words were smothered against his lips. He tried to press his tongue past her lips. She wouldn't part them, and in a frenzy of need, he nipped her bottom lip and, when she cried out, plunged his tongue past her lips.

Heat shot through her. She surged against him, struggling to break free, but when she did she felt his hardness against the thin fabric of her gown and knew her struggles were exciting him even more.

He cupped her breast, and when she cried out, he pulled the front of her dress lower and began to caress her with the palm of his hand. She fought herself as well as him, fought with all the strength that was in her not to give in to him, or the heat—oh God, the heat that ran like electric wires through her body.

He took a throbbing nipple to tug and to squeeze, and when she cried out, he took her mouth again. His voice thickened as he moaned, *"Cara. Cara mia."*

He let go of her wrists so that he could reach down and tug the tight slit skirt up over her thighs. She heard the material rip, heard the snick of his zipper, of his trousers being pulled over his hips before he yanked her panties down.

Then the hot feel of his skin before his mouth covered hers again. "I hate you," she whispered. "Hate—"

"I know. I know."

She gripped his shoulders and raked her nails across his skin. He moaned his pain into her mouth and then he was inside her, hard and wild, his body writhing in a frenzy of need against hers.

She fought him—and the terrible passion that threatened to overwhelm her—but it was no use. He held her there, surging against her until, with a cry of need, she lifted her body to his.

He sought her mouth, supping from it like a man about to die of thirst, and all the time his big body moved against hers. It was too much, too wild, too primitive. For him. For her.

He plunged and withdrew, to plunge again and again. The breath rasped in his throat. He held nothing back as the feeling mounted and grew, until it was past bearing.

She was out of control, lost in this moment of the most supreme ecstasy she had ever known. She cried aloud into the darkness of the night, close to fainting from sheer pleasure when it happened for her and she soared like a wild bird up and up into the endless darkness.

He took her cry and with one great surge exploded inside her, thrusting against her again and again, until with the strangled murmuring of her name he collapsed over her.

Slowly, slowly, their breathing evened. Slowly, slowly, Nicky became aware of where they were, of the damp earth against her back, of the drifting clouds and the slip of silver moon above. She felt the beat of Carlo's heart against her breast and knew that this time had been different. This time he had held nothing back. This time he had given all of himself.

But to whom had he given it? To her or to Isabella?

And with the thought, a pain unlike anything she had ever known clutched at her heart and she began to weep.

CHAPTER ELEVEN

They didn't speak on the way back to the house. Carlo held her hand very tightly, as though afraid she would run from him again. But Nicky was too mentally and emotionally drained to run. When they reached the house and she faltered at the foot of the stairs, he picked her up in his arms and carried her.

Once in their sitting room, he placed her on the black leather sofa. "There's a chill in the air," he said. "I'll light a fire."

She watched him bend to strike a match to the chips and logs that had already been laid. One of the sleeves of his evening jacket was torn at the shoulder; his trousers were grass stained and caked with dirt. The impeccable Dr. Santini, she thought.

She looked down at the blue gown. It, too, bore grass stains. The bodice was torn and had slipped over one shoulder; the slit skirt was ripped to her waist.

The fire caught and Carlo turned to look at her. "I'll get you a robe."

A moment later he returned. He helped her take the dress off and wrapped her in his robe.

"We have to talk," he said.

Nicky shook her head. "Tomorrow—"

"Not tomorrow. Now."

He sat beside her on the sofa, and when she would not look at him, he cupped her chin and made her face him. "We can't let this wait, Nicolina."

"I don't want to talk to you."

"I know you don't, but there are things that have to be said."

"What?" she asked, her eyes flashing with anger. "That the only reason you married me was because I look like your dead wife?"

His head jerked back as though she had slapped him. "That wasn't the only reason," he said.

Nicky turned away from him. "Wasn't it?"

"Nicolina..." He hesitated. "If we are to go on from here, there are things you must know and understand."

She looked at him, and for the moment her anger was replaced by a deep anguish. "I can't bear it," she whispered. "I don't want to hear about Isabella, about your life with her."

"If I can stand telling, then you can stand to listen. You have to know the way it was." He took her hands in his, and held them tightly when she tried to pull away.

"I met Isabella at a medical conference in Rome," he said. "She was engaged to a colleague of mine, and she had come to the dinner at the end of the conference with him. When she walked into the banquet room, every man there turned to stare. As for me..." He shook his head. "I was stunned by her. She was the most beautiful woman I had ever seen. My colleague introduced us. Isabella and I talked, we flirted, and when the dinner was over she left with me."

"Did you sleep with her that night?" Nicky asked, her voice taut with all that she was feeling.

"Yes," he said. "I slept with her."

Nicky closed her eyes and leaned back against the sofa. She didn't want to listen to any more of this. It was too painful. It was tearing her apart.

"We were married a month later," he went on before she could stop him. "I brought her home with me, here to the Casa Santini." He let go of Nicky's hands and turned to stare into the fire. The only other light from the room was from the lamp on the desk. His face was shadowed; there were lines she had not seen before, a haunted agony in his eyes that in spite of the way she felt made her want to reach out and touch him.

"In less than six months I realized I had made a terrible mistake," he said. "Isabella changed. Or perhaps she had simply stopped pretending. She was self-centered and vain. She spent money like it was water slipping through her fingers. She flaunted her beauty and flirted, as she had flirted with me, with every man she met. My friends, my colleagues..." He ran a hand across his face as though to wipe away a painful memory. "I think now that she had already started having affairs, but I didn't believe it then. I told myself I could change her, that because I loved her I could make her into the woman I wanted her to be. We traveled to the States, to Israel and Egypt, anywhere Isabella wanted to go. By the time we returned to Italy, I honestly believed that she had changed. But she hadn't."

He reached for Nicky's hand again, and though she tried to pull it away, he would not let her go. "She started an affair with someone I knew. When I found out I went a little crazy. I wanted to kill him...."

The grip of his hand was painful, but Nicky didn't pull away.

"Maybe I wanted to kill her, too," he continued in a voice made hoarse by all the emotions raging through him. "At first she denied the affair, then she admitted it and begged me to forgive her. She swore it was over, that she'd have nothing more to do with the man who had become her lover."

He looked at Nicky. "I believed her. God help me, I believed her."

"It wasn't over? She hadn't ended it?"

"No, she hadn't ended it. When I accused her again, she laughed in my face. I asked her to leave but she refused. She loved Casa Santini and her life here. She said she would live here forever. That's when she moved out of our rooms up to the third floor."

The third floor. The room that was locked had been Isabella's. Suddenly the heat in the room was suffocating; she was so warm, it was difficult to breathe.

"The last year of our marriage was a farce," Carlo said. "And then . . . then there was an accident. I don't know how it happened. No one knows. But Isabella fell..." He took a shuddering breath. "She fell from the third-floor window and broke her neck."

For a long time there was no sound in the room, only the crackle of flames in the fireplace. Then a log dropped, shattering the silence. And Nicky said, "Why did you marry me, Carlo?"

"Because I . . ." He shook his head as though to clear it. "The first time I saw you, there at the pensione when you were so ill, it was like looking at a younger image of Isabella. And later, when you got out of the hospital and I began to know you—when I realized you weren't anything like Isabella—I began to think that I could make you be her, a better, nicer her. The woman I had wanted her to be."

He dropped his head into his hands. "I must have been mad," he said. "It wasn't fair to you."

"No, it wasn't," Nicky said in a cold little voice. "You made me dress like her. You made me cut my hair so that I would look more like her. There was never any *me*, Carlo. There was only Isabella."

"No," he said. "That's the way it was in the beginning, but that's not the way it is now. However it may have started out, for whatever reason I married you, I know now that it hasn't been like that for a long time. Tonight, when we walked into the Andrettis', I suddenly knew what a terrible thing I had done by trying to make you over into Isabella's image. I've never been so ashamed, so sorry about anything in my life."

With gentle fingers he brushed the bangs away from her forehead. "Let your hair grow back the way it was when I first met you," he said, and tightened his hand around hers. "Tonight when you ran away from me, when I knew you had found out the truth about Isabella, I felt as though my whole world had come crashing down. And I knew—" He tilted her face so that she had to look at him. "And I knew how much I loved you, Nicolina." He shook his head and with the barest suggestion of a smile said, "Nicky. Only Nicky now, yes?"

She turned her head away. How could she believe him after what he had done? How could she forgive him?

She moved as though to get up off the sofa, but he held her back.

"When you ran into the maze and I ran after you, I was mad with fear that I had lost you. That's why when I found you . . . that's why I had to have you, why I made love to you there." He took her shoulders and made her face him. "It wasn't the image of Isabella I made love to tonight, Nicky. It was you."

"And the other times? Our wedding night?"

She waited for him to answer, and when he didn't, she tried again to get up. But he held her back. "Do you think it could have been like it was between us tonight and so many other other times if I didn't love you? If you didn't love me?"

"I don't know," she said quietly. "I don't know anything any more."

He got up from the sofa and, taking her hands, pulled her to her feet and put his arms around her. "You're my wife," he said. "You mean everything to me."

And when she didn't answer, but simply stood unmoving in his arms, he said, "Come," and taking her hand, led her into the bathroom. He took the black robe off her and turned on the water in the shower. When she stepped into it, he stripped out of his own clothes and came in beside her. She tried to move away from him but he wouldn't let her. "I'll make it up to you," he said. "I swear I will."

She didn't respond, she only stood there with the warm water coursing over her body, naked, inert, feeling nothing.

When he turned the water off, he dried her and carried her to their bed. He lay beside her and took her in his arms, but he made no attempt to make love, only held her until at last, her head cupped against the hollow of his shoulder, she slept.

During the next few days Carlo did everything he could to make up for having hurt her. As he had in Venice, he wooed her with flowers and gifts. One evening at dinner she remarked to Elizabetta how much she liked her pearls, and the next day Carlo presented her with a string that was almost an exact replica.

But it wasn't pearls Nicky wanted; she wanted him to love her because of who she was, and though he had said he did, she did not believe him.

It helped to have Elizabetta at the dinner table each night, for though Nicky and Carlo had not spoken again of what had happened at the Andretti party or of what he had told her later, it was there between them. The ghost of Isabella, Nicky thought sometimes when she was alone. She stands between us as though she were really here.

There were so many things that made sense now: the shock on Elizabetta's face the first time she had seen her. The way Luigi, the gardener, had looked at her. The expression in the jeweler's eyes when he'd dropped the loupe. And the people at the party, the way they had stared at her.

She was grateful to Stefano Ponti for having told her the truth, and though she had not mentioned his name to Carlo, she thought about him from time to time. He was an attractive man and he had been kind to her, but because Carlo didn't like him, she didn't expect to see him again. So she was surprised when, a week after the Andretti party, Stefano Ponti sent her flowers with a note that read, "Congratulations on your marriage. I hope to see you soon."

The bouquet was on the table in the entrance hall when Carlo came home that evening. "The flowers I sent today?" he asked.

"No." And just for a moment, although she wasn't sure why, Nicky was tempted to lie. "No," she said. "Signor Ponti sent them."

"Send them back."

"What?" Nicky looked at him, surprised. "But why?"

"Because I don't want him sending you flowers."

"He sent them as a friendly gesture, to offer congratulations on our marriage. It would be rude to send them back."

A muscle jumped in his cheek and she knew he was fighting for control. "Throw them away," he said. "I do not want them in this house."

She did not tell him that on the following day, she wrote a thank-you note to Stefano Ponti. Nor did she tell him of Ponti's call to thank her for her note.

Except for that brief flare of anger at her having received flowers from Ponti, Carlo, in the days following the Andretti party, did everything he could to reassure Nicky of his love. When she resisted his attempts at lovemaking, he seemed content to simply hold her. Several times a week they went out to dinner, and on the days when Elizabetta felt well, she accompanied them.

One such night, when they returned home and had retired to their rooms, Carlo said, "How would you like to go to Capri?"

"Capri?" Nicky looked up from the book she had been reading.

He nodded. "I thought a change of scene might be good for both of us. We could drive, perhaps spend a night in Sorrento, leave the car there and go by boat to Capri." He offered a coaxing smile. "It's a beautiful little island, perhaps the most beautiful in the world."

Nicky put her book down. She shook her head, but before she could say anything, Carlo said, "We'd only be gone a week. I've already spoken to Dr. Tacchia and he can take over for me. We can leave this weekend—if you'd like to, I mean."

"I don't think so, Carlo. I know Elizabetta is feeling better but I don't want to leave her."

"We could ask her to join us if you like. Rosa could come, too, so that Elizabetta would have someone with her at night. Would you like her to come with us?"

"Yes, I would, if you think she's well enough to make the trip."

"I'm sure she is." He smiled. "I can't tell you what it means to me that you and Elizabetta get along so well, that you're so thoughtful of her. Isabella . . ." He shook his head. "You're very different from her," he said in a low voice. "There are times when I don't know how I ever got along without you."

And when she didn't answer, he said, "If Elizabetta agrees to go to Capri, will you come?"

Nicky hesitated, then at last she said, "Yes, if Elizabetta agrees."

They left for Sorrento the following Sunday morning. Rosa, who sat in the back with Elizabetta, was so excited she couldn't stop chattering. They stopped often to rest, had a pleasant lunch in Avezzano, and reached Naples in the late afternoon.

"There's Vesuvius," Carlo said as they rounded a curve in the highway, and Nicky saw the volcano in all its brooding glory there above the Bay of Naples.

Nicky was glad now that she had come, and pleased that Elizabetta and Rosa were with them, for though Carlo had done his best to make things up to her, and though she tried to be pleasant, especially when Elizabetta was with them, there was a part of her that could not, would not unbend. As far as she was concerned, Carlo had been living a lie, pretending she was someone else. She was not sure she would ever forgive him for that, or that she could ever bear to have him touch her again.

At sunset they were on a winding road, climbing high into the hills past Ravello. Farther on, and all along the Amalfi Drive, were incredibly beautiful views of the sea.

When Nicky asked, "Can we stop for a moment?" Carlo pulled to the side of the road. They got out of the car and went to stand at the edge of land overlooking the sea.

It was almost too beautiful to be real. The sky caught fire and the blue became a fiery red shot with rays of pink and yellow, and the yellow sky changed the color of the water so that the deep blue-green turned golden in the reflecting rays of sunset. Suddenly, inexplicably, Nicky felt the sting of tears. And something more. A softening deep inside her, a giving way of the coldness that had grown around her heart since the night of the Andretti party. She wanted to be held. She wanted to be in love again.

"Nicky?" Carlo put an arm around her shoulder. "What is it?"

But she only shook her head, unable for a moment to speak.

"Tell me," he said.

She wanted to, wanted with all her heart to turn to him and say, "I want it to be like it was in Venice when I thought you loved me. I want to love you again...."

But she could not and so she said, "I'm silly. I weep at beautiful sunsets."

"There are times when I have looked at the bay from here when I, too, have wanted to weep. This part of the road is one of the most beautiful in Italy. It makes me happy that you see it as I do, for Italy is your country now."

"Is it?" Nicky looked away, and before he could say anything else, she went back to the car.

By the time they reached Sorrento, Elizabetta was tired. Nicky went up to her room with her to make sure that she and Rosa were comfortable.

"Rosa and I will eat in our room tonight," Elizabetta said. "You and Carlo have dinner by yourselves. Tell him you want a shamefully expensive meal in a romantic restaurant overlooking the sea. Perhaps..." The older woman hesitated. "Perhaps it is my imagination, but I think things have not been too good between you and Carlo. I've felt tension and I've seen your unhappiness. I don't know what's bothering you, Nicky, but perhaps while we're in Capri you and Carlo will resolve whatever it is." She took Nicky's hand. "I said once that you were like my granddaughter, but you mean even more than that to me. You're the daughter I never had, Nicky, and it hurts me to see you so unhappy."

"I'm—I'm not unhappy," Nicky murmured, trying to hold back her tears. "I'm just a little homesick. Or maybe I'm tired and Capri will help." She kissed Elizabetta's cheek. "Why don't you rest for a little while before dinner. Call me if you need anything tonight."

"I will." She patted Nicky's hand. "Now go and do something romantic. I'll see you in the morning."

Something romantic, Nicky thought as she left Elizabetta's room and went a few doors down to the room she would share with Carlo.

She showered and changed, and when she was ready, she and Carlo left the hotel.

They dined on the terrace of a restaurant that overlooked the sea. In the distance they could see the necklacelike trim of lights that stretched all along the Bay of Naples, the firefly glow of fishing boats, and in the shadow of the moon the outline of Vesuvius. All of it so beautiful, so perfect. If only...

"You've been very quiet all day," Carlo said, breaking in on her thoughts. "Are you all right?"

"Yes, of course." Nicky took a sip of her wine. "Thank you for bringing me here. It's very lovely."

"I'm glad you're enjoying it, Nicky. You'll like Capri, too." He reached across the table and took her hand. "There are so many things in so many places I want to show you. We've never really had a honeymoon, so if you'd like, we'll go to Greece in the spring, to Mykonos perhaps, and Corfu. Unless there's somewhere else you'd rather go."

Nicky was silent for a moment. "I've been thinking about going back to Florida," she said.

"To Florida?" He stared at her. "Surely you can't be serious."

She lowered her eyes. "I'd like to get away for a while, Carlo. Back to where I belong."

"This is where you belong. Here in Italy with me."

"Do I?" A sigh quivered through her. "Do I, Carlo?"

"Of course you do."

She shook her head. "I don't know," she murmured in a voice so low he could barely hear her.

The dinner was served. It was delicious, but neither of them ate more than a few bites of it. I've spoiled tonight for him, Nicky thought. I didn't want to, I didn't mean to, but I don't think I can go on with this pretense of a marriage. Carlo had married her only because she resembled Isabella. And she had married him... Even now she wasn't sure why. Because he had swept her off her feet? Because she had a deep-seated need to feel loved and protected?

Because when he kissed her she never wanted him to stop. And because, even in the short space of time she had known him, she had fallen desperately in love with him.

He had said that he loved her, but she was not sure she believed him, not while he was still haunted by the ghost of Isabella. Isabella the beautiful. Isabella the unfaithful wife.

She looked out across the water and knew that there had never been a night as beautiful as this, and she wanted to weep for the love that had been lost, and the love that never had been.

As soon as they finished dinner, Nicky said she wanted to check on Elizabetta.

"I'll take a walk then," Carlo told her. "I'll stop in and see her when I return and meet you in our room later."

"I'm a little tired." She didn't quite meet his eyes. "I may be asleep by the time you come back."

"Then of course I will not wake you," he said with the suggestion of irony in his voice.

She went to Elizabetta's room. Rosa answered the door. "The signora is asleep," she whispered.

"Very well," Nicky said. "If you need anything in the night, don't hesitate to phone our room."

"I won't. *Buona notte, signora.*"

"*Buona notte,* Rosa."

Nicky went to her room. She started to turn the lights on, then stopped. With the light of the moon and the lights from the terrace below, she could see well enough. She dropped her handbag on one of the chairs and stepped out onto the balcony. The view from here, as it had been from the terrace of the restaurant, was breathtaking. The night was soft with promise, the air scented with jasmine and gardenia.

It was a night made for love.

She leaned with both hands on the railing of the balcony and looked pensively out at the water. Longing . . . she felt such longing. . . .

She heard the door of the room open and close. Then the soft tinkle of a music box and the sweet, sad, oh-so-Italian strains of "Sorrento." Her hands tightened on the railing. She took a breath, then turned and saw Carlo standing on the threshold of the open door.

"I thought you might like a souvenir of Sorrento." He put the box down on the table near the open doors. He waited, but made no attempt to go to her.

She looked at him and felt again the ebbing away of the coldness, the crumbling of the walls she had built around her heart. For a moment she didn't speak, then she held out her hands.

He reached her in two strides and with a cry pulled her into his arms. "Nicky," he said. "Oh, Nicky."

The dearly familiar arms held her and warmed her. He kissed her and his mouth was gentle, as though his slightest touch might bruise. Only when she whispered, "Carlo," did the kiss deepen with the tentative touch of his tongue to hers. And when she answered that touch, he tightened his arms around her and pressed her close.

It was like coming home after a long absence, being warmed by a fire after the rain, the slow awakening when the body has slumbered too long without feeling.

"Do you know how much I want you?" he murmured against her lips.

"As much as I want you," she whispered.

"Forgive—"

She stopped the words with a kiss, a kiss that told of hunger and of need. And when at last they parted, he picked her up and carried her to their bed.

"Let me undress you," he said. "Let me do everything for you."

And when he had stripped her of her clothes, and himself of his, they lay in their bed together, gently holding, gently kissing, putting off for a few moments that fierce coupling they both wanted. And when it came it was as it had been that night in the maze. Nothing was held back; he gave, she gave, and in that last supreme moment they held each other tightly and muffled their cries against each other's mouth.

"Love, oh love," he said. And held her while she slept.

The next morning they took the boat for Capri.

CHAPTER TWELVE

The days in Capri were the happiest Nicky had ever known. For the first time in their marriage she felt that there were no secrets between herself and Carlo.

It had hurt to learn that he had first been attracted to her only because she resembled his dead wife, and that when he had married her he had tried to turn her into the image of Isabella. He had done a great wrong without thinking of the consequences for her, and that was hard to forgive.

But because she loved him, she had to try.

From what he had told her, his marriage to Isabella had been bad almost from the beginning. She'd had an affair, she had moved out of Carlo's bed and she had almost ruined his life. She had said she would never leave the Casa Santini, or Carlo, and in a way that was difficult for Nicky to explain, she felt that if she walked away from Carlo now because of Isabella, that Isabella would have won.

She wasn't going to let that happen. She loved Carlo and she was determined to make this marriage work.

In the days that followed she began to see a side of him she had not seen before. As though he had at last freed himself of hidden demons, he frowned less and smiled more. He was attentive and loving. He was everything she wanted him to be.

Reluctant to leave Capri, they extended their stay another week so that they could explore this most beautiful of islands. He showed her the palaces where emperors and rich Romans had lived. They took a boat to the Blue Grotto and in the darkness of the cave swam off the boat and kissed underwater where no one could see.

At night, with the scent of jasmine drifting through the open balcony doors, as well as the soft music of mandolins from a nearby café, they made love. They kissed each other in every secret, tender place, and rose together to heights of unbelievable passion. When the lovemaking ended, they slept close and touching, her head against his chest, their fingers entwined. And if in the night he turned to her with a whisper of need, she opened her arms to receive him.

She had never been so happy, so utterly filled with love.

And because love is for sharing, they shared their love with Elizabetta. Every morning they had breakfast with her on the terrace of her room. When the elderly woman felt well enough, they strolled along the waterfront, stopping often to rest at a sidewalk café for a sherry or a coffee.

Day by day, Nicky became closer to Carlo's grandmother. And though she loved her mother and knew that Eleanora, in her way, returned her love, for the first time in her life she felt the presence of a real mother figure. She loved Elizabetta, wanted to do things for her and care for her.

When Carlo said, "It's nice of you to spend so much of your time with my grandmother," she looked at him, surprised.

"But I love her," she said. "I enjoy being with her."

"You're sure?" Carlo hesitated. "I have to go to a conference in Rome in two weeks. I'll be gone for only three or four days and I'd planned on asking you to come with me. But now I'm wondering if you'd mind staying with Elizabetta. I know she appears to be better, but the fact of her illness really hasn't changed. I'd feel happier about leaving if I knew you were with her."

"Of course I'll stay with her," Nicky said.

He put his arms around her. "I love you," he whispered against her lips. And holding her away from him, he brushed the bangs back off her face. "Your hair is beginning to grow and I'm glad. I liked it the way it was when we first met. I'm sorry I made you cut it. I'm sorry about a lot of things."

"That's behind us," Nicky said. "We never have to talk about it again."

On their last night in Capri, Elizabetta insisted that Carlo and Nicky have dinner alone.

"This is one of the most romantic islands in the world," the Italian woman said. "And here you are, spending almost all of your time with me. It isn't fair. I insist that tonight the two of you have a splendid meal in a splendidly romantic restaurant. Somewhere where there is music, yes?"

"But we want you with us," Nicky objected.

Elizabetta waved an imperious hand. "I'll brook no argument. I have already made a dinner reservation for you for eight o'clock."

Carlo put his arms around her and kissed her cheek. "I love you, *Nonna,* Grandmother," he said.

"And I love you, my boy." She patted his cheek. "The two of you go and have a good time. Rosa and I will be perfectly fine right here."

And reluctantly, because she remained adamant, they agreed.

The restaurant was on a hilltop overlooking the harbor. There were flowers on the table when they arrived, with a note from Elizabetta that read, "May your last night in Capri be very special."

As they were reading it, a waiter appeared with a silver bucket of champagne. "Dom Perignon," he said. "It was ordered when the reservation was made."

And when he had poured it, Carlo raised his glass and, touching it to Nicky's, said, "To our last night in Capri."

"And to Elizabetta," she answered.

They sipped the champagne and held hands across the table. They ate grilled fish stuffed with shrimp and crab, and left it half-finished to dance to "Arrivederci Roma."

"It's been a wonderful week," Nicky said. "I'll never forget it."

"Nor will I." He kissed her gently, unmindful of the people around them. Tightening his arms around her, he whispered, "I love you, Nicky."

"As I love you," she said.

They danced for a long time before they returned to their table. And when they had had a cappuccino, they left the restaurant and walked arm in arm along the waterfront. Finally, somewhere after midnight, they returned to their room for a night of love.

The next morning they left Capri.

The trip back to the Casa Santini tired Elizabetta, and she took to her bed as soon as they returned. Carlo examined her and afterward said to Nicky, "She'll be fine after a few days of rest. Please don't worry."

But Nicky did worry. She spent long hours every day with Elizabetta. She read to the older woman from the verses of Dante, for that is what Elizabetta wanted to hear.

"As one, who from a dream awaken'd straight,
All he hath seen forgets; yet still retains
Impression of the feeling in his dream;
E'en such am I; for all the vision dies,
As 'twere, away."

"As 'twere away," Elizabetta said with a sigh when Nicky had finished reading those particular lines, and her gaze lingered on the photograph of Gianfranco beside her bed.

She spoke often of him now, recalling the early days of their marriage, the trips they had taken, the joy they had shared over the birth of their first child. Again and again she looked at the photographs in the album she kept on the table beside her bed. Again and again she showed Nicky pictures of her husband, and Nicky always said, "How handsome he was. How happy you must have been."

"Oh, yes," Elizabetta always answered. "Oh, yes."

A few days after their return from Capri, Annamaria Tacchia called to invite Nicky to lunch, but Nicky, reluctant to leave Carlo's grandmother, suggested the other woman have lunch at the house. Annamaria accepted and the two of them had a pleasant time together. During lunch Annamaria brought up Stefano Ponti's name.

"Do you see much of him?" she asked. When Nicky shook her head, Annamaria's dark eyes sparkled with curiosity and she said, "But why? He lives next door. He's absolutely charming, and so good-looking." She giggled. "Too good-looking, yes? Perhaps Carlo is jealous of him."

"Oh, I doubt that," Nicky said. But she remembered Carlo's anger when he'd seen the flowers Ponti had sent a few days after the Andretti party. She had not told him that another bouquet had arrived the day after their return from Capri, or of the phone call the following day.

"We must get together," Ponti had said. "Carlo is away so much of the time that it must be lonely for you. Can you come for tea some afternoon? Tomorrow, perhaps?"

"I'm afraid not," she had answered. "Carlo's grandmother isn't well. I like to spend my time with her."

"Oh dear, I am sorry. I want so much to show you my house...." He'd paused. "And perhaps you'd like to see the tunnel that runs between my place and yours."

That had piqued Nicky's interest, but still she declined. She would not dream of visiting Stefano Ponti, even though he was a neighbor, without telling Carlo. And Carlo, for whatever reason, didn't like Ponti. That made a visit with the other man out of the question.

"No," she said to Annamaria, "Carlo isn't at all jealous. He and Signor Ponti are only acquaintances, not friends. There's a high wall between the two estates, so we never see him."

When Annamaria left, Nicky walked her out to her car. They agreed to meet again the following week, when both their husbands would be in Rome, and kissed each other's cheeks, as was the custom of Italian women.

Carlo seemed pleased that night when she told him how much she'd enjoyed Dr. Tacchia's wife.

"You must see her again," he said. "Next time, though, why don't you meet in a restaurant? It would do you good to get out more."

"But I don't like to leave Elizabetta," Nicky replied. "She hasn't looked well since we've returned from Capri. She doesn't want to walk in the garden anymore, or have lunch with me in the dining room. She just wants to stay in her room, to rest or read or look at her photographs. I'm worried about her, Carlo."

"Yes, so am I, but there really isn't a great deal any of us can do, Nicky. Your spending time with Elizabetta will help her more than anything right now."

"I worry about your leaving when she isn't well."

"Nothing will change in the few days I'll be gone. Meantime you have Dr. Glannini's number. If there's anything you feel uncertain about, call him and he'll come."

"All right," Nicky said.

But she could not help her feeling of unease when Carlo left for Rome the following day.

The rain began in the middle of the night. By morning it had developed into what the local newscasters called a tropical depression, with a forecast of winds between sixty to seventy miles an hour.

Nicky got up early, and as soon as she was dressed, went to Elizabetta's room.

"She's still asleep," Rosa whispered when she let Nicky in. "The rain kept her awake most of the night."

"I'll come back after breakfast," Nicky said. "If she awakens and wants anything before I return, please come and tell me."

And when Rosa assured her that she would, Nicky went back down the corridor to the dining room. The rain was fierce, blown by winds that seemed to grow stronger every minute. It slashed hard against wooden shutters that banged and rattled in protest.

When the cook brought in Nicky's omelet, she said, "It is a wicked *tempesta, signora*. They say it comes in from the Adriatic Sea." She shook her head and her dark Italian eyes were solemn. "I do not remember a day such as this. It is a day of evil portent. Bad things happen in storms like this one. You must stay close to the house today. Do not venture out."

"I have no intention of venturing out." Nicky took a bite of her omelet, and wanting to change the subject, said, "This is delicious, Maria. Why don't you fix another one and I'll take it in to the Signora Elizabetta when I'm through."

She finished the omelet, and by the time she'd had her second cup of coffee, Maria returned with a tray.

"Do you want me to help you?" the woman asked.

Nicky shook her head. "No, I'll take it in. *Grazie,* Maria."

She picked up the tray and started out of the dining room just as a blast of wind hit the house. The shutters banged, the chandelier swayed and suddenly the lights flickered and went out. With the shutters closed, the room, like the whole house, was in darkness.

"Dio mio!" Maria cried, and quickly blessed herself. "I will get some candles."

Nicky stayed where she was, clutching the tray, but before Maria could return with the candles, the lights came back on. Worried that if Elizabetta was awake she might be frightened, Nicky called out, "I'm going to the signora's room," and hurried from the dining room.

When she knocked at Elizabetta's door, Rosa let her in, and Nicky saw that Carlo's grandmother was awake.

"Che tempesta!" she muttered. "What a terrible storm! It feels as though the whole house is going to topple."

Nicky put the tray down on the table next to the bed. "The radio called it a tropical depression. I'm afraid it's going to be like this for most of the day."

"If it is it will ruin the garden." Elizabetta clasped her pale hands together. "My poor roses," she fretted. "What will happen to my poor roses?"

"They'll be all right," Nicky assured her. "Luigi will trim them after the storm and in a few days they'll be as good as new."

"You're not going out anywhere, are you?" Elizabetta asked, her anxiety heard in her voice.

"No, of course not." Nicky tucked a napkin around Elizabetta and placed the tray on her lap. "We'll spend the day together. We'll read and—"

"The shutters are banging!"

"I know, dear."

"Are they all securely fastened?"

"I'm sure they are."

"Tell Sergio to check them and make certain that he does."

Nicky looked at Rosa, who hovered nearby looking almost as anxious as Elizabetta. "All right," she soothed. "Just as soon as you've had your breakfast." She put a spoonful of sugar into Elizabetta's tea. "We're going to be fine," she said. "I'm sure the house has weathered worse storms than this."

"The last storm was terrible...." Elizabetta picked nervously at the sheet. "The wind...the wind took the trees. It tore away shutters." She covered her eyes with her hands and the thin blue veins stood out like the lines on a road map against her white skin. "Ah, *Dio*," she cried. "Ah, *Dio*."

Nicky sat on the bed and put her arms around Elizabetta. "You mustn't do this to yourself," she said. "It's only a storm. Everything's going to be all right and I'll be here with you."

"But the wind... It frightens me so, Nicky." Elizabetta began to cry and her thin body shook as though with a chill. "You must tell Sergio...tell him to close the shutters."

"I will, dear."

"And you...Nicky, you must see to the shutters on the third floor. You, not Sergio."

"The third floor?" In as calm a voice as she could manage, Nicky said, "When I went up there before, one of the doors was locked. I'll need a key."

"I have it." Elizabeth lowered her voice so that only Nicky could hear. "I keep it hidden so that no one—no one..." With trembling hands she pulled open the drawer in the table next to the bed and began to search among scattered papers, a rosary, a brooch, a few letters, and at last she whispered, "Here! Here it is!"

She handed the large brass key to Nicky. "Make sure the window and the shutters are tightly closed, because if they're not..." She looked at Nicky, her eyes redrimmed, frightened. "Lock them," she said. "Be sure to lock them."

"I will," Nicky assured her. "But I'm not going to leave until you relax." She eased Elizabetta back against the pillows and took her hands. "You mustn't upset yourself like this. It isn't good for you."

"All—all right. I'm all right now. It's just that—that storms like this upset me." She touched Nicky's hand. "You're a good girl," she said. "You'll take care of everything, won't you?"

"Of course I will," Nicky promised. "Now eat your breakfast, and when I come back I'll read to you."

A blast of wind shook the house and a shudder went through Elizabetta's body. "Go," she implored. "Go quickly. And—and be careful."

Though Nicky didn't want to leave the elderly lady, she nodded and hurried out of the room. At the foot of the stairs leading up to the other floors, she ran into Sergio.

"The Signora Elizabetta would like you to check all of the windows and shutters on this floor and the next," she said. "I'll check the third floor."

"The third floor? But I'll be glad to do it, *signora*."

Nicky shook her head. "No, that's all right, Sergio. I'll take care of it."

The lights flickered and went out again, but only for a moment. Nicky hesitated, then ran quickly up to the second floor. At the bottom of the next flight, she hesitated again. Then, squaring her shoulders, she slowly climbed the stairs. When she reached the top she opened the door. Only a little light filtered into the large entry, and she wished she had thought to ask Sergio for a flashlight. She certainly didn't relish the thought of being up here alone in the dark. She'd check the windows and the shutters and get back downstairs just as quickly as she could.

She went into the small bedroom, then the sewing room and the playroom. The windows and shutters were all tightly closed. One of the shutters in the large bedroom was clacking, but when she checked it she saw that the boards had come loose. There wasn't anything she could do about it, but she would remember to tell Sergio to have it fixed.

The room at the turn of the hall was next. She stood at the door, not sure why she felt a sudden reluctance to enter. Then, telling herself she was being foolish, she unlocked the door and went in.

The door slammed shut behind her. She swung around, then stood for a moment without moving. The storm sounded stronger here, the wind fiercer. She reached behind her and felt along the wall for a light switch. A shutter banged hard. She mumbled, "Where's the light?" and when at last she found it, sighed with relief and switched it on.

The room was large. Her first impression was of blue, all shades of blue. Pale blue walls. Darker blue velvet chaise longue. Bright royal blue satin spread on the big four-poster canopied bed. A life-size painting above the bed of a woman dressed in blue.

A shutter slammed so hard that the chandelier above her head began to sway, tinkling as each crystal pendant moved against the others. The effect was an eerie kind of music, more discordant than pleasant. With a shiver, Nicky turned away and saw that the window was half-open. The blue lace curtains were blowing in and the heavy drapes were soaked.

She hurried forward to close the shutters that were banging against the side of the house, almost out of her reach. She leaned out of the window to grasp one side. The wind was strong, blowing and swirling in gusts that threatened to topple her. She reached out for the shutter and a gust of wind caught her. The blue curtain, like a clinging wet ghost, blew into her face, blinding her for a moment. She tried to thrust it away, when suddenly it was as though a hand were against her back, pushing her forward. Pushing her...

She cried out and tried to grab the edge of the window, but the wind was strong, far stronger than before. She looked down and saw the ground below. Half in, half out of the window, she fought with all of her strength against the raging wind, the rain slashing at her face while an invisible force pushed...

"No!" she cried, and with a surge of strength, managed to pull herself back into the room. She went down on her knees, gasping, and crawled to the bed. There she grasped a bedpost and pulled herself erect.

The lights flickered and went out.

She clung to the bedpost, afraid to move, afraid to let go. But the rain was still blowing in. Forget about the shutter, let it bang. But the window—she had to close the window.

She ran across the room and slammed it shut just as a terrible crash of thunder shook the house. She was hurrying back toward the bed when lightning, like a bright flash of fire, illuminated the room. And in that flash of brightness, Nicky looked up at the portrait above the bed. The portrait of Isabella.

She screamed. Screamed and screamed and couldn't stop screaming, because it was as though she were looking at a portrait of herself.

The screams became a whimper, and still Nicky stood there frozen, legs weak, heart racketing against her ribs, unable to look away from the portrait of Isabella.

But...was it Isabella or was it she, Nicky, transformed into the other woman? The woman who had been Carlo's wife. The two wives. Isabella and Nicky. Which was which? Am I her or is she me? A sob rose in her throat. "Dear God," she whispered. "Dear God."

Then she felt it—the sharp sense of someone else in the room. A waft of smoke. And perfume, the kind of perfume a woman like Isabella would use, the scent sweet, heavy, cloying.

A sob rose in Nicky's throat. She turned, and like a person gone suddenly blind, staggered toward the door, arms out, fighting her way through the darkness of her terror and the terrible howl of the wind behind her.

There came another rumble of thunder and through the noise the sharp tinkling of the chandelier. She looked up. It swayed back and forth, back and forth as though trying to loosen itself. Centuries-old boards and mortar creaked, and as Nicky watched, a wide crack split the ceiling. She put a hand up as though to shield herself, and with a cry sprinted toward the door.

The chandelier crashed to the floor behind her, throwing crystal splinters in every direction. She felt a sharp sting on her cheek as a crystal shard hit her.

Blind with fear, she reached out, found the door. With frantic hands she searched for the knob, turned it, jiggled it, but the door wouldn't open. She looked back at the room just as another bolt of lightning zigzagged across it and lighted the portrait.

Isabella watched her with an enigmatic smile. As though . . . as though the two of them shared a dreadful secret.

Spots danced before Nicky's eyes. She felt herself beginning to slip . . . to slip . . .

"*Signora! Signora!* Are you in there?"

Nicky grasped the knob. "Luigi!" she cried. "Get me out of here! Get me out."

She heard him pounding on the door, heard the squeak of the knob, and grasping it with both hands, she twisted as hard as she could.

He flung the door open. They stared at each other. "Are you all right, *signora?*" he asked.

"Yes, I—I . . ." With a cry she pushed past him and ran, ran as though all the demons of hell were after her.

Only when she reached the bottom of the stairs did she stop, because her legs would no longer hold her. Shaking as though with a chill, she sank down, head against her knees, and closed her eyes.

But she could still see Isabella, smiling that enigmatic smile—the smile of a secret they both shared.

CHAPTER THIRTEEN

She was in the sitting room off the bedroom when Carlo phoned that night from Rome. "I heard about the storm near Florence," he said. "Are you and Elizabetta all right?"

"Yes, we're fine."

"What about the house?"

"We lost one of the trees and a few shutters, and a window was broken in the kitchen. Other than that we're all right."

"I was worried."

"Were you?"

"Of course." He sounded surprised. "Is anything wrong?"

"Why would anything be wrong?"

"You sound a little strange."

"You're imagining things."

"Am I? Yes, well, perhaps I am. I'm sorry, Nicky, but I'm not going to be able to return tomorrow. A colleague of mine has a patient in Genoa he wants me to see. If everything is all right there and if Elizabetta isn't any worse, I'll go with him to Genoa tonight. The patient is going to need bypass surgery and Dr. Marzari has asked me to assist. I'll be away at least a week. Are you sure you don't mind?"

"Why should I mind?" There was a part of her that knew she was being abrupt, but she couldn't seem to help it.

"Nicky . . . ?"

"I'll take care of things here," she said.

"You're sure nothing's wrong?"

"Quite sure."

"I miss you, Nicky."

She gripped the phone, but the words she wanted to say wouldn't come.

"Nicky?"

"Have a good trip," she said.

"I'll call tomorrow night from Genoa. Give Elizabetta my love."

"I will."

"Arrivederci, cara mia."

"Goodbye, Carlo."

When Nicky put the phone down she stood for a moment beside it, a puzzled frown furrowing her brow. She wasn't upset because Carlo was going to Genoa. Why had she acted the way she had? What was wrong with her? She'd call him back, tell him she loved him. Tell him . . . But when she reached for the phone, a wave of dizziness overcame her. She gasped and caught the scent of perfume, the same sweet, cloying perfume that had pervaded Isabella's room.

She fought her fear and told herself she was only imagining the scent. Maybe the perfume Isabella had used still lingered upstairs in her room, but not in here, not in her and Carlo's rooms. She'd been spooked by the storm, by Isabella's portrait. That was all.

She touched the small bandage on her cheek where she had been cut by a shard of glass from the falling chandelier, and knew that if she had not darted away in time, she would have been directly under the falling glass. Clutching the back of a chair, she closed her eyes and had a sudden vision of herself crushed and bloody under the weight of the chandelier.

The scent of perfume came stronger, heavier. It filled her nostrils, drugged her senses. She felt weak, ill, and knew she had to get out of here, had to have air. "Leave!" a voice inside her head screamed. "Do it now. Do it quickly."

She covered her nose with her hand and stumbled from the room toward the stairway. She took great gulps of air, and when she had composed herself, went down to Elizabetta's room to tell her good-night.

"You look pale," the elderly lady said with a look of concern. "Are you all right, my dear?"

"Yes, I—I'm fine. A little tired, perhaps. It's been a long day." Nicky took a steadying breath. "Carlo called a little while ago to see how we were. He asked me to give you his love. He's going to be away longer than he expected because he has to go to Genoa to assist in a surgery."

"That's too bad, Nicky. You'll miss him, won't you?"

"Miss him? Yes, I—I suppose I will."

Elizabetta cocked her head as though puzzled. "Is anything wrong?" she asked.

"No, no, of course not."

"You look worn out. Why don't you get some rest? I'm better now that the storm has passed. Rosa has gone to fix my tea, and as soon as she returns we'll settle in for the night."

She held her hand up to Nicky. "Sleep well, my dear," she said.

But Nicky didn't sleep well. Tired as she was, it was a long time before she fell asleep. And when she did, it was to dream dreadful, frightening dreams.

The cardinal in bloodred robes sat on a golden throne and pointed his bone-thin finger at the tormented woman who knelt at his feet. "She must die," he hissed.

The knight raised the sword above his head. She looked up at the blade shimmering in the sunlight, saw its sweeping descent and tried to cry out. But the only sound was a muted, mewling whimper.

Nicky sat straight up in bed, shaking as though with a fever. Sweat covered her body. Without thinking, she reached for Carlo. But Carlo wasn't there—he was in Genoa and she was alone.

"Be calm," Nicky told herself. "It's only a dream. A dream . . ." She thought of the woman who lived . . . no, who *had* lived upstairs on the third floor, and a shiver of fear ran through her. Think of something, anything. Say a prayer.... "Now I lay me down to sleep, I pray the Lord my soul to keep...."

Curled in a fetal position, eyes closed, she willed sleep to come.

It came with a dream even more terrifying than the first had been.

Tangled vines reached out for her. She ran toward the refuge and the terror of the maze, arms out in front of her, running blindly in the terrible green darkness. Silence like the silence of a dream surrounded her. Please oh please oh please...somebody, somebody. Bony hands reached out for her; the cardinal, the knight, the hand-

some one on the black stallion, sonorous voices intoning a funeral chant, "Take her, take her, take her...."

She came abruptly awake, awake to the smell of the sweet and cloying perfume. Oh, God, what was happening to her?

"Fight," a voice inside her head whispered. "Fight or all will be lost."

She got up and went into the sitting room. She turned on all the lights and opened a window. The smell of night air drifted in, pure and clean and fresh. She stood by the window, breathing deeply, and aloud she said, "Okay, so you had a bad dream. But you're awake now. There are no ghosts of men—or of women—long dead. No sweetly cloying scent. No sounds that go bong in the night."

But just in case, she spent the rest of the night on the sofa in the sitting room.

The next morning Nicky had breakfast with Elizabetta in the small dining room that overlooked the garden. The sun was shining and the grass after the rain was as green and new as spring.

"But my roses," Elizabetta lamented. "I know they're ruined."

"Perhaps some of them are, but I'm sure that in a few days Luigi will have everything looking just fine again. As soon as we've eaten I'll have a look. Would you like to come with me?"

Elizabetta shook her head. "I couldn't bear to see the garden now. Later, perhaps, after Luigi has put things to right, I'll take a look. But you go, Nicky. And as soon as you've seen how it is, you will come and tell me, yes?"

"Of course I will."

"We'll meet for lunch then?"

"Yes," Nicky said. "For lunch."

And when they had finished breakfast, and she had helped Elizabetta back to her room, Nicky went into the kitchen. Maria was there, seated at the kitchen table, peeling potatoes for supper.

"Buon giorno," the cook said when she saw Nicky. "Can I get you something? A cup of tea or..." She stopped. "Are you all right, *signora?* You look a bit pale. Is anything wrong?"

"No, no, nothing. I came for a basket. I'm going into the garden to pick some flowers."

"The baskets are behind the door in the pantry. I'll get one for you."

"No, I can get it. I..." Nicky stopped. Her expression changed. "Yes, do," she said. "And quickly."

Maria looked startled, but obediently put down the pan of potatoes and went to the pantry. "Here you are, *signora,"* she said when she returned.

"And garden shears," Nicky said impatiently. "Obviously, if I'm going to cut flowers, I'll need garden shears."

"I—I'm sorry, *signora."* Hot color flooded the cook's cheeks.

And when Maria had given her the basket and the shears, Nicky, without a thank-you, turned and hurried out to the garden.

Most of the heartier flowers had survived the storm, but as Elizabetta had feared, many of her roses had been lost.

"Buon giorno, Signora Santini." Luigi tipped his hat. "What a storm that was. The garden was in terrible shape when I came out this morning. But you tell the signora not to worry. Luigi is going to fix and soon everything will be as it was before the storm. You tell..."

But Nicky had passed him by without speaking.

She went farther into the garden. The dahlias were in bloom and she filled her basket with them before she moved on to a deeper section of the garden she had never been in before. There were hedges here, a scattering of flowers, and a high stone wall with a gate half-hidden by climbing ivy.

As though compelled by an invisible force that pulled her forward, Nicky went toward the gate. "Yes, go on. Go on," a voice seemed to whisper in her ear.

She lifted the latch and, opening it, found herself in another garden. This must be part of the Ponti estate, she mused, and smiled a bit because she knew she was trespassing.

It was very pretty here in a tangled kind of way, all vines and trees and scattered patches of wildflowers. She liked the untended, carefree look, preferred it, actually, to some of the more orderly gardens she had seen. Perhaps she'd start a garden of her own. Perhaps...

"Aha!" The voice came from almost directly in front of Nicky. She took a step back, startled, as Stefano Ponti emerged from behind a tree.

"Caught you, did I?" he said with a laugh. And she suddenly found herself thinking how handsome he looked, quite dashing in white trousers, a navy shirt with a silk ascot, and a navy-and-white blazer.

"I was wandering in our garden and I saw the gate." Nicky smiled. "What's the penalty for trespassing in Italy?"

"A whiskey and soda, if you're caught."

"It's just past twelve. Isn't that too early for a drink?"

"Not on this side of the wall." He took her arm. "Come along. We'll have one of the servants bring something out for us." He glanced down at the flowers in her basket. "Dahlias," he said. "They were Isabella's favorite flowers, too."

Isabella? A chill ran down Nicky's spine, but before she could speak, Ponti took the basket from her and, linking his arm through hers, led her back through the garden toward the house.

Smaller than the Casa Santini, the gray-stone, two-storied villa was set back among shaded trees and pristine lawns. As they drew nearer, Nicky saw the fountain that faced the house, its water bubbling up to sparkle in the sunshine. And in the center of the fountain, facing her, the life-size figure of the naked Bacchus, god of wine and pleasure.

"Handsome, isn't he?" Ponti said.

Nicky felt a hot flush of color in her cheeks. Then she laughed and said, "How pagan!"

Ponti laughed with her. "Of course. I had a stonemason that calls himself a sculptor copy it from the Bargello National Museum. I thought it added a dramatic touch..." He paused and looked down at Nicky, and tightening his arm a bit on hers, said, "For a bachelor like me who loves both pleasure and wine, as well as beautiful women, of course."

"Of course," she said, and laughed.

"Ah, here is Giovanni." Stefano gestured to the tall, slender man coming toward them. "Just in time," he said. "Would you bring us two whiskeys with soda please. With ice for the signora." He turned to Nicky. *"Si?"*

"Si," she said, and laughed again.

He took her arm again and led to a small garden shaded by willows at the side of the house with lawn chairs under a wisteria-covered pergola. "Here we are."

He motioned her to a chair. "Do sit down. The drinks will be along in a moment or two."

"I really shouldn't. Carlo is away. I suppose I shouldn't leave his grandmother."

"But there are maids, yes? Surely they will see to her. Besides, it's time we got acquainted. I want to hear all about you. Where are you from?"

"Miami," she said. "I'm from Miami, Florida." And soon, prompted by him, she found herself telling him about her job, and about Eleanora and her latest husband.

"Your mother sounds charming. And she lives in Brazil, you say? An exciting place, especially at carnival time. Have you ever been there?" When Nicky shook her head, he said, "You must go. Rio is one of the most exciting cities in the world." He leaned forward and, resting a hand on her knee, said, "I'd like to be the one to show it to you."

Nicky drew back as though startled. "Signor Ponti..." she started to say, but stopped when she saw the man Giovanni approaching with a tray laden with snacks and drinks.

"Caviar," Stefano said. "How nice. Thank you, Giovanni."

"Will there be anything else, *signor?*"

"Not at the moment. But in a little while we'll want another drink."

"Very good, *signor.*"

Nicky took a sip of her drink. "It's good," she said.

"Yes, isn't it?" Ponti leaned back in his chair. "Whiskey and soda was Isabella's favorite drink." He spread a bit of caviar on a cracker, added a dollop of onion and handed it to Nicky. "And I must say she could certainly drink her share of them." He sighed and said, "Her death still grieves me."

Nicky set her glass down on the table between them. "You said she fell from a third-floor window."

"Fell? Yes, that was the story." He cocked an eyebrow and in a sardonic voice said, "But one doesn't really know unless one was at the scene." He looked at Nicky. "Does one?"

"Was there..." She hesitated. "Was there ever any doubt that it was an accident?"

"Doubt? Yes, there was doubt. Everyone knew there'd been trouble between Isabella and Carlo for months." Ponti took a sip of his drink. "There was an inquest, of course, but the Santinis are a powerful family and it was little more than a formality." He looked at Nicky over the rim of his glass. "You asked if there was ever any doubt that it was an accident. The answer is yes, in my mind there's a great deal of doubt."

Nicky looked at him, her eyes wide with disbelief. Was he suggesting that Carlo had pushed Isabella from the window? Surely he couldn't be serious.

"There was a storm the day Isabella died," he went on. "Much like the one we had last night. Carlo and the servants testified that apparently..." He raised an eyebrow. "That apparently Isabella had reached out of the window to close a shutter and had fallen to her death."

A storm? Nicky stared at him. She picked up her drink and, without thinking, drank almost half of it.

"Her neck was broken," Stefano went on. "But other than that there wasn't a mark on her. She was as beautiful in death as she had been in life." He looked at Nicky. "Does Carlo ever talk about her?"

"No," she said quickly. "No."

"Perhaps I shouldn't either. But Isabella..." Ponti sighed. "She was a very special woman, Nicky. She loved life more than anyone I've ever known. And parties. How she adored parties. She could dance all night, drink a great deal and still look absolutely gorgeous." He paused to light a cigarette, then hesitated and said, "I'm sorry, would you care for one?"

"Yes, thank you."

He lighted it for her. "I didn't know you smoked."

Nicky smiled. "Didn't you?" She inhaled and let the smoke out slowly. "Please go on," she said.

Ponti leaned back in his chair. "I don't want to speak badly of Carlo, and of course I don't blame him, but he was insanely jealous of Isabella. Wherever they went, men flocked around her and it drove Carlo crazy. He was wildly in love with her...." He stopped. "Dear me, what am I doing? You don't want to hear about his first wife. It's insensitive of me and I'm sorry."

He looked up and said, "Ah, here's Giovanni. Finish your drink and have another, one more to celebrate the sunshine after the storm."

Nicky drained her glass and the manservant took it.

"When you come back with a refill, bring some of those little sausages and a bit of cheese," Stefano said. He touched his glass to Nicky's. "To my beautiful new neighbor. I hope this is only the beginning of..." His lips quirked in a smile. "Of a delightful friendship."

Nicky took a sip of the fresh drink, and knew that it should be her last. She wasn't used to drinking anything stronger than wine. She really shouldn't.... But the sun was warm on her face and it was pleasant to sit here under the wisteria-covered pergola with an attractive man. And Stefano Ponti was attractive. "Let go of your inhibitions,'' a voice inside her head seemed to say. "What harm can it do? Carlo is away; he doesn't need to know."

Giovanni returned with the little sausages and the cheese and two more drinks. "I've prepared lunch," he said. "Would you like me to serve it here or in the house, Signor Ponti?"

"In the house, I think," Stefano said. He turned to Nicky. "Perhaps you would like to call Elizabetta."

"Elizabetta?" Nicky stared as though seeing him for the first time. "I told her I'd have lunch with her."

"But surely she won't mind if you don't. You can telephone from the house and tell one of the servants—"

"No, no, I..." Elizabetta! she thought. Elizabetta needs me. She pushed back her chair and stood. "I really can't," she said.

"Very well then, I won't insist, if you promise we'll do this again soon." He took her arm. "Come along, I'll walk you to the gate."

They crossed the pristine lawn and went back through the tangled trees and overgrown garden. At the gate he stopped. "Please come again soon." He took her hand and brought it to his lips, then turned it and touched his tongue to her palm.

A remembered sensation. A faint shiver that started at the base of her spine grew and spread.

"Stefano?" she whispered, but before he could reply she turned and ran back through the gate into the garden of the Casa Santini.

Annamaria called a few days later. "Can we get together for lunch?" she asked. "I have to go into Florence to pick up a suit I ordered. We could make a day of it, shop and have lunch, maybe get our hair done."

"I'd love to," Nicky said.

"Is Carlo still away?"

"Yes, in Genoa. He expects to be back at the end of the week."

"I'm sure you miss him."

"Of course."

"I'll pick you up at ten. Is that all right?"

"Yes, that's fine."

When Nicky replaced the phone, she tried to quell the guilty feeling she'd had ever since the other day at Stefano Ponti's. She'd had too much to drink, and not wanting Elizabetta to see her, had gone straight to her room, with instructions to one of the maids to tell Carlo's grandmother that she had a headache and was resting.

She had been chagrined and ashamed of herself when she had appeared at dinner that night. To make up for it she had spent a great deal of her time the next few days with Elizabetta.

Carlo called every night. "I miss you very much," he said. "I cannot wait to get back to you."

"When do you think you will?"

"By the end of the week. Saturday at the latest. We'll do something special, *cara mia*. Dinner and dancing, yes?"

"Whatever you want, Carlo."

"You know what I want, *carissima*." And when Nicky didn't answer, he said, "Nicky? Nicky, are you there?"

"Yes." She tightened her hand on the phone. "Yes, Carlo, I'm here. And yes, I'd love to go out on Saturday night."

"*Bene, carissima.* Until then."

Annamaria arrived a little after ten the following morning. They went first to the shop to pick up the suit Annamaria had ordered. While Annamaria was paying her bill, Nicky picked out material for three suits, two for evening, one for street wear.

"*Three* suits!" Annamaria said with a nervous giggle. "They're terribly expensive, Nicky. Are you sure Carlo won't mind?"

"Quite sure." Nicky shrugged. "Now I need something to wear for Saturday night."

"I know just the place," Annamaria said, linking her arm through Nicky's.

When they reached the shop just off the Via dell' Oriuolo they were taken into a small salon, and when asked if they would like tea or perhaps something stronger, Nicky said, "A martini, please. Very dry, with two olives."

The refreshments were served—tea for Annamaria, the martini for Nicky—and the parade of clothes began. Nicky chose a short, metallic-threaded red dress, a short black tulle, a shocking pink silk jumpsuit, and for Saturday night, a strapless black silk chiffon with a center slit that came to the upper thigh.

"*Dio mio!*" Annamaria said, looking shocked. "It's very revealing, no? Do you think Carlo will like it?"

"I like it," Nicky said. "That's what matters."

A helper took the clothes to Annamaria's car, then the two of them went to lunch. The restaurant was elegant, the food delicious. And Nicky had another martini.

"I'd like to get my hair cut," she said.

"It's very pretty the length it is now."

"But I like it short." Nicky took a sip of her drink. "And lighter."

They went to the salon where Carlo had first taken her. The operator Annamaria had made an appointment with came to greet them. And the same hairstylist—Enrico? Yes, that was his name—greeted Nicky.

He was wearing a jumpsuit today, too, bright red to match his hair. And he had as many gold chains around his neck and gold rings on his fingers as he'd had before.

He gave a delighted squeal when he saw her. "You look *meraviglioso*," he cried. "Absolutely marvelous. But even better when Enrico is through, yes?"

"Yes." Nicky smiled. "I want my hair cut exactly as you cut it before, and a bit more blond. *Si?*"

"But of course, *si*." He draped a pink-and-white cape over her. "It will be my pleasure to make you even more beautiful than you already are."

The cut came first. "A bit shorter," Nicky said. "With the same fringe of bangs."

Then the color. "Be sure it's *very* blond," she instructed.

Next came the blow-dry, a touch of the curling iron, the brushing.

Enrico rested his hands on Nicky's shoulders. "Yes?" he asked.

Nicky studied her reflection in the mirror. The reflection smiled back at her. She touched her short blond hair. *"Bene,"* she said. *"Multo bene."*

CHAPTER FOURTEEN

Carlo arrived home at ten on Friday night. Nicky was in the sitting room off their bedroom, curled up on the black leather sofa when he opened the door and called out, *"Dov'e mia sposa bella?* Where is my beautiful wife?"

Lazily Nicky uncoiled, and straightening the skirt of her blue satin peignoir, stood to greet him.

"Buona sera, Carlo," she said. "I thought you weren't going to return until tomorrow."

"I took a late flight." He dropped his suitcase and hurried across the room. *"Dio,* how I have missed you!" he said.

Her lips twitched but she didn't respond.

"I couldn't stand another night away from you, *carissima."* He put his arms around her and kissed her, his mouth hungry against hers. "I'm not going to leave you again," he murmured. "The next time I have to travel, you will come with me. I..." He stopped and held her away from him. "What have you done to your hair?"

"I had it cut and lightened." She stepped out of his embrace, and going to the desk, took a cigarette out of the package and lighted it. "I went back to Enrico. He does such good work, doesn't he?"

"You're smoking!" Carlo frowned. "I've never seen you smoke before."

"No, I don't suppose you have." She lifted her shoulders and the blue satin peignoir fell open to reveal the almost-transparent gown beneath. "I like one occasionally, especially with a drink, and of course at bedtime." She smiled a slow and knowing smile. "It is bedtime, isn't it, *amore mio?*" Stubbing her cigarette in a heavy cut-glass ashtray, she came to him and wound her arms around his neck. "Come to bed, Carlo. Yes?" She opened his jacket and began to unbutton his shirt. "It's been too long," she whispered. "I don't want to wait a moment longer."

She kissed him. Her breath was hot, her tongue like quicksilver against his. She cupped his bottom to bring him closer and moved in undulating motions against him.

"Nicky... ?" With a strangled cry, his mouth still against hers, he backed her up to the black leather sofa, pressed her down on it and began tearing at his clothes. This was a side of her he'd never seen. It surprised even as it excited him. Nicky wanted him as he wanted her. *Dio,* what a wonderful homecoming.

She took off her robe and the sheer gown and held her arms out to him. *"Amore,"* she said. "Come to me now. Make love to me again."

There were no preliminaries. She wanted no gentle touchings or tender words. It was raw sex, wild, uninhibited. He thrust hard into her and she cried out, *"Si, amore! Si,* the way I like it."

Fingernails dug into his shoulders. She lifted herself to him, moving hard and fast. But it wasn't enough; she wanted more. Gripping his shoulders, she forced him to roll so that she was on top. In control. The way she wanted to be. She moved against him, but when she felt his body begin to tighten, she said, "No!" and stopped all movement.

"Don't!" he cried. "Don't stop!"

She smiled a slow, secret smile. "But you have to wait," she said, without a hint of passion in her voice. "Waiting humbles you, Carlo."

"Nicky...?"

"Nicky?" She laughed, then like one possessed began to move against him, head thrown back, bracing herself, digging her nails hard into his shoulders. And when his body rose to hers and he cried out in an agony of release, she laughed again.

When Nicky awoke the next morning she was alone. She lay for a few moments without moving, trying to remember what had happened the night before. Carlo had come home. He'd left his suitcase by the door and then... Then what? She sat up and rubbed her eyes. Had they made love? Yes, of course, they must have. But why didn't she remember? Had she slept so soundly afterward that she couldn't recall what had happened?

Feeling uncertain and uneasy, Nicky sat up and reached for her peignoir. The satin was smooth against her fingertips, but strangely enough, she didn't remember buying it.

She put it on and went into the bathroom, where she showered and washed her hair. When she came out of the shower, she frowned at her reflection in the mirror. Why in the world had she let Annamaria talk her into cutting her hair again? Carlo hadn't wanted her to cut it, he'd wanted it to grow longer, the way it had been when they were married. She shook her head. Well, it would grow and she'd never let anybody talk her into having it so short again.

Back in the bedroom, she put on a pair of dark gray slacks and a light gray silk shirt. When she went to the dresser to get a belt, she saw a tissue-wrapped package, and opening it, she found a silk scarf in variegated shades of turquoise, green and blue. She held it to her face for a moment, liking the feel of it against her skin, then draped it around the neck of her shirt.

Anxious to thank Carlo for his gift, she turned and hurried out of the room.

He and his grandmother were having breakfast on the terrace. Elizabetta looked up when she saw her, and raising a hand in greeting, said, *"Buon giorno,* here you are at last. And just in time. We were about to start."

"Buon giorno." Nicky went to Elizabetta and kissed her cheek. And with one hand on Elizabetta's shoulder, said, *"Buon giorno,* Carlo."

"Nicolina," he said, and nodded.

"Did you sleep well?"

"Not really."

"Oh?" She took a chair across from him. "But why? You must have been tired from your trip."

"I was."

She looked at him uncertainly, puzzled by his coolness. "Perhaps you were overtired. Sometimes that happens."

"Yes, I suppose it does."

She fingered the silk scarf at her throat. "Thank you for this," she said. "It's lovely."

"I'm glad you like it." He looked away from her as Maria came out to the patio.

"Melone," the cook said. "Eggs and sausage. And I will bring more coffee."

"Grazie, Maria." Elizabetta smiled. "It's nice to have everything back in order again, isn't it?" She squeezed Carlo's hand. "And it's wonderful to have you back, my boy. Nicky and I missed you, especially during the storm. It was quite dreadful—the wind blowing, shutters bang-

ing. Nicky went up to the third floor to make sure the shutters there were securely fastened and..." She hesitated, napkin against her lips, then said, "I'm afraid there was an accident."

"An accident? Where?"

"In...Isabella's room. The chandelier fell. I heard the crash and I thought..." She pressed the napkin to her lips again. "I was so afraid it had fallen on Nicky."

His face went white. *"Per Dio!"* he exclaimed, looking at Nicky. "You could have been killed. Why did you go up there? And what in the hell were you doing in Isabella's room? I've asked you not to go up to the third floor. Why would you deliberately go against my wishes?"

"Because I asked her to," Elizabetta said before Nicky could answer.

"You know I don't want anyone in Isabella's room. Nicky could have been hurt. *Ay, Dio,* she could have been killed."

"I—I didn't think." Two bright spots of color rose in Elizabetta's pale cheeks. "The shutter was banging and I—I was so upset..." She dropped her head into her hands. "I'm sorry," she whispered. "Sorry."

"It wasn't your fault." Nicky shoved her chair back and hurried to kneel beside the elderly woman. She put her arms around her and said, "There's nothing to be sorry about. Please don't be upset." She glared at Carlo. "How could you?" she murmured. "How could you speak to your grandmother that way?"

He stood and rested a hand on Elizabetta's shoulder. "Forgive me, *Nonna.* It's not your fault. I had told Nicky not to go up there. She should have known better."

"You mustn't blame Nicky," Elizabetta whispered.

"All right, Grandmother. I'm sorry."

"I'd like to go to my room now."

"Aren't you feeling well?"

"I'm a little tired, that's all." She patted Nicky's arm. "Don't look so worried. I'm quite all right. I only want to rest for a little while."

Carlo helped his grandmother to rise, and with an arm around her waist, accompanied her back into the house.

Nicky watched them go, angry because Carlo had spoken so harshly to his grandmother, and to her. There were so many things she didn't understand. Why had Carlo seemed upset this morning? And why had he reacted so strongly when he'd found that she had gone up to the third floor in the storm? Was it because the room had been Isabella's? Because, in spite of what he had said, there was a part of him that still loved his dead wife and the room was sacrosanct, a shrine to her memory?

Or was it because he hadn't wanted her to see Isabella's portrait and know how very much they looked alike?

And why had she herself been acting so strangely? Why didn't she remember anything about last night? This morning, when she had gone through the sitting room on her way downstairs, she had noticed a package of cigarettes on the desk. Curious, because she had never seen Carlo smoke, she'd picked it up, and then she'd seen the crushed-out cigarette in the glass ashtray, a cigarette with lipstick on it.

So many things were happening lately that she didn't understand. The day after she and Annamaria had gone to Florence she had looked at the new clothes hanging in her closet and it was as though she had never seen them before. Why had she chosen them? Why?

She was still sitting on the terrace, staring out at the garden, when Carlo returned.

"I'm sure Grandmother will be fine after she's rested for a bit," he said as he sat down. "What about you, Nicky? Are you all right?"

"Me? Yes, of course."

"When did you start smoking?"

"I don't remember."

Carlo looked at her, puzzled. He refilled his coffee cup from the pot on the table and said, "I had a walk in the garden early this morning. Luigi told me you were prowling around after the storm, checking on things."

Nicky clenched her hands together in her lap.

"He said you went to the far end of the garden, where the gate to the estate next-door is."

"Yes, I . . ." She swallowed hard. "I stumbled on it by accident and I—I went through to see what was on the other side."

"And?" he prompted.

"I ran into Signor Ponti."

Carlo frowned, a frown that warned she should not hold anything back.

"I had a drink with him, in the garden near the house."

The frown deepened.

"He's really very nice."

"Is he?"

Nicky stood and faced him. In a quiet voice she said, "I don't know what the trouble is between the two of you, but Stefano is a neighbor and—"

"Stefano?" He got up and, facing her, asked, "What's happening to you? Why are you behaving this way?"

"What way?" she asked. "I don't know what you mean."

"Your hair, for one thing. You knew I wanted you to let it grow. And your smoking. Is that something *Ste-*

fano has been teaching you?'' He gripped her shoulders. ''You're not to see him again,'' he said gruffly. ''Do you understand?''

Confusion clouded her mind. She shook her head as though trying to clear it. ''Please let me go,'' she said.

''Do you understand?''

''Yes!'' she cried. ''All right. Yes.''

He let go of her and turned away. ''All of a sudden I don't know who you are. Last night you...'' He looked back at her. ''Who are you, Nicky? Who are you really?''

''Who do you want me to be?''

He stared at her. Then, without a word, he went back into the house. In a few moments she heard his car start.

She dropped her head into her hands. ''Carlo,'' she whispered. ''Help me. Help me.''

But he wasn't there to hear her whispered cry.

Later that afternoon, when she and Elizabetta had finished lunch in Elizabetta's room, Nicky took a book and went to sit out on the terrace. And that is where Stefano Ponti found her.

''Here you are,'' he said. ''I've come to return your basket and to bring you some fresh dahlias out of my garden.''

''Thank you,'' she said a bit nervously. ''The flowers are beautiful.''

''I mentioned that they were Isabella's favorites too, didn't I?''

''Yes.'' She didn't want to be reminded of Isabella, and she was upset that Ponti was here, because if Carlo found out he'd be furious. But she had been a guest in Stefano Ponti's garden and now he was returning her basket and bringing her flowers. There really wasn't anything else she could do but invite him to sit down.

And when he did she said, "May I offer you a drink?"

"That would be nice." He gave her one of his best smiles. "If you'll join me."

"I really don't make a habit of drinking during the day."

"Just one?" he coaxed.

"All right, just one. Would you..." Nicky hesitated. Then, deciding that Carlo would be upset whether she invited Stefano Ponti in for a drink or had it out here on the terrace, and that it was only simple courtesy to ask, she said, "Would you like to come in?"

He nodded. "I haven't been here since before Isabella died. I'd like to see the old place again."

"Then we'll have our drinks in the library. It's cool there in the afternoon. Come along."

When they were inside, she preceded him down the hall, and when they reached the library she asked, "What would you like? Whiskey and soda?"

"Brandy, if you have it."

"Of course." She poured his drink, hesitated, then poured a splash of brandy for herself.

"To your health," he said, and touched his glass to hers.

"And yours." Nicky took a sip of her drink and felt a pleasurable warmth when it trickled down her throat. She took another sip and began to feel more relaxed. She really couldn't understand Carlo's antipathy toward Stefano Ponti. He was a charming man. And he certainly was attractive.

"Cigarette?" he asked, and when Nicky nodded, he took a flat gold case out of the breast pocket of his jacket, opened it and took out two cigarettes. He put both of them in his mouth, lighted them with one match, and holding her with his gaze, placed one between her lips.

She'd seen a man do the same thing in an old Bette Davis movie on the late-late show. She'd thought it romantic then, and thought it just as romantic now.

Smoke wafted through the room and with it she caught the scent of Isabella's perfume. But now it seemed to her that the scent wasn't all that unpleasant, that actually it was rather nice, exotic, and yes, rather sexy.

She leaned back in her chair and smiled at Stefano. "Tell me about yourself," she said. "Have you ever been married?"

He shook his head. "I'm afraid I've never been that fortunate."

"In love?"

"Only once."

"What happened?"

He looked at the glowing end of his cigarette. "I lost her."

"I'm sorry."

"So goes life." He looked at Nicky. "Would you like me to show you the tunnel leading over to my place?"

"The tunnel?"

"You remember, I told you about it before."

"Yes, of course." She ground out the cigarette. "I'd love to see it. Which room is it in?"

"This room."

Nicky looked around. "But I don't see a door."

Ponti laughed. "You can't have a door opening a secret tunnel, *cara*. It has to be behind a sliding panel or a bookcase. Or..." He crossed the room and stopped before the life-size painting of a bewigged Santini ancestor. "Or a painting," he said. "You simply touch the brass nameplate here at the bottom of the portrait..."

The painting swung around.

"And voilà," he said. "The secret tunnel."

Nicky jumped to her feet. "I can't believe it," she cried. "Let me see."

He opened the door. "Wait a moment. There's a switch here somewhere. Yes, here it is." He motioned Nicky forward. "Have a look," he said.

She gave a nervous laugh. "How long do you think it's been here?"

"Probably since the days of the Machiavellis. Certainly for three hundred years. That's when my place was built."

"Did everyone know about it?"

"The Pontis and the Santinis did. I imagine all sorts of devious plots were hatched in the tunnel, and many a secret liaison was arranged there beneath our two houses."

"Do you ever use it?"

"Of course."

"For a devious plot or a liaison?"

Stefano smiled. "What do you think?"

"I think..." She hesitated. The scent of the perfume was stronger now. It permeated the room, giving her a heady feeling. She took another, bigger sip of her brandy. "I think you're an interesting man, Signor Ponti, and that maybe..." She laughed up at him. "And that maybe I want to know you better."

He took a step closer and brought her free hand to his lips. "That can be arranged, my dear." He brushed his lips across her palm. "My very dear Signora Santini."

And again, as she had that day in the garden, Nicky felt a slight chill at the base of her spine, a sensation that, while frightening, was pleasurable.

He looked at her and his dark Italian eyes were intense. "If you ever need me," he said, "if you should ever feel in danger and you can't reach me any other way, remember the tunnel."

"Danger?" A quiver of fear trembled through Nicky. "Why would I be in danger?"

"I don't know, Nicolina. But just in case. Yes?"

"Stefano..." She shook her head, not understanding. What was he talking about? Why should she be in danger?

But before she could ask, he said, "Wouldn't you like to see where the tunnel leads?"

"I—"

"No, she would not!" Carlo stood in the doorway of the library, his face tight, his eyes burning with anger.

Ponti let go of Nicky's hand. With a forced smile he said, "I was showing her the tunnel."

"Get out!"

"Really, Carlo—"

"Get the hell out of my house!"

"Carlo..." Nicky took a steadying breath. "Signor Ponti returned the flower basket I'd left when I visited. I asked him in for a drink and he showed me the entrance to the tunnel."

"Leave us," Carlo said without looking at her.

"But—"

He swung on her. "Go up to our room," he said. "Immediately."

"I—"

He took a step toward her and there was an expression in his eyes she had never seen before, a rage so intense that suddenly she was afraid. Putting her glass down, she backed away, hands in front of her as though to protect herself.

The scent of perfume was stronger now, overpowering, sickening. Couldn't they smell it? Was she the only one who could? She swayed and grasped the back of a chair for support. "Listen," she said, desperate for him to understand. "Something's happening. I—I don't know what it is, but—"

"I told you to go up to our room." His voice was quiet with menace. "Now, Nicky..." The words hung in the perfumed air, threatening. Dangerous.

She looked at Carlo, then at their neighbor, and with a muffled cry ran out of the room.

Carlo glared at Stefano Ponti. "I want you to leave my house," he said. "If you ever return, if I ever see you with Nicky again, I will kill you. Do you understand?"

"Perfectly." Ponti, one eyebrow raised in a sardonic gesture, brushed a piece of lint off the sleeve of his navy blue jacket. "Would you like me to close the door to the tunnel or shall I leave it open in case you want to come through in the night and stick a dagger in my heart?"

"Don't tempt me," Carlo said in a voice of deadly calm. "Get out of here, Ponti, before I change my mind and do it now."

Ponti raised his shoulders. "Don't think it hasn't been lovely," he said. "And do make my excuses to Nicky and thank her for the drink."

Carlo took a step forward.

"All right," Ponti said. "I'm going."

The door of the library closed behind him. Carlo stood where he was for a few moments before he crossed to the door leading into the tunnel and closed it. Slowly the anger faded from his eyes, to be replaced by a haunting look of unbearable anguish. He sank into a chair and covered his eyes with his hands.

Was history repeating itself? Was it starting all over again, just when he'd thought he'd put the past behind him?

In Nicky he had found a new love, a new life. The sadness and the turmoil of the years before were behind him. With her he had a chance to begin again, to find happiness at last. Had he been wrong about her? Had he been fooled a second time?

At last, with a heavy heart, Carlo went out of the library and slowly climbed the stairs.

He found her curled up on their bed. She raised up when she heard him come into the room. Her eyes were swollen from crying.

"We have to talk." He took his jacket off and folded it over a chair before he came to sit on the edge of the bed. "We can't go on this way," he started to say. "We—"

But before he could go on, Nicky flung herself into his arms. "Help me!" she cried. "Help me!"

"What...?"

"I don't know what's happening to me. I do things, I say things... I'm sorry I went to Signor Ponti's home. I'm sorry I drank and I'm sorry he came here today." She began weeping uncontrollably.

"All right," he said stiffly. "We needn't discuss it right now."

"But you don't understand," she whispered between her sobs. "Sometimes I don't remember things." She pointed to the blue satin peignoir at the foot of the bed. "I don't remember buying it. I don't remember beginning to smoke." Tears were streaming down her face. "I don't even remember whether or not we made love last night."

His eyebrows drew together. "You don't remember?"

She shook her head. "I think I'm losing my mind. I smell her perfume and—"

"Whose perfume?"

"Isabella's. Ever since that day in her room, the day of the storm. I tell myself I'm imagining it, but the scent is so real it sickens me. And when I smell it I—I do things I don't mean to do." Nicky grasped the front of his shirt. "You're a doctor, Carlo. Help me."

"You're exciting yourself. You're imagining things."

He didn't believe her. Oh, God! God! She started to shake, shake with a terrible chill that had her teeth chattering and her body in spasms.

Alarmed, he put his arms around her. "You're overwrought," he said. "You're upset because you went into Isabella's room and saw her portrait. That's my fault. I should have had it removed a long time ago. I'm sorry I didn't. I'll have workers come in. They'll redo the room and take away the painting."

"It won't help," she said through teeth she tried to keep from chattering. "Nothing will help me now."

"Nicky, stop this. You must stop." He put his arms around her and pulled her closer.

Nicky looked up at him. Their faces were close. She touched his lips. "Oh, Carlo," she whispered. "Carlo, I'm so afraid."

And suddenly he believed her, at least he believed that *she* believed that strange and unexplainable things were happening. In this moment, close in his arms, she was his Nicky again, the Nicky he loved.

He kissed her gently, and some of the anger and despair he had felt when he walked into the library and found her with Stefano Ponti faded. Her mouth was soft and sweet, her body warm against his. She murmured against his lips and her arms crept up around his neck, gentle arms to hold him as he held her.

"Carlo," she whispered. "Oh, darling, I love you. I love you so much."

He stroked the hair back from her face. "What's happening to us, Nicky? Why have you been seeing Stefano Ponti? I don't understand."

"Nor do I." She clung to him. "Hold me, Carlo. Please, just hold me."

He kissed her and the slow sweet rise to passion began. She began to fumble with the buttons of his shirt and he said, "Wait, I'll do it," and sat up so that he could take it off.

Nicky put her arms around his bare shoulders. Before he could stop himself he winced and drew away.

"What is it?" she asked, startled. "What's the matter?"

"Nothing." He shook his head. "It's nothing."

"Let me see." Nicky knelt beside him. "Your back! Carlo, what happened? You've got scratches. Deep scratches. How did you get them?"

"You did it," he said quietly. "Last night when we made love."

"Me?" She looked at him. Her eyes went wide with shock. "No," she whispered. "Oh, no."

Then her eyes lost their focus, and before he could catch her, she fainted and fell back against the bed.

CHAPTER FIFTEEN

"Nicky! Nicky!" Carlo cradled her in his arms. "Speak to me!" When she didn't respond, he slapped her gently to try to rouse her.

Her eyelids fluttered.

"Car—Carlo?"

"Si, amore mia. Si."

"I fainted?"

"Yes, Nicky."

"But I—I've never fainted in my life. What happened?" A look of horror crossed her face. "Those scratches on your back. You said I made them."

"That's not important now. Don't think about it."

Nicky struggled to sit up. "But don't you see?" she said, her voice rising with shock. "I don't remember! Oh, my God, I don't remember!" She gripped his hand, fighting for calm. "I know you don't believe me, Carlo, but I swear to you, I have no recollection of making love last night."

He wanted to say something to help her. But what could he say? Her shock when she'd seen the marks on his back had been real, so real she had fainted. She'd also said that she didn't remember buying the blue satin robe or starting to smoke. And something about perfume. Did she expect him to believe that somehow Isabella was causing these things that were happening to her? That was preposterous.

"I think you were frightened when you went to Isabella's room," he said, trying to be reasonable. "You were up there alone during a bad storm, and the lights went off, *si?*"

"Yes, but—but the perfume. I didn't imagine that."

"Didn't you?"

Nicky pulled away from him. "No, I didn't. Nor did I imagine that the chandelier fell, or that if I hadn't jumped out of the way it might have killed me."

He took her hands in his. "Very likely the chandelier had started coming loose from the ceiling a long time ago, Nicky. Years of wind and rain have weakened the roof up there. That's why it fell. There weren't any evil spirits just waiting for you to come in."

"Weren't there?"

"No, Nicky." Carlo stroked the back of her hand. "I know you saw Isabella's portrait in her room and I'm sorry."

Nicky looked down at the hands holding hers, and in a voice so low he could barely hear, she said, "I thought when I saw the portrait that you hadn't wanted me to see her room because you were keeping it—the room, I mean—as a shrine to her memory."

"A shrine?" Carlo shook his head. "*Per Dio,* no! Isabella may have lived here at the Casa Santini during the last year of her life, but in every sense of the word we were separated. After she moved up to the third floor we rarely saw each other. We lived completely separate lives."

He got up from the bed and went to stand in front of the windows that overlooked the balcony. For a few moments he didn't speak, but at last he turned back to Nicky and said, "I told you that Isabella had been having an affair, but I didn't tell you that it was with Stefano Ponti."

"Stefano?" Nicky looked at him, stunned.

"That's why when I saw you with him in the library I thought... I thought history was repeating itself. That the two of you—"

"No!" Nicky, her face stricken, started up from the bed. "How could you even think such a thing?"

"She would meet him in the tunnel," he went on. "And go from there to his place. When I saw you standing there with him I thought that you..." He shook his head, unable to go on.

Nicky went to him. "I know that there's something strange going on with me. And I know I've acted badly. But you have to believe me when I tell you that there will never be another man for me." She cupped his face between her hands. "I love you, Carlo. Only you. Whatever has happened, whatever it is that's happening to me, that is the one absolute in my life. I love you."

He gazed into her eyes, then with a cry he brought her close and held her as though he would never let her go. "Don't ever leave me," he said.

"I never will."

He kissed her, and it was as it had been that night in Venice, coming from Torcello. He savored her mouth with slow, sweet kisses, and his arms came around her as though to shelter her from a fear she didn't understand. When she brought a hand up to caress his cheek, he took it and gently kissed each finger, then rained soft kisses over her face, her eyes, her cheeks, the tip of her nose. He trailed a line of moist pleasure down to her throat and her ears before he took her mouth again.

And when she swayed toward him, he picked her up and carried her to their bed.

For a long time they only held each other, satisfied with the deep kisses, the quiet touching.

He leaned his head between her naked breasts, content to feel her warmth against his face. But when he turned to kiss her there, their bodies grew heated with desire and they could no longer wait.

It was a gentle coupling. He kissed her when their bodies joined and they began to move together in perfect rhythm. When at last, in a voice made hoarse by all that he was feeling, he said, "Yes, *cara mia?* Yes?" Nicky lifted her body to his. And in that moment of completion she knew with shining clarity that at last they were truly one.

"I love you," she whispered against his mouth. "Only you, Carlo. Forever you."

They spent the rest of the afternoon and evening in their room. They spoke of things they had never talked about before. When they became hungry, he called downstairs for sandwiches and wine. Afterward they bathed together in the black marble tub, her back against his chest, her eyes closed, drifting on a sea of contentment in the scented, steaming water.

Warm water. Warm him. Soap-soft hands caressing her breasts. In a little while she turned so that she could touch the shoulders she had scratched, and rising on her knees, she healed the scratches with her lips.

He put his arms around her and knew that this was the Nicky he had fallen in love with, this sweet and gentle creature here in his arms. But what of last night? Who had she been then? With a chill he remembered the earlier years with Isabella, and how, not always, but often enough so that afterward he had been disturbed by it, she had lost all control during lovemaking. Like a wildcat she had scratched and bitten, and yes... God help him, there had been times when she had excited him almost to the state of collapse.

And last night? Had there been a moment of recollection in the middle of making love with Nicky? A bright flash of remembrance of another time with Isabella?

A terrible feeling of horror twisted hard in the pit of Carlo's stomach. If Nicky had been telling the truth when she'd said she didn't remember last night, then something was terribly wrong.

He tightened his arms around Nicky. She had given him her love with total trust and an innocence of heart, and he had tried to change her into the image of Isabella, Isabella who knew so little about what loving someone meant. He would never forgive himself for what he had done to Nicky, and he would spend the rest of his life making up to her for the harm he had done her. He would protect her from . . . from what? The unseen presence of a wife dead these past two years?

He was a medical man. He didn't believe in ghosts or that the spirit of a dead woman could possess another woman's body. But something was happening to Nicky, and he didn't know what it was or how to explain it.

When at last he helped her out of the tub, he carried her to their bed. "Sleep, *cara mia,*" he said, and in a little while, cradled close in his arms, she slept.

But Carlo didn't. He listened to her breathing, and in the dim light of the room, watched the rise and fall of her breasts. Something very strange was going on; he had to find out what it was.

When Nicky awoke the next morning, Carlo, fully dressed, was sitting on the side of the bed.

"You're leaving?" She sat up and rubbed her eyes. "Why didn't you wake me?"

"Because if I had I'd have been late for work." He smiled and kissed her. "Besides," he said, "you need to rest." He brushed the fair hair back from her forehead. "How do you feel? Any dizziness? Anything?"

"No, Carlo, I'm fine." She yawned. "Have you had breakfast?"

"Had breakfast and looked in on Elizabetta. I told her you were asleep and that you'd see her later." He glanced at the bedside clock. "It's late, Nicky. I really have to go." He kissed her again. "Workmen are coming tomorrow to check the roof and the ceiling in the room on the third floor. Other workmen will take away the chandelier and the furnishings. Meantime—" He shook his head. "Meantime, Nicky, I don't want you up there. All right?"

She looked at him, troubled, hesitating before she answered, "Don't worry. I'll see you tonight."

"As early as I can make it." He lifted his hand in a salute. "*Addio,* Nicky. Until later."

She sat propped up on her pillows, her brow furrowed in thought, until she heard his car start out of the driveway. Then, with a resolute expression on her face, she got up and threw back the sheet. Like a soldier going into battle she went to the closet and took out a pair of blue jeans and her red-and-white-striped T-shirt. Carlo had said the workmen were coming tomorrow and that they were going to take away the chandelier and remove the furnishings. Which meant they were also going to take away the portrait of Isabella. If they were, there was something she had to do first.

Either she was losing her mind or a force of evil had been let loose in the Casa Santini. She had always considered herself a fairly rational, fairly intelligent, modern woman, stable and sensible, rarely given to flights of fancy. She liked Halloween as well as the next person, but she didn't believe in ghosts and goblins. But—and the *but* was a big one—something very strange was happening to her and she was going to find out what it was.

She went into the sitting room, walked over to the desk, picked up the cigarettes and threw them into the wastebasket. Then she went out of the room and closed the door behind her.

At the foot of the stairs leading up to the third floor she stopped and took a deep breath. "Okay," she said, bracing herself. "Let's go!"

Up the stairs, open the door, go down the hall. Eerie, dimly lit, it smelled damp and musty after the rain.

Past the small bedroom, the sewing room, the playroom and the Machiavelli bedroom. All the way down to the end of the hall. Turn. Walk up to Isabella's room as though her heart wasn't beating like a wild thing in her chest and her knees weren't threatening to buckle.

Hand on the knob, one deep breath. Count to three. Another deep breath, and before she could change her mind, Nicky flung the door open.

In the dim light she could see the shattered shards of glass from the fallen chandelier. She stepped around it, and not looking at the portrait above the bed, went directly to the window. She opened it, then the shutters. The curtains ruffled in the breeze. Fresh air, she thought, to help chase the ghosts away.

She turned back to the room and looked up at the portrait of Carlo's first wife. Isabella looked down at her with the same enigmatic expression in her blue eyes as before, sardonic, patronizing. And it came, that first faint drift of perfume, clogging her nostrils, dizzying her so that she had to grasp the edge of the bed to steady herself.

"No!" Nicky said aloud. "I won't allow this to happen. You can't do this to me, because I won't let you." She glared up at the portrait, and stabbing a thumb at her chest, cried out, "*I'm* Carlo's wife, not you. I'm not going to let you spoil what we have with your expensive perfume and your—" A sudden gust of wind swept into the room. The door slammed shut, the shutters banged.

The scent of perfume was stronger. Carried on the wind, it filled the room and enveloped her in its cloying sweetness. She fought against it with all of her strength, and said, "No! I refuse to let this happen! I refuse to believe you can do this!"

The wind was stronger now, swirling around the room with an almost hurricane force, like a live and deadly presence of evil. The curtains stood straight out; the shutters slammed against the house. She thought of Elizabetta. Elizabetta would hear the noise and it would frighten her. She had to close the shutters.

She fought her way toward the window, grasped the edge of the sill and, leaning out, grabbed for one shutter and swung it back. Now the other one. The curtains flapped like sleeves on invisible arms and twisted around her body. She got the shutter, but before she could manage to swing it back and close it, the curtains swept around her, blinding her as they had that other time.

With a muttered curse, Nicky stepped back. She grasped the curtains in both hands and ripped them down off their rods into a tangled mess on the floor. Breathing hard, she went back to the portrait and, hands on her hips, glared up at Isabella.

"Tomorrow you're going to come down," she shouted. "And that will be the end of you. You're out of Carlo's life and out of mine. I love him and he loves me, and together we're going to beat you, Isabella. We're going to beat the Billy-blue-hell out of you."

With that Nicky turned and went to the door. And when she slammed it shut, she didn't look back.

She had no more nightmares. She no longer smelled the scent of Isabella's perfume. She wore blue jeans when she wanted to, and shoved the too-flashy dresses and the blue peignoir to the back of her closet.

Workmen came to repair the roof, others to take away the broken glass of the chandelier. Nicky stood at her window and watched them carry out the furniture from Isabella's bedroom. And the portrait. She had no idea what was going to happen to it, but as long as it was out of the house, she didn't care.

Carlo was considerate and loving. He talked about a second honeymoon in Greece, but both of them knew it would have to be postponed because of Elizabetta. That was their only cause for concern now. More and more, Carlo's grandmother stayed in her room. She slept a great deal, and when she was awake, spent her time looking at her photographs.

"I'm so concerned about her," Nicky told Carlo.

"I know, *cara*. But there really isn't anything we can do. She's been like this before and she's always come out of it. Perhaps she will this time, too."

But Nicky could tell by his voice that he didn't think she would.

"I hate this kind of a rain," Carlo said one morning as he was dressing for work. "The roads will be slick and the highway to Florence will be jammed with traffic."

"Then stay here with me." Nicky adjusted the silk scarf he had brought her from Genoa over the shoulders of her white shirt. Then, turning to him, she wound her arms around his neck. "I'll make it worth your while, Doc."

He growled against her mouth. "Don't tempt me," he said, and let her go.

"Drive carefully."

"I will." He hesitated at the door of the dining room. "I'm worried about Elizabetta, Nicky, so if I can I'll get back early. If there's any change, call me at the hospital."

"I will, Carlo." She kissed him. "I'll stay with her," she said. "Try not to worry."

When he left, she went directly to Elizabetta's room. Carlo's grandmother was awake and fretful. She wanted her photographs, so Nicky took the album and put it across her lap. She leafed through page after page, then, with her hand resting on Gianfranco's photograph, went to sleep.

Nicky returned to Elizabetta's room at noon. They had a sherry together, then lunch, with Nicky coaxing Elizabetta to "take just one more bite." And after they had eaten, Nicky took the volume of Dante's poems, which Elizabetta never grew tired of hearing, and read until the older lady nodded off.

She had just tiptoed out of Elizabetta's room when one of the maid's called out to her, "*Signora!* There is a phone call for you."

"I'll take it in the library," Nicky said.

She went into the library and picked up the phone. *"Pronto?"* she said. "Hello?"

"This is Stefano," the voice on the other end said.

She frowned. She didn't want him calling here. After learning that he was the one who'd had an affair with Isabella, she wanted nothing to do with him.

"How are you, Nicky?"

"I'm fine, thank you."

"I've been worried about you."

"Worried? Why?"

"Since that altercation in the library when Carlo discovered us together." He lowered his voice until he was speaking almost in a whisper. "You don't know Carlo like I do."

"Maybe I haven't known him as long, Signor Ponti, but I assure you, I know him a great deal better than you do."

"You only think you do, Nicky. That afternoon in the library was mild. I doubt that you've ever seen Carlo really angry, angry enough to kill. That's why I've been worried. Why I..." He hesitated, then almost in a whisper, said, "I have something I must tell you, Nicky."

"What is it?"

"I can't discuss this over the phone. I have to see you in person. Is Carlo home now?"

"No, he's at the hospital."

"You could come through the tunnel. I'll meet you halfway."

"No. Absolutely not."

"It's about Carlo, Nicky. About Isabella. I know how she died. If you refuse to meet me I'll be forced to go to the police."

"The police?" Panic stopped the breath in her throat. All sorts of thoughts ran round and round in her head. Carlo. Isabella. He had been aware of her deception, her infidelity. How it must have twisted his soul. But surely he couldn't have...

"Isabella fell," Nicky whispered into the phone.

"Did she?" The voice was soft, insidious. "Are you sure, Nicky? Are you really sure?"

She clutched the phone.

"I don't want anything to happen to you. Meet me, Nicky, because if you don't..."

The words hung in the air, threatening ruin, disaster.

She closed her eyes. "All right," she said. "I'll meet you."

"As soon as you can. I'll be waiting."

She took a breath to steady herself. "I'll come right away," she said.

CHAPTER SIXTEEN

Carlo tried to focus on what the speaker was saying about the latest design in pacemakers, but his attention wandered. Time and again he looked at his watch, feeling restless, anxious without knowing why. Deep down in his gut he had a terrible intuition that something was wrong. Was it Elizabetta? He looked at his watch again. It was a little after three in the afternoon. If Dr. Allocca didn't finish this up soon...

"Now to the second phase of my presentation," Allocca said.

Carlo pushed his chair back. "I'm sorry, Doctor, but I'm afraid you must excuse me. Something pressing..."

He didn't wait for their questions. He simply got up and hurried out of the room. At the nearest nurses' station he reached for the phone and dialed home. It rang three times before Rosa answered.

"Let me speak to my wife," he said.

"She isn't here, *signor.*"

"Is my grandmother all right?"

"Yes, Dr. Santini. As a matter of fact, the Signora Elizabetta got up and dressed for lunch today."

"Thank God," he murmured under his breath. Then, "Do you know where my wife is?"

"She went into the library a little while ago to take a phone call. If you'll wait, I'll try to find her."

"No, that's all right. But please tell her I'm on my way home."

He put the phone down. He should have felt relieved, but he didn't. What in the hell was the matter with him? Why did he feel this compelling need to get home?

It was still raining when he wheeled the car out of the hospital parking lot and headed back to the Casa Santini.

Nicky stood for a moment, undecided. She didn't want to go down into the tunnel to meet Stefano Ponti. But he'd said if she didn't he would go to the police. He had insinuated that Carlo was responsible for Isabella's death, but that was impossible. Carlo wasn't capable of murder. He couldn't have killed Isabella. That was unthinkable.

Perspiration broke out on her forehead. She thought of how angry Carlo had been when he'd found Stefano Ponti here in the library with her. There'd been a look of such dark rage on his face when he'd advanced on the other man that for a moment she'd been afraid he was going to do the man bodily harm. If he felt that way about Ponti, what must his anger have been toward Isabella? Could he have been angry enough to kill her?

In the deep recesses of her mind a small voice whispered, "He might have. He might have."

She had to find out.

She pulled off the scarf Carlo had brought her from Genoa and blotted at the perspiration on her face. Then she got up, went to the painting of the bewigged ancestor and pushed on the nameplate at the bottom of the frame. The painting swung out. She reached for the light switch and looked down at the stairs that led below.

She started down.

Twenty narrow steps, thirty, forty and more. The passageway was no more than three feet wide, maybe six feet high. She'd never been claustrophobic before, but she didn't like this. The light was so dim she could barely see in front of her. The stone walls were damp, the floor of the tunnel sloping and irregular.

Ponti had said the tunnel had been here since his family had built its villa next to the Santinis. Three hundred years ago? Four? Who had built it? For what purpose? What dark schemes had been plotted here? What evil had transpired? What trysts arranged? What murders done?

Shivering with cold and fear, Nicky went slowly forward. She heard a scratching noise and shrank back against the wall. A rat scurried in front of her. For a moment she froze where she was, her back against the damp wall, her heart pounding with fear of the unknown. But she had to go on, on farther into the dimly lighted tunnel.

At last the passageway became wider. Ahead she saw a brighter light and hurried toward it.

"Nicky?" Ponti called out. "Nicky, is that you?"

"Yes," she called back, and hurried toward the voice. She didn't like Ponti, but it would be a relief not to be alone.

"A little farther," he said, "Keep coming."

She hurried her steps, anxious to be in the light again, and saw him there ahead of her. He was in a room with torchlike lamps on the stone walls. There was a love seat, two straight-backed chairs, a table.

And on one wall the portrait of Isabella.

"Here you are at last." He came toward her, arms outstretched.

Nicky backed away. "The portrait," she said. "How did you get it?"

"From the dealer Carlo sold it to." He smiled. "This was our secret place, you see—Isabella's and mine. Sometimes when we were too impatient to wait we made love here in this room." He sighed. "It brings back many memories, having you with me now, Nicky."

She started to edge back the way she had come.

"Are you afraid?" Ponti shook his head. "But you have nothing to fear from me. I only want to protect you. I care about you, Nicky. Don't you know that?" He reached for her hands and drew her closer into the circle of light.

"I've been concerned ever since that night at the Andretti party when I saw your resemblance to Isabella. I knew then why Carlo had married you, and I was afraid..." He tightened his hands around hers. "Oh, my dear, I was so afraid that the same thing that happened to her would happen to you."

Nicky tried to pull away. "You don't know what you're talking about," she protested.

"Oh, but I do. I know the way Carlo treated poor Isabella." He looked up at the portrait. "I fell in love with her the moment we met. She was so vital, so incredibly alive." His face tightened with inner rage. "Carlo killed her. He—"

"No!" Nicky tried to pull away, but he wouldn't let her go.

"He killed her because he knew she was in love with me, and then he found you because you looked like her. That's the only reason he married you, Nicky. You know that, don't you?"

"That's not true!"

"Isn't it?" His eyes were intent on hers, as though by the sheer power of his gaze he could convince her. "We both loved her," he said, "but it was me Isabella loved, not Carlo. That's why he killed her, Nicky. That's what you have to understand."

"But I don't," she cried. "I don't believe you."

"Come with me to my house now and I promise that I won't let what happened to Isabella happen to you."

She stared at him, shaken. Carlo couldn't have killed Isabella. He wasn't capable of murder. Was he? She looked up at the portrait as though it could tell her that what Ponti said was a lie, and heard a voice inside her head whisper, "Carlo is proud. Think how that must have hurt him to know Isabella was in another man's bed, doing all the things with someone else she had done with him."

Nicky yanked her hands free, but before she could move away, Ponti grabbed her and pulled her onto the love seat.

"Don't fight it, *cara mia*. Don't fight what we feel for each other."

"I feel nothing for you," she cried. "Get away from me!"

"No, *cara,* no. Carlo took Isabella from me, but I won't let him take you. We will be lovers. I'll take care of you, Nicky. Only love me. Love me." He pushed her back against the pillows and half covered her body with his.

"You're mine now," he whispered. "I'll make you as happy as I made Isabella."

She screamed, but when she did he ground his mouth against hers to silence her, and held her so that she couldn't move.

Tires squealed to a stop on the graveled driveway. Carlo jumped out of the car and sprinted toward the house. He flung the door open and called out, "Nicky! Nicky, where are you?"

Sergio hurried toward him. "What is it, *Dottor?* Is something wrong?"

Carlo threw his briefcase down on a hall table, and fighting for calm, said, "Have you seen my wife?"

"No, Dr. Santini."

"Where is Rosa?"

"I believe she's in your grandmother's room. Shall I get her for you?"

"No, *grazie,* I'll find her."

He turned away and hurried down the corridor to Elizabetta's room. He knocked, and when Rosa opened the door, said, "Is Nicky here?"

"Carlo?" Elizabetta smiled at him from her chair. "You're home early. Is anything wrong?"

"No, nothing's wrong. How are you feeling?"

"Quite good, actually. I thought I might join you and Nicky for dinner this evening."

"That would be splendid, *Nonna.*" He ran a nervous hand through his hair. "Where's Nicky? Have you seen her?"

"Not since lunch. Rosa said you called asking about her. Perhaps she's still in the library. You're sure nothing is wrong?"

"No. I don't know. I have a feeling..." He shook his head. "It's probably nothing." He kissed her. "I'll see you at dinner, yes?" He started out the door.

"If there's anything I can—"

But Carlo had already turned and hurried out into the corridor.

He ran toward the library. The door was closed. He opened it, calling out as he did, "Nicky? Nicky, are you in here? Where are..." He stopped. The door to the tunnel was open. *Ay, Dio!* Had she gone into the tunnel or had Stefano Ponti come here?

He ran into the room. The scarf he had brought Nicky from Genoa lay on the floor at the entrance to the tunnel. He picked it up and crumpled it into a wrinkled ball. Then, with a cry of rage, he ran toward the steps leading down into the tunnel.

Nicky fought as hard as she could, but Ponti was like a man possessed. "Don't you see?" he said over and over again. "You are Isabella come back to me. This is our destiny. We belong together."

"No!" she cried. "Let me go! Let me go!"

He pressed hot kisses against her lips and reached under her shirt for her breasts. She hit him with all of her force against the side of his head, and when he let her go, she scrambled off the love seat and ran toward the entrance to the tunnel.

He went after her, caught her and brought her back. "Don't fight me," he said. "I don't want to hurt you. I only want to love you." He grabbed her wrists and, holding them behind her back, pressed his body to hers. "Carlo will never know," he whispered. "It will be like it was before."

She smelled it then, the sweet and cloying odor that filled her nostrils and made her stomach go weak with nausea.

"Isabella," he said. "My Isabella."

"No!" The cry tore from her throat. "I'm *not* Isabella!"

He pushed her back against the love seat. Her knees buckled and she screamed. Screamed until she felt as though her lungs would burst. Screamed though she knew no one could hear.

He'd been a fool, a blind fool. She had betrayed him just as Isabella had. But she was worse than Isabella because she had pretended to love him. He would never forgive her for that.

He raced through the tunnel. He would kill Ponti. This time he would kill—

He heard something and stopped, straining to hear. A scream? Yes! Nicky! Nicky screaming for help.

He sprinted ahead. Had he been wrong? My God, was she in danger, crying out for him?

He ran on, stumbling in his haste, cursing aloud in his agony to get to her.

Light ahead. The room where Ponti and Isabella met.

He saw Ponti. Nicky. Everything in the flash of a microsecond—the love seat and the chairs. The portrait of Isabella. Stefano and Nicky struggling together. He had her pinned against the love seat. Her shirt was torn; there was a red mark on her cheek. She struck out at Ponti again and again, screaming, "Stop! Let me alone! Let me—"

With a terrible cry of rage, Carlo sprang at the other man. He got an arm around Ponti's throat and yanked him away from Nicky. Ponti tried to swing around, and when he did, Carlo hit him, a blow that sent his enemy staggering backward. Before he could recover, Carlo was on him again, slashing him with blow after blow. Ponti fell and Carlo fell with him, pummeling with vicious fists until Ponti's face was bruised and bloody.

Nicky staggered up from the love seat. "Stop!" she cried. "Carlo, stop. You're going to kill him."

But he was past hearing, past reason. Here was the man his wife had been unfaithful with. The same man who had attacked Nicky. He felt a dull redness in front of his eyes and his hands closed around Stefano Ponti's throat.

"Carlo! Stop!"

But he was deaf to Nicky's cries, deaf and blind to anything except the need to kill this seducer of women, this... Suddenly there was a sharp sting of pain across his back. He swung around and saw Elizabetta, the cane in her hand raised to strike again.

"Get away!" he cried.

"Not until you stop!"

He hesitated.

"I won't let you kill him."

"Grandmother—"

"No!" She struck him a blow across his shoulders. "He isn't worth killing. Let him alone."

The dull redness disappeared from behind his eyelids. He let Ponti go, and like a man gone suddenly lame, staggered to his feet.

Ponti gasped and clutched his throat. And Nicky, weeping hysterically, rushed to Carlo.

"Thank God you came," she sobbed. "Thank God."

He grasped her shoulders and shook her. "Why did you come down into the tunnel?" he shouted. "Why?"

"He—he told me if I didn't he'd go to the police about—about you. He said—he said that you'd killed her. That you'd killed Isabella."

"And he did!" Ponti struggled to a sitting position. "He did kill her. He pushed her out of her bedroom window to her death. He—"

"No!" Elizabetta's voice cut like a burning sword. "It wasn't Carlo. I'm responsible for Isabella's death."

The three of them stared at her. Carlo put a hand on her arm. "No you didn't, *Nonna*," he said gently. "Isabella fell during the storm, when she was trying to close the shutters. You had nothing to do with her death."

"Yes, I did!" Her voice rose. Her face was chalk white and her eyes, so like Carlo's, burned with a zeal he had never seen before. "I thought something was wrong this afternoon when you returned. I went into the library, and when I saw the door to the tunnel open I knew this was where you were." She turned her gaze to Nicky. "Where you both were, and I knew I had to come down."

"*Nonna,* please. You're exciting yourself. Come and sit down."

She shrugged his hand away. "I've lived with this for two years," she said in a shaky voice. "It's time the truth came out. You must listen to me. You must!"

Nicky put an arm around her waist. "All right," she said. "But come and sit down, Elizabetta. Please, dear. Come, I'll help you."

And when she had helped Elizabetta to the love seat, she knelt beside her. "Tell us if you want to," she said.

In a shaky voice Elizabetta began. "I went to Isabella's room that day because I knew she was having an affair with Stefano." She looked at him. "Your family and mine have been neighbors for more than three hundred years. You were Carlo's friend and you betrayed him."

"I couldn't help it," he rasped, his hand on his throat. "She was so beautiful...." He shook his head, unable to go on.

Elizabetta turned away from him. "I went to her," she said to Carlo. "I told her I knew of the affair. I begged her to stop and she laughed in my face. She told me I was an old fool and to mind my own business. She said...she said she would sleep with whomever she chose and there wasn't anything you could do about it."

She reached for Nicky's hand and clung to it, as though to a lifeline. "The window was open, the shutters were banging and the rain was blowing in. I said, 'Please don't do this to Carlo. He's a good man and he loves you.' But she laughed at me and I..." She looked at Carlo, her face twisted with the agony of the need to tell him how it had been. "I wanted to hurt her the way she was hurting you. I struck out with my cane...." Her voice was low as she struggled for the breath to finish what must be said. "I raised it," she whispered. "She stepped back and... she fell. And screamed..." Elizabetta covered her ears with her hands. "And there was only me to hear."

Her face was ashen and still she fought to speak. "Forgive me. Carlo, please. Forgive—"

He knelt beside her. "It was an accident, *Nonna*. There's nothing to forgive." He clasped her wrist so that he could feel her pulse, and when he did, he looked at Nicky and bit his lip. *"Nonna..."* he said. *"Nonna?"*

She fell back on the love seat.

"Elizabetta!" Nicky cried.

The paper-thin eyelids fluttered. Lips tinged with blue moved as though she were about to speak. Then she gasped, and it was over.

"Do something," Nicky cried. "Carlo, do something!"

He reached for the pulse in Elizabetta's throat, waited, then shook his head. "She's gone," he said gently.

Nicky leaned her face against the pale, still hands and let the tears fall.

Carlo rested his hand on her shoulder. Then he helped her to rise. And when he did, she looked up at the portrait of Isabella.

Only a portrait. Paint on canvas, nothing more. The truth had been told, the ghosts of the past had been laid to rest.

It was over; the future lay ahead. She put her hand in Carlo's. And knew that though this was an ending, it was also a beginning. They had each other, and their love. They had only just begun.

* * * * *

And now from Silhouette Shadows
an exciting preview of

FOOTSTEPS IN THE NIGHT
by Lee Karr

CHAPTER ONE

An ominous rumbling of thunder accompanied the clouds darkening the Irish countryside. Maurie Miller stood by the window in the small boarding house room she had rented, looking out on a steep slate roof where masses of green-black ivy clung to the stone exterior. Her gaze followed the landscape stretching away bleakly in the relentless drizzle. She turned away from the window. There had been nothing but rain since she'd stepped off the plane at Shannon International Airport two days ago.

Exhausted, she lay down on the narrow bed and drew the knitted coverlet over her. *At least I'm here,* Maurie thought. *Tomorrow I'll begin the search for my roots.* On the edge of sleep, she heard Mrs. Duffy, the landlady, talking in her rich Irish brogue to the new boarder, Daylan O'Shane. The voices faded, and all Maurie heard was the hypnotic brush of rain on the roof.

She didn't know how long she'd been asleep when a strange awareness came over her. She could hear the rain peppering the windowpane, but another sound pushed its way into her consciousness. A music box. A tinkling melody mingled with the sound of hushed voices. Must be the landlady and the new boarder outside her door, with a music box, she thought lazily, her eyes still closed.

She pulled the coverlet up over her shoulder, but the familiar feel of knitted yarn had changed to a caressing softness. Her fingers slid over a soft down-filled quilt.

With a start, Maurie raised her head and stared at a satin pillowcase embroidered with the initials C.C. And suddenly she realized she was lying on the middle of a wide bed fashioned with a high headboard and four carved posts.

Slowly she sat up. *I'm dreaming,* she thought on some detached level. The tiny farmhouse bedroom had changed into an enormous bedchamber with richly paneled walls and a high ceiling ribbed with elaborate moldings. Mullioned glass windows spanned a wall framed by swags of deep green draperies. Only a modern television console built into the wall facing her was at odds with the castlelike bedchamber.

I'm dreaming. Awake and yet still dreaming. She couldn't quite see into the far corners of the room. She lay back down, closing her eyes. In a moment, she would awaken. The dream would be gone, and she would be back in her narrow bed in the little room, with the smell of roasting meat and potatoes floating up from the kitchen as Mrs. Duffy prepared dinner. Yes, in a minute she would wake up. She could still hear the pattering rain...and the music box. A lilting tune. She tried to place it. Irish? English? "Londonderry Air." That was it.

A childish giggle made her slowly turn her head. Two figures sat on a chaise longue against one wall of the room. A gray-haired woman smiled down at a child sitting on her lap. The dark-haired little girl giggled as she watched a horse on a music box go around and around.

Maurie tried to speak, but couldn't. With concentrated effort, she threw back the quilt and slid her legs over the edge of the bed until her feet brushed a plush carpet. A rain-laden wind splashing against the windows brought a bone-deep chill to her body, and she shivered, hugging herself. She was startled to find herself wearing a long blue nightgown and matching bed jacket.

The woman looked up. "Oh, Mrs. Fitzgerald, you're awake. Feeling better, are ye? Hollie, dear, Mommie's awake." She carried the child over to the bed. "Give yer mommie a kiss, sweetie."

The little girl clung to her nanny's neck and buried her face in the plump woman's neck.

"'Tis just childish shyness, Mrs. Fitzgerald," apologized the woman. "Yer being sick and all. The little one doesn't understand that her mother—"

"No...I'm not...her mother," Maurie murmured. Her voice sounded different. "I'm Maurie Miller. Maureen Miller."

"Go on with yer." The woman gave a nervous laugh. "Yer've been ill, and things are a bit mixed up fer ye, that's all. Yer be Dawna Fitzgerald—Mrs. Oliver Fitzgerald, and mother of wee Hollie here."

"No, I'm not." *Why can't I wake up?* "I am not Mrs. Fitzgerald." Maurie tried to explain that this was all a dream, but a rush of incoherent words made her put her hands to her face. The sudden British accent in her own voice was unmistakable. Where was her own American speech? Why was a stranger's voice coming out of her mouth? *It's only a dream. Only a dream ...* "I'm Maurie ... Maurie."

The little girl looked into Maurie's face, and as if she beheld a stranger in her mother's bed, she began to cry.

"Hush, darling. Yer mommie's just having a bad spell. We'll call the nurse. Miss Doughty will take care of her." The nanny flung an anxious look to Maurie as she clutched the child and hurried from the room.

Maurie walked around the bed to a light switch as if she'd known exactly where it was located on the wall. She stood there in her bare feet and fancy clothes, letting her gaze travel the room. She moved over to a dressing table and stared at her reflection in the mirror. The face was her own, but different. *As if I've been ill.* The arched eyebrows had the same uplift over azure eyes, but she'd never worn her hair like this, long, with soft waves flowing over her shoulders.

"Dawna! What are you doing out of bed! Look at you, standing there shivering. For heaven's sake, don't you want to get well?" a young woman wearing a petal pink sweater over a white nurse's uniform scolded her impatiently. "Now you get back in bed. It's time for your medicine."

"No, I... You don't understand...."

"No argument, Dawna, or I'll call Oliver. And you know how short your husband's temper is—especially when you insist on being difficult. I don't know why you make it so hard on yourself. It's very stupid of you, Dawna."

"I'm not Dawna." Maurie's voice quivered. When would the nightmare end?

"You're not well," the nurse said with a hint of satisfaction. "No one would be surprised if your melancholy drove you to some unfortunate behavior. Something dreadful could happen—any day." The slender woman handed Maurie two pills and a glass of water. "Take them, Dawna. Now."

No, I'm not... Maurie silently protested, but she was unable to speak. As if she were used to obeying the nurse's tone of voice, she swallowed the pills.

"Good girl," Miss Doughty said in a falsely bright tone. "Are you cold, Dawna? I'll turn up the heat a bit. I don't think I'll ever get used to this miserable wet climate. We had rain in London, but it didn't have this bloody never-ending chill, day after day. The sun would come out and dry up everything, remember?''

"I've never been to London—I'm an American," Maurie protested in clipped British tones. "This is just a horrible nightmare."

"Your husband is running out of patience, Dawna. This new little subterfuge will only infuriate him more." With that pronouncement, the nurse flounced out of the room, and Maurie heard a key turning in the lock.

A half-opened door at one end of the room caught her eye, and she hurried toward it. A bathroom. Once again, Maurie's fingers seemed to know just where the light switch was. Her head ached, and her limbs felt light, as if the pills were beginning to take effect. She saw another door at the far end of the spacious bathroom. She walked over to it. The shiny brass knob felt cold as she clasped it and turned it slowly. Cautiously she let the door swing open before she stepped into an adjoining bedroom.

A man stood with his back to her. He held a cigarette in one hand and a sheaf of papers in the other. A brocade smoking jacket stretched across his broad shoulders. She must have made a sound, because he swung around. His expression hardened the second he saw her, and a flash of cold impatience flickered in his deep-set, piercing brown-black eyes. He had black hair and a precisely trimmed mustache that added to the rigidity of his unsmiling lips. "What are you doing out of bed, Dawna?"

He must be Oliver, Maurie thought on some detached level. "This isn't real—I'm not Dawna. I'll wake up...."

"That does it. My patience has run out." His glare was contemptuous. He threw down the papers and stamped out his cigarette. "I won't have my wife talking gibberish!'' he said and clenched his fists. ''You're no good to anyone this way, Dawna. I'm going to call the doctor. There's a sanitarium—''

''Listen to me!'' Panic swelled up and choked her. ''I'm a college professor from the States. Twenty-nine years old and not married. You are *not* my husband! I don't have a child. I'm not married.'' She heard herself explaining that she'd been born in Ireland and taken to America by adoptive parents, that she was here to search for her roots.

His face flared with anger. ''You like to torment me, don't you? You delight in thwarting me at every turn. I'm warning you, I've had enough of your stupid stubbornness.''

As he took a threatening step toward her, Maurie backed up. Frightened, she spun around to flee but lost her balance. She went down on one knee, her cheek hitting the edge of the door. She screamed loudly—

Her arms flailed beneath the knitted coverlet that lay over her. A pounding on the door vibrated through the small room and brought her straight up in the narrow bed. She was back in her room.

''Open up!''

Someone was knocking on the door. Maurie staggered to her feet and crossed the room. With shaking hands, she slipped back the simple bolt and opened the door. Standing there was Daylan O'Shane—who had the same raven hair as the threatening Oliver. Arched eyebrows shadowed his dark eyes, and in a terrifying moment, his face and the one in her dream mingled. Panic-stricken, she tried to shut the door, but he blocked it with his leg.

Maybe she wasn't awake at all. . . .

Take 4 bestselling love stories FREE

Plus get a FREE surprise gift!

Special Limited-time Offer

Mail to Silhouette Reader Service™

3010 Walden Avenue
P.O. Box 1867
Buffalo, N.Y. 14269-1867

YES! Please send me 4 free Silhouette Shadows™ novels and my free surprise gift. Then send me 4 brand-new novels every other month, which I will receive months before they appear in bookstores. Bill me at the low price of $2.96 each plus applicable sales tax, if any.* That's the complete price and—compared to the cover prices of $3.50 each—quite a bargain! I understand that accepting the books and gift places me under no obligation ever to buy any books. I can always return a shipment and cancel at any time. Even if I never buy another book from Silhouette, the 4 free books and the surprise gift are mine to keep forever.

215 BPA AKZH

Name	(PLEASE PRINT)	
Address	Apt. No.	
City	State	Zip

This offer is limited to one order per household and not valid to present Silhouette Shadows™ subscribers.
*Terms and prices are subject to change without notice. Sales tax applicable in N.Y.

USHAD-93   ©1993 Harlequin Enterprises Limited

**Silhouette Books
is proud to present
our best authors,
their best books…
and the best in
your reading pleasure!**

Throughout 1993, look for exciting
books by these top names in
contemporary romance:

DIANA PALMER—
Fire and Ice in June

ELIZABETH LOWELL—
Fever in July

CATHERINE COULTER—
Afterglow in August

LINDA HOWARD—
Come Lie With Me in September

When it comes to passion,
we wrote the book.

BOBT2

Fifty red-blooded, white-hot, true-blue hunks from every State in the Union!

Beginning in May, look for MEN MADE IN AMERICA! Written by some of our most popular authors, these stories feature fifty of the strongest, sexiest men, each from a different state in the union!

Two titles available every other month at your favorite retail outlet.

In September, look for:

DECEPTIONS by Annette Broadrick (California)
STORMWALKER by Dallas Schulze (Colorado)

In November, look for:

STRAIGHT FROM THE HEART by Barbara Delinsky (Connecticut)
AUTHOR'S CHOICE by Elizabeth August (Delaware)

You won't be able to resist MEN MADE IN AMERICA!

What a year for romance!

Silhouette has five fabulous romance collections coming your way in 1993. Written by popular Silhouette authors, each story is a sensuous tale of love and life—as only Silhouette can give you!

Three bachelors are footloose and fancy-free... until now.
(March)

Heartwarming stories that celebrate the joy of motherhood.
(May)

Put some sizzle into your summer reading with three of Silhouette's hottest authors.
(June)

Take a walk on the dark side of love—with tales just perfect for those misty autumn nights.
(October)

Share in the joy of yuletide romance with four award-winning Silhouette authors.
(November)

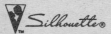

A romance for all seasons—it's always time for romance with Silhouette!

PROM93

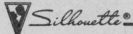